D1707379

Get your sneak peek and free
book...

scan me

Or go to www.jenniferalsever.com/free-book

Garfield County Libraries
Carbondale Branch Library
320 Sopris Avenue
Carbondale, CO 81623
(970) 963-2889 · Fax (970) 963-8573
www.GCPLD.org

i

BURYING

EVA

FLORES

JENNIFER ALSEVER

The Flores File: Video Interviews
NOW

September 25

Sophia Palmer (senior at Paonia High School): Lemme just say, I *didn't* kill Eva Flores.

Ethan Switalski (senior at Paonia High School): Soph came running to my house after the whole sheriff thing, and I knew it looked bad for her. That *stupid* curse. God... I just... [Exhales, looks out the window and stops talking.]

Sophia: The sheriff's office... I... [Pause.] After everything that went down, I knew they'd think it was me. I mean, I knew it. Right? But I'm *not* a murderer. I'm not an arsonist.

Ethan: They kept her there for hours, interviewing her. Probably illegal with no lawyer and stuff. So when she came to my house, she was literally shaking.

Sophia: I was just driving by when I saw the sheriff's car and fire truck. So I stopped on the side of the road to watch. [Bites her lip, looks at her hands.] I mean, who wouldn't do that?

Ethan: Soph kind of, you know, stumbled through my door. Said she'd been talking to Sheriff Rawlings. For like, forever. And he was being all nice, trying to get her to confess to some gruesome crime or something. Anyways, Sophia's all, *I'm too young to go to jail.*

Sophia: I just kept staring at the lodge—it was like passing by a car wreck and you can't look away. The black grassy field, so weird, so burnt. It snaked its way up to the river. Literally scorched the pine trees, circled the lodge. I couldn't stop looking. There were these black holes on the edges of the roof. But then I saw Dakota's dad, and he saw me. I sank deeper into my seat.

Delta County Sheriff Geoffrey Rawlings: I saw her right away. She pretended not to notice, but I wanted to talk to this girl. I'd heard stories about her. Mostly from my own kid.

Ethan: I guess he knocked on her window.

Sophia: He scared the shit out of me. [Covers her mouth.] Sorry. [Takes a sip of tea from a ceramic mug.] But he did.

Sheriff Rawlings: I motioned for her to roll down the window.

Sophia: I kind of froze.

Sheriff Rawlings: That was it. That two-second delay in rolling down the window? I knew I needed to interview Ms. Palmer.

Sophia: It's funny how some things just stay with you. That moment. [Looks to the corner of the room.] I remember the little rattle of the window when I rolled it down. And then when the smoky air came into my car... I don't know. My brain was moving in slow motion. He said, "You're friends with that Eva girl, now, aren't you?" I just shrugged. I mean, I wasn't friends with her. He asked me why I was sitting out there.

Ethan: It took like an hour to get her to stop shaking. She just kept on repeating *I didn't do anything*. I knew that. Me and Morgan knew that. But it was like, I don't know... Like she was trying to convince *herself* that she didn't do something. Like the more she said it, the more she could control things again... That damn journal.

Sheriff Rawlings: After our talk that night, we found them. The journal. The Snaps. The texts. The bloody jacket. Unwinding this story all took time. As you'll see. But I think the kids just honestly made up some crazy story.

Sophia
MOTIVE

Then: March 24

The broken steamer screamed like a high-pitched kettle, but Sophia's mind drifted away as she watched her.

Eva Flores.

The way she flicked her blue hair over her shoulder. The way she leaned over her iced latte and sucked on the straw without touching her fingers to the cup. It was obvious, just by looking at her, that Eva's life oozed ease and comfort. She owned her future, and she didn't realize the beauty of that.

Sophia imagined striding into The Wheel wearing a cowboy hat and Lone Ranger mask, walking up behind Eva, touching her shoulder.

Eva looks up and smiles before Sophia pulls out a pair of gleaming silver scissors. And snip, snip, she cuts the blue strands off her head. Eva's face is aghast, and slowly she shrinks into the red plastic chair because she, too, is made of plastic.

Ethan's voice snapped her out of the fantasy. "You know, she thinks you're in love with her." His red hair hung in strings by his face.

"Whatever," Sophia said, once again aware of the steamer's ear-piercing screaming noise. "She's just ... so..."

"Hot?" Ethan wiped down the counter with a white cloth.

Sophia turned to Riley, who was making a latte. "You gonna fix that or not?"

Riley bugged her eyes out at Sophia.

"You're holding it wrong," Sophia said.

Riley let go of the black button on the latte machine, and it stopped screaming.

"Yup, she thinks you're enamored of her ethereal beauty," Ethan reiterated with sarcasm. He didn't look up, just kept wiping the same spot on the granite countertop.

It was what they did. Wipe the same things over and over. Try to look like they were really working. But really, The Wheel was not busy enough to require three baristas working in a shift. Sophia was waiting for Zeb to figure out that he was paying too much, that he wasn't making enough money in a small town like Paonia, that he didn't really need Ethan and Sophia, and that the two talked more than they worked. She figured Zeb would see that Riley was the only one present, making lattes—unlike Sophia, who secretly made decaf for customers who acted like assholes.

But Zeb liked Sophia and Ethan. He trusted them. They ran the place, so he could keep his low-key lifestyle and go rock climbing and fly fishing.

Sophia glared at Ethan. "Well, that's what she wants to think. She acts like just because she's got the whole TikTok thing that she owns the town."

"That's because she does." He watched Riley put a couple of dishes into the dishwasher.

"It pisses me off," Sophia said, leaning against the counter.

"God, you're so salty about *everyone*," he said.

Sophia stared at him for a couple seconds, wondering if she really was irritated with everyone all the time. If she really *did* hate everyone.

"You *do* hate people," he said, reading her mind.

"I don't hate people…Just most people," she said.

He glanced up and flicked his head to the left. She turned around, following his gaze to see a regular Karen type on the other side of the counter with one hand on her hip, waiting. Mid-thirties, completely self-absorbed, wearing Lululemon yoga pants and a matching jacket. Just waiting. You knew she was truly irritated because she would glance up and then frown again at her phone.

"The usual," she said through a saccharine smile that faded immediately after the words left her mouth.

Sophia nodded and turned before bumping Riley out of the way. When the nonfat, oat-milk, double-shot-espresso, two-shots-of-vanilla latte was complete, the knockoff espresso machine flashed messages on the screen: "Frucy breakfast" and "Cheese bruger."

Ethan watched the screen and chuckled. "Where the hell did Zeb get this machine?"

"eBay?" Sophia turned and handed the drink to Karen, who flashed her gleaming smile—read, fake—spun on her heel, and grabbed her toddler's hand. He had some weird name like Cosmo or something.

"You're still butt-hurt about what she did to you," Ethan said.

"That whole thing changed no one's opinion of me." Sophia leaned her back against the counter, her usual position. "No," she said quietly, "but really. Eva's just—"

She glanced to her left and stopped. There she was: Eva, standing directly in front of her with that perfectly shiny Smurf-like hair. Holly Stephenson and Lydia Roan flanked her.

Sophia could feel the weight of their united gaze. Holly scanned the necklaces that laced Sophia's throat: the black ribbon choker, the long silver chain of crystals bound by wire, the silver star. Eva studied the ink-drawn gargoyle on

Sophia's forearm and gazed blankly at her black Rolling Stones T-shirt. Whenever Ethan saw Soph in it, which was often, he always mimicked it—with an open mouth and flat, extended tongue. She would end it with a slap of his forehead.

Sophia directed a steady gaze back at Eva, eyelids heavy, a look that always forced people back on their heels. A look that worked.

Holly stepped up to the counter, inching past Eva. "I'd like the burrito." She extended her credit card. Her fingernail polish was a sparkly blue.

Sophia glanced at the card but didn't take it. Her voice was monotone. "Do you want green chile or red?"

"I want—"

"Both," Eva interjected, leaning into Holly's hair. "You want both."

Holly's face withered, and she nodded swiftly. "Yeah, I guess I want both."

It turned Sophia's stomach. She knew what that felt like, how Eva tried to take the reins. And what happened when you didn't let her.

"You always let your friends order for you?" Sophia asked.

Holly's eyes were wide, like a creepy antique doll. Eva, who had been looking at her phone, glanced up and scoffed. Sophia made the burrito and continued eavesdropping while the girls talked.

"Wow, your hair's so long, Hols." Eva lifted a few strands of Holly's blond, shoulder-length hair with her fingertips.

Holly self-consciously petted her own hair. "Yeah, mad split ends."

Eva smirked, raising her brows before she looked away. Holly wilted. Sophia remembered the way Eva had tried that with her, five months earlier. Eva had been the new girl—and already wildly popular because of her stupid dance videos. In each clip, she had a plastered smile and a taut, tan tummy. For some reason, she'd taken a unique interest in Sophia. Too close, too fast. And then Eva unleashed vengeance.

Sophia handed the plate with the smothered burrito to Holly.

Eva leaned a hip on the counter and gazed at Sophia. "Nice car out there," she said, tossing her head toward the window, where Sophia's refurbished 1976 Datsun was parked on the street. Eva glanced at her friends, and a small smile inched up one side of her cheek.

Sophia gazed at her with a blank, hard face. Inside, she was boiling. Eva was *not* calling her old car "nice."

"Says the girl who's riding in a brand-new Range Rover," Lydia said, nudging Eva with her elbow.

"When did your parents get it?" Holly asked, wide-eyed. "You didn't—"

"It's awesome," Lydia sang.

"I know, right?" Eva looked back to Sophia for some sort of affirmation. "You're, like, a mechanic... You can appreciate expensive cars, right, Sadie?"

Eva was one of those people who tried to pretend she didn't remember you or your name. Even if you lived in a tiny town, even if you sat next to her in Spanish, even if you had a locker next to her. Even if you regularly served her nonfat, one-pump, double-shot vanilla lattes in a restaurant that she visited nearly every day. Even if she had practically been glued to you for a period of time.

Even if she tried to ruin your life.

"Sophia."

"Yeah. It's a good brand, right?" Eva nodded and grinned, pulling on the beaded jade mala necklace that swung at her belly, bared by a midriff tank top.

"It's lit." Lydia's voice was ridiculously low for a teenaged girl.

Sophia just gazed at Eva blankly.

The three girls turned away and settled at a table in the

corner. Eva glanced back over her shoulder with a gloating expression. "Can you *even* imagine working here?" she asked her friends not-so-quietly.

Eva brushed her hair over her shoulder and looked up at Sophia with big round brown eyes before "accidentally" bumping her drink onto the floor. The iced latte flooded the floor, oozing like a river, wrapping around the legs of their chairs, and pooling beneath their feet.

"Oh, no!" Eva said dramatically before looking over at Ethan and Sophia, shrugging with a smile through gritted teeth. "Ooops."

Ethan rolled his eyes and turned his back to them, leaning on the counter. He unlocked his phone. Riley's head was inside the microwave oven, where she scrubbed it with a noxious-smelling bleach cleaner.

Sophia turned to Ethan. "If I throw a stick, you think Eva'll leave?"

"Not a chance," he said, staring down at his phone.

"She's like..." Her voice trailed off. She had to stop talking about her.

"Uh-huh," he said, distracted. Sophia caught a glimpse of his screen; he was on SnapChat again.

Neither of them moved to clean up the mess. Sophia figured she'd let the three sit amid the sticky puddle as long as possible.

When the girls were gone, Ethan turned to Sophia, slapped her on the back. "Ready to clean up, Sadie?"

He laughed. Sophia didn't.

"Dude, you check out that car I found online?" he asked. Sophia didn't hear him.

The Flores File: Video Interviews
NOW

Riley Neuman (senior at Paonia High): They had no idea I existed. I mean, I worked with those guys at The Wheel forever. Saw them three times a week.

Ethan: Riley? Oh god. She was our punishment. She's a freaking racist. Homophobic. She has serious issues.

Riley: I worked beside those two every day. Of course I was listening to everything. Not that they would know. To them, I'm just "the girl in the back, washing dishes." No ... more like they don't even know I'm a person. I'm just ... this void to them.

Ethan: It was kind of like Eva and her girls hung out at The Wheel just to piss off Soph.

Riley: Sophia *hated* Eva. I mean, I could have written a book about all the trash she talked about her. I'd say she was obsessed with her. But most people were.

Ethan: Sure. Soph kinda went off about Eva after she and the girls left The Wheel that day. But yeah, I'm not gonna lie—she was a little overly focused on Eva... But don't tell her that. *Please?*

Riley: She just went on and on about Eva: "*Eva brings so much joy ... when she's gone.*" And all that. Ethan probably didn't hear. If I remember, he was too focused on his phone. [Scoffs.]

Ethan: What? Who? Who was I talking to? Just some guy. Somebody. So yeah, I was distracted. But it was nothing new for Soph to be all riled by Eva. I maybe hoped ... that she was into her. That it was just, like, a crush. But it turned out to evolve into more...

Riley: I mean you'd expect *Ethan* to be gay—just the way he, I don't know, hung out with girls?—but the guy he was into, who came in for coffee? He was like, I don't know, like *normal.* Some guy from out of town. But anyway, I was listening to them the whole time. They forgot. Sophia didn't even know. That was kind of my magic, right? She didn't even know I listened to them. *Ever.* I heard *everything.*

2

Sophia
SHARP SCISSORS

Then: March 29

The camera lens focused in and out, zooming in on the tin can, the chaotic jumble of red ribbon, the random scraps of brightly lined fabric, the crinkled tin foil, the tip of an overturned coffee cup. The objects sat delicately on top of a blown-up photo of a snowflake.

Confusion atop silent beauty. The shutter snapped in rapid succession, and Sophia lowered the camera to look at her images in the viewfinder. She smiled before carefully replacing the lens cap and placing it on the card table. A breeze blew her hair, the ends of which had once been indigo but now faded to a green.

"Did you defrost the chicken?" The staccato sound of her mother's voice swept through the white tent.

"Yeah, Ma," she said. "On the counter."

Sophia stood up, stepping over her props in the corner of the tent, and wove around the gold and blue satin floor pillows. A waft of spicy incense struck her as she ducked through the opening of the tent and lumbered toward the rocky path to their tiny home. The tall grass whispered to her bare knees.

Inside, Sophia opened the kitchen cupboard to retrieve a can of corn. "I thought we could just throw them in the oven before I pick up Dylan from work," she said.

When she turned around, corn in hand, she stopped still. Her mom sat at the bar, on a wobbly stool, with a far-off expression on her oval face. Dark black lines ran from her eyes to her cheeks. Mascara. She had been crying. Her mom never cried.

Sophia set the can down. "Ma?"

Her mom's eyes jolted to attention, pulled back from a distant time and place.

"You okay?" Sophia asked. "You're—"

"Oh." Her mom sat up straighter, licked her fingers and began wiping away the streaks. "Nothing."

Sophia sighed and rolled her eyes. "Right."

A yawning bit of silence stretched between them, and Sophia finally turned away, yanking open a drawer, searching for a can opener.

"I got fired," her mom said finally.

Sophia stopped and looked up. Her heart sank to her stomach. *Not again.* She had just started to feel safe again, *human*, really, where she wasn't on free lunch anymore at school. The paycheck from her after-school barista job helped, but the pressure had been off. It hadn't been up to her and Dylan to ensure money kept flowing into the house.

Sophia stared at her. Her insides twisted, but she kept her face still as stone.

"Oh, don't look at me like—"

"Like what?"

"Don't fight with me, girl," her mom said. "That's not what I need right now. It's not my fault."

Sophia turned away and slapped the can opener on the corn, yanking the crank to open it. She felt her skin take on a flinty veneer, the hardened vibe she gave to the world. Inside, she was broiling, feeling the same chaos as her photographs. *Art mimics life? Or vice versa?*

"Why?" she asked with her back turned to her mother.

"Hendy hit on me." Her voice sounded tired. When Sophia turned around, her mom's face was in her hands. "I swear, I didn't do nothing."

Her boss Hendy was a slime bag. Sophia had known it the first time she met him, at the Christmas party just two weeks after her mom took the job. She'd seen the way he eyed her, his gaze lingering on her hips, tracing her shape. "You and your mom look like sisters," he had said that night, the side of his top lip twitching. It had made Sophia feel dirty.

That night, Sophia had kept her gaze on Hendy's shiny forehead, knowing it would make him as uncomfortable as she was—there was no way he wasn't self-conscious about the fuzzy ring of meager hair that formed a horseshoe on his head.

Hendy had gazed across the party at her mom again. "Yeah, she looks awesome."

"She's smart," Sophia had said, turning away. Undoubtedly smarter than *him*. If only she hadn't gotten knocked up when she was eighteen. In another universe, her mom would have been *this guy's* boss.

"She shoulda been a model."

And you should be in jail, she had thought. She heard about all the sketchy stuff he was doing in the office: over-billing clients, lying on documents about their taxes. But Hendy was the only lawyer in Paonia, and he held the keys to whether or not they would pay the rent. And now, he had finally put the moves on her mom and ruined everything.

"What'd he do?" Sophia felt like an angry older sibling, like she wanted to take her rage out on that jerk. "You should sue his ass."

"I'm not gonna do that, hon." Her mom stood up. "He

was a perv. I knew it. I *knew*. But it was a good job. Don't worry about it."

"There's something called MeToo."

"Don't." Her mom's voice was sharp like a whip, and it always set Sophia in line.

Sophia's stomach lurched. "Did he—"

"No." Her voice was sharp, and she shook her head and waved her hands in front of her face, disgusted by the thought. "No, no, no. He just made an ultimatum. You know? I mean. Yeah, that's it. I'm done. I'll find another job."

Her mom spun around and disappeared into the bedroom. Sophia stood there, livid that this freaking asshole could wield so much control over their lives.

She imagined Hendy pawing at her mom, saying she was a "good employee."

Then she let her imagination off its leash.

Sophia bursts into the musty office, grabbing him by the collar and crashing his head onto his oak desk, kneeing him in the balls. He crumples to the ground, gasping for air. Then, her mom comes up from behind, kicks him in the back, and the two of them grab a stack of cash off the lobby counter and walk out the door.

"Sophia—" Her mom's voice shook her out of the fantasy. She was hidden in the bedroom, undoubtedly readying to shower. To wash the scum of that guy off her body. "Thanks for cooking. For everything."

"No problem." Her voice was quiet. The reality wasn't quite like the fantasies in her head. Nothing was like those stories.

The cool can of corn still in her hand, she held the can opener and gazed out the window to the back lawn.

Mrs. Ratner, withered and tiny in her polyester pants, squatted in front of the small chain-link fence. Sophia squinted. What was her little old landlady doing? Oddly, she was clipping the edges of the grass with scissors. Just regular kitchen scissors. The old woman looked up at Sophia, as if she knew she was being watched, and smiled beneath a wide-brimmed hat. It wasn't the smile of a sane woman. It was the smile of a woman who was old—so, so, old—and clearly losing her mind.

She was the one person Sophia and her family had in their corner. A little old woman named Mrs. Ratner, who kept her rents at 1980s rates. A little old woman who was now clipping the lawn with scissors.

The week before, she had tacked up a blue tarp onto her side of the chain-link fence, explaining that she didn't want the neighbors' grass to get any of the water that might spray from her property's sprinklers. Now the water pattered against the tarp as the woman clipped each blade of grass.

Sophia's phone dinged.

Ethan:
come over

Sophia:
making dinner

Ethan:
i found me a car

Sophia:
k

Ethan:
dude selling it is certified creeper tho

Below the message was a photo of a rusted blue 1968 Mustang. Flattened tires. Dented roof. A faceless man wearing a low-tipped cowboy hat stood next to it. She had just set her phone down when it dinged again. Growling, she picked it up.

Ethan:

its cool AF

we gotta check it

The Flores File: Video Interviews
NOW

Jennifer Palmer (Sophia's mother): My Sophia? Recently? You know, Soph didn't really say much. Once she hit high school, those earbuds went in. [Pause.] I *am* assuming that you're going to clear her name of all this. By doing all these interviews.

Dylan Palmer (Sophia's brother): She's the best little sister. She always picks me up from my job at Don's. I'm a bagger there. I get twelve dollars an hour.

Ethan: Soph is dope. I hate that all the focus and suspicion is on her. If you knew her, you'd think it was stupid. She's been my best friend literally since ninth grade. So yeah. She has this look like maybe she'd punch you in the face if you said something wrong. I figured I wanted that girl on my side.
Morgan and me? We've been tight since elementary school. She and I—she wore these thick glasses, oh my god, you wouldn't believe—but she was all badass on the playground. She busted in and ripped these kids off me one time. They were older. Two of 'em pinned me down. [A few moments of silence pass. Rubs his face with two palms.] Yeah, so they... They held my eyelids open and spit in my eyes. So anyway. It's like the three of us have this

15

unspoken vibe where we... I dunno. [Nods several times.] We just get each other.

Morgan Spittler, PHS senior: I know Soph seems like a bitch. But she's not. She's got this tough look about her. It's like this exterior that's like a walnut shell, something like that, you know? But she's low-key cool. Always there for you a hundred percent. Well. I mean. She's ... made some big mistakes. But she's good.

Dylan: She makes me dinner. Every night. Never forgets me at Don's.

Jennifer: [Scoffs.] To be honest, I'm getting a little tired of all this focus on Sophia. She works hard, she helps me with Dylan, she's so independent. [Pauses, before leaning into the camera with raised eyebrows.] I know what you think about her and that girl, Eva. But she wouldn't do that. She's a *good* kid. A complex kid? Sure. Different? Hell yeah, and I couldn't be happier about that. But she's no murderer. [Looks away, frowns.] And yeah, to tell you the truth, I'm not interested in doing this interview anymore. [Stands up.]

Dylan: Sophie told me she found magic that made wishes come true.

3

Sophia
REVENGE

Then: March 30

When Sophia got home from school the next day, her mother sat at the table, squinting through a pair of grocery-store readers. The kitchen smelled like fresh-baked bread.

"What're you doing, Ma?" Sophia asked.

"Taking all my single earrings and making necklaces with them," she said, before biting her lower lip and slipping a silver bead through a wire. On the table, she'd lined up four different earrings: a silver hoop, a fake turquoise stud, a red and brown feather, and one with twisted beaded gems. Her mom was notorious for losing just one earring.

"Why are you suddenly baking bread and making jewelry?"

"Cash." She glanced up and winked. "No job yet. I'll sell these at the meditation tent."

She tied the wire with scissors, grasping one end between her lips. "Star said the women in class … they want this stuff."

Her mom's friend Star Caperson often showed up at the meditation tent in the back yard and did free psychic readings for tourists. Sophia didn't believe in that shit, but her mom said she was often spot on. "Did she get that marketing tip from the spirit guides?" Sophia asked.

Her mom rolled her eyes. "She *does* know strange things happen in this world that we don't understand." She sang the words.

The refrigerator was fairly empty, outside of a jug of milk, two yogurts, a package of bologna, and a shriveled apple. Sophia shut the door and filled up a water glass instead before leaning her back against the refrigerator.

Sophia studied her mom's straight posture, mirroring how she seemed to weather adversity. Her mom's own dad had left her when she was a baby and her mother died when she was eighteen. Not long after, Sophia's mom met Jordan, Sophia's dad, and six weeks later, she became pregnant with Dylan. Two years later, she had Sophia. Her dad split for a while before coming back into the fold a few years later, only to take his young family on a rollercoaster ride—until abandoning them and running off to "find himself."

Her dad complained that her mom wasn't his soulmate. She was "lost" and drinking too much. Sophia disagreed. She thought her dad was an arrogant prick.

"It sucks, you know," Sophia said.

"Wha? You don't like this one?" Her mom frowned and held up a long opal-colored beaded necklace with a dangling gemstone at the bottom. "The color, I know... It's all I had—"

"No, it sucks that Hendy did this to you."

Her mom set down the necklace.

"Well..." She let out a heavy sigh. "I'm not going to let folks keep me down."

So instead, she's going to make jewelry and bake bread. The injustice of it all made Sophia want to hit something.

"Hendy's a perv."

"Hendy's got ... problems." Her mom waved her hand.

"I just want to—"

"I don't want that kind of negative energy in here." She added another bead to the string.

"But I'm serious, Ma," she said. "You should get even."

"We're not like that." Her mom's voice trailed off as she held up the necklace, checking to see if each side looked even.

"*You* might not be like—"

"Sophia Marie!" Her mom's voice was ice water. She scowled. "Just go if you're gonna be like that. Go!" She flicked her hand and returned to the beading.

Sophia's stomach growled. Swiftly, impulsively, she took off her rows of thrift-store necklaces with beads and wire-wrapped crystals, the rows of silver and leather bracelets, and the thick turquoise ring her dad had worn on his pinky finger. She placed them on the table in front of her mother.

"Soph, you don't have to do that," her mom said, pushing away the jewelry. "Those are yours."

"Donating to the cause." She turned and left the kitchen. Over her shoulder, she added, "They'll sell. Good shit."

That night, Sophia dressed in all black and crept toward Hendy Ferguson's office on Grand Avenue. She knew it was risky, but she *had* to do something. That guy, with his lawyer machismo, *deserved* it. A cool breeze fluttered her hair, and the sounds of laughter rippled from the restaurant down the way.

Then she spotted his silver Volvo. The same one he'd driven her mom home from work in; the same one in which he'd wrapped his arm around the top of the passenger seat as he spoke to her. She'd watched that night from their kitchen as her mom politely spoke to him, inching closer to the door. He had teeth like a wolf.

Sophia saw movement through his office window with the bent metal blinds. It wasn't as if her mom could call a lawyer about sexual harassment. He was the only guy in town. So plan B it was.

Squatting low, she unzipped her backpack and removed a gleaming pocket knife, the one she used to cut up branches and metal for her photos. With quick jabs, she stabbed the front tire of his car, before scraping the blade along the sides of the newly washed car. The squeal of the knife made her heart expand, giving her a weird sense of joy.

Hendy's laughter echoed through the open window, prompting Sophia to pause, a pulse of lightning fear freezing her.

"Don't you worry," he said. "The people who did this will pay. You got me, babe." He was talking on the phone. His voice faded, indicating he was moving away from the window, and Sophia returned to her handiwork.

Swiftly, she stabbed each of the other three tires. The blade stuck tight on her last extra slice, and she had to thrust her body back to remove it from the rubber.

She glanced up again from her crouch and then ran. Something moved in the distance. Sophia paused and squinted in the dark. She could make out a shape outside The Wheel. *Must be Riley.*

She better not say a word.

She wasn't a criminal. She was only ensuring that Hendy got what he deserved.

The Flores File: Video Interviews
NOW

Manny Flores (Eva's stepfather): Eva had so many friends. Everyone knew her, and she changed lives on TikTok. [Clears throat. Pauses. Looks off to the corner of the room.] Everyone wanted to be her. Maybe not the smartest girl, but she had the Flores flair.

Becky Flores (Eva's mother): She could have been a model. If she were thinner—and if she had taken my advice.

Manny: [Nodding.] She was hot, she was influential, a powerhouse. She could've been a powerhouse.

Lydia Roan (Eva's best friend): Not everyone knew her like I did.

Holly Stephenson (Eva's former best friend): No one knew her that well. She kind of put up a wall.

Lydia: She was a moth. [Hesitates.] I ... I mean. What do they call it? They call it a moth to a light or something?

Holly: She had this vibe where everyone wanted her approval, needed it. She was just thirsty, always flexing. Everyone wanted to be liked by her... I know *I* did. Everyone did. If Eva wanted something, you didn't say no.

Lydia: Write this down. [Leans forward and points.] Sophia Palmer killed her.

Holly: I mean, from the outside, everything looked all fine and good. But I know it wasn't. She wouldn't tell you that. She was like a vault. But...

Lydia: It was Sophia. I told the police, too. I don't know why she's not in jail.

Holly: If you want to find Eva, go talk to Aidan Voinovich. He was always watching her.

4

Sophia

JUNKER

Then: April 2

Sophia looked at Randolph as she put her cereal bowl into the dishwasher.

"Why the hell does Eva sit in the cafe every single day I work? It's like she wants to *watch* me clean up her messes..."

She tossed the milk carton into the nearly empty refrigerator and kicked the door shut. "As if she'll wear me down somehow, some way, so that I'll just fawn over her. *Oh, Eva, you're amazing!*"

Randolph leapt off the table and hissed in response. His green slit eyes looked like a scowl.

"You have no clue what it's like to be human," she said, glaring back at him.

He hissed again, and she kicked her foot in the air, swatting him away. "Stupid cat."

Her mom always warned her that Randolph avoided her because she called him names like *stupid* and *loser*.

Her phone buzzed, revealing a photo of Dylan, with his lopsided grin and bright eyes. It was 6:10 p.m. Like clockwork.

"Yo," she said.

"You can come get me now, Soph," he said in a singsong voice. She never understood how Dylan managed to live his life in the best of moods. He was a light breeze on a hot day. You couldn't help but welcome his presence. He probably made Sophia a better person than she really was.

In fact, he was the antidote to who she often was. If she woke up in a bad mood or grew sick of people after a shift at The Wheel, his presence was enough to make those feelings evaporate. She rarely saw him when he wasn't enamored with a bug on the ground or thrilled to get whipped cream in his coffee.

She remembered only one time when he had cried. He must have been twelve. A group of kids had shoved him up against the brick wall behind the grocery store; they smeared peanut butter across his forehead and called him "retard." Sophia punched one guy in the face, even though he was five years older, and they all ran off. But it couldn't erase the shame that spilled across his face. It was as if his soul had actually shattered, or at least cracked.

Sophia waited for her brother for several minutes in the empty parking lot of the grocery store with the engine of her 1976 Datsun humming. She loved the square angles of the dashboard and the way the car jiggled when she shifted gears. She mindlessly petted the blue embossed leather door—retro '70s—that she had reupholstered after finding the rig on Craigslist for $500. She loved the way the car smelled. The only way she could describe it was *old*. Like newspapers and grandpas, a bit of attic must and years of dirt ground into carpet.

She'd spent six months fixing up that car. She'd spent hours beneath the greasy underbelly, dirt falling into her mouth. Spent days searching for specialty parts on the Internet, spent weeks adding new carpet, seats, a transmission and carburetor.

She'd meticulously sanded the outside, fixing rusty holes with Bondo, before watching her paint job cook at the body shop for hours. She'd picked up the basics from auto shop class at school. She was the only girl in that class, and every boy kept trying to do everything for her—until she'd ripped the dipstick out of Marc Richardson's hands and growled that she was there *to learn too.* Then they all backed off. Her neighbor Ray, who must have been like sixty and could have been a rocket scientist if he had gone to college, helped her with her Craigslist Datsun project. The seller was an idiot: he couldn't figure out why the car didn't run right, but she figured out quickly it was just a vacuum leak. Her $500 car was probably worth four grand.

As Sophia waited, Star Caperson waddled through the parking lot, frizzy hair bouncing and long chiffon cardigan billowing behind her. Sophia looked away, pretending not to see her. She wasn't up for a long conversation about planets and horoscopes.

Nonetheless, Star appeared at the car door. "It's my shining Sophia!"

Sophia rolled her eyes. There was nothing shining about her, but Star saw the best in everyone. They chatted about her mom, and Sophia told her that Ma got fired because her boss was a jerk.

"Oh." Star hung onto the word for a long time with a furrowed brow. "I'll have to give her a jingle. Maybe I can do some psychic readings at her tent."

"Or you can just use your psychic stuff to help her win the lottery?" Sophia laughed.

"Oh, if only wishes came true," Star said, and she placed a warm palm on Sophia's elbow, where it rested on the window's edge.

Sophia wondered if this woman would feel the boiling helplessness she felt beneath her skin. *No, she's just a charming charlatan.*

Star's thin face shifted from a friendly smile to surprised wide eyes.

"What?" Sophia asked.

"Oh dear," Star said slowly, clenching Sophia's elbow tighter. "The spirits ... they'll come to you." She nodded and gazed off in the distance. "You may have no choice but to comply."

"Huh?" Sophia asked. A twinge of irritation shot through her. *God, Star was weird.* Sophia wondered how her mom even hung out with her.

She spotted her brother strolling out of the grocery store and across the oil-stained pavement. "Um, yeah, here's my brother. I gotta go." *Perfect excuse.*

Star waved goodbye with three fingers and wandered to her own car, and Dylan jumped inside Sophia's. He didn't seem to notice the exchange. The door closed with a tinny sound, and he swung a plastic bag in front of her face. She grimaced and pushed it away. He unloaded a pile of small yogurts, cheese, ham, and other past-due items his boss had pawned off on him. She didn't care that they were expired. They took what they could get.

"So, how'd it go?"

He dropped the bag on the floor and slowly, methodically, pulled the seatbelt across his lap. Following the ritual clicking sound of the seatbelt, he looked up and smiled. "Oh, real good, sis."

She put the car into gear, and the engine jiggled the whole car. She glanced in the sideview mirrors that were so small they were a quarter of the size of modern cars.

"I bagged eleven-point-two people's groceries."

"Eleven point two?"

"Yeah, one guy realized he didn't have enough money, so he had to put it all back. But he got two candy bars."

Sophia smiled and turned up the hill toward Ethan's house.

"Another lady had twenty-four oranges and five tubes of toothpaste! Another lady bought pumpkin seeds and sprouts and a buncha Kombucha."

This laundry list of groceries purchased happened after every shift, offering a window into how her brother saw the world. Sophia appreciated that he wasn't so hung up on the sideways glance of a stranger, or the fact that he didn't get long enough breaks, or the fact that his feet hurt when he stood too long, or even that he had to work by that mopey clerk Greg Mayhew, who smelled like fish. (At least he smelled like that when Sophia was in class with him the previous year.) Dylan was all about the simple pleasures of doing good work and adding up the value he brought at the end of the day.

She turned onto Highway 133, headed east.

"Where we going, sis?"

"Ethan wants me to stop by."

He did a fist pump into his stomach. "Morgan gonna be there?"

"Maybe."

"Yes!"

Sophia's friends passed her People Test, not just because they were solid to her, but because they were genuinely kind to Dylan. They never acted as if he was different, and that made them rise to the top, above everyone else in Paonia.

The path to Ethan's house from the driveway was covered in tall, smelly weeds surrounded by piles of dirt. Ethan's dad had torn up the lawn one afternoon the previous summer and built a small garden in the corner filled with sugar snap peas. The peas withered on the vine, and his father never did anything to deal with the rows and rows of turned up dirt that looked as if a colony of moles had taken over.

Inside, dust particles sprinkled the scant sunlight through

dirty windows, and the two of them wove through piles of unfolded laundry and past a dozen five-gallon buckets of water that Ethan's dad always kept in the hallway "just in case" there was a fire.

His dad's two little dogs, Roger and Thelma, hovered at her feet. Roger's tongue was permanently hanging out of the side of his mouth. And Thelma looked like a chemo patient: skinny and balding.

Sophia knocked on the bedroom door with a thud, calling out to her friend. "Yo."

"Yeah, open," he said.

She swung open the door, and it was like entering an entirely different house. Ethan kept his room tidy: clothes in drawers, books and notebooks set neatly on his desk, his bed always made with a crisp black comforter pulled up tight. The room looked like a hotel room in some ways, as if he wasn't getting too comfortable there, wasn't prepared to stay a second longer than he had to after graduation.

He sat on his bed, legs crossed, with a laptop open. Ethan refurbished laptops, while Sophia refurbished cars. He got his first computer when he was seven, and by eleven, he'd broken into the local Girl Scouts website and managed to get himself forty-one boxes of free cookies. He once told Sophia that he even dreamed in code.

"What's up?" Dylan asked, giving him knuckles.

Sophia plopped down on the other end of the bed. "Your dad ever getting rid of that water?" she asked.

"Nope," he said. "He's not getting rid of the shovel he keeps on the roof of his car either, or throwing out the suitcase."

"Suitcase?" Dylan asked.

"He keeps an extra suitcase filled with water and granola bars wherever he goes," Sophia said.

"Don't forget the porta potty in his car," Ethan added, not looking up from the keyboard.

"If the world does fall apart, then your dad won't get very far," Sophia said.

Ethan looked up and frowned. He shut the computer.

"He's so out of shape. He's like become part of the couch," she said, laughing.

Ethan stood up quickly. "Let's get going."

"Where?" Dylan asked, following him out of the room.

"On an adventure. We're looking for a car I saw on TikTok," Ethan said.

Sophia sighed and slowly crawled off the bed to follow. Ethan was always on that app. She, on the other hand, had pretty much broken up with her phone. She'd deleted her social media apps and was loath to download anything—certainly not TikTok. It had taken a couple months to get used to it, but she felt lighter somehow now, free of this nagging pull on her brain to pick up her phone.

A few weeks later, she'd become engrossed in refurbishing the Datsun and her art blossomed in her mind. She'd made twenty-four pictures that she was really proud of—hours spent arranging chaotic sprinkles of objects atop of other images. The silhouette of a girl in silver velvet fabric mixed with cutout pictures of rusted hubcaps. She placed muddy hand-prints on it, along with a dollar bill.

Another piece sold for two hundred and fifty dollars at her mom's mediation tent: A giant canvas covered in torn maga-zine photos in the shape of a sports car. It looked as if it was spewing jagged snippets of magazine-model body parts. Eyes peered out from the tires, and painted skeletons scattered the bottom of the piece.

The three of them crammed into the Datsun, and Ethan sat in the tiny back seat, his knees up to his chin and his red hair brushing against the roof. He held his phone in between his knees, typing.

"What is it?" Dylan asked.

"It's a '68 Ford Mustang," Ethan said.

Sophia didn't respond.

"Does it have lotsa rust?" Dylan asked. He'd helped Sophia plenty of hours while she fixed up her car, and other days he'd just lie on the grass and stare at the clouds, listening to her while she worked.

"Rust?" Ethan squinted at the picture. "Looks like it."

"What about an engine? It's gotta have an engine."

"Nope. No engine." Ethan laughed and looked up at Sophia in the rear-view mirror. "Is that a problem?"

"That's a big, big problem." Dylan scrunched his face up.

"We'll put magic into it and make it run," Ethan said.

"Magic? Like, real magic?" Dylan asked.

Sophia grunted. She hated it when people distorted her brother's sense of reality. He may have had the body of a man, at age twenty, but he had the mental age of an eleven-year-old. One time, Morgan told him that if he ate macaroni and cheese, his face would turn bleach white. He still wouldn't eat it years later, even after Sophia told him Morgan was joking.

The car gurgled as it climbed the winding hill that led to all the wineries popular among tourists with little yapping dogs.

"I don't know about magic," Ethan said. "But we'll see what we can do about this car. With any luck, Soph here will help me build an excellent vehicle and, after graduation, I'll be outta here."

Dylan looked out the window. "I'd miss you."

Sophia didn't respond. She loved fixing up her car, but whatever Ethan had in mind would take months. And she had some more pressing things at play. Her mind settled on her mom, sitting on the bar stool at home, scanning the Internet for another job. She did the guided meditations in the tent out back, but only on weekends, and that wouldn't be enough. Sophia would have to pick up more hours at The Wheel. But with school, she wasn't sure how many more she could work.

Burying Eva Flores

She turned up the music—an indie band she recently discovered. The car wound around bend after bend on the dirt road, past horses and cows, stretching cottonwoods and waving tall grass. Dylan hummed along to the song.

They came to a brick house that looked like a mansion and almost glowed in the sunset.

Morgan came running out of the house in flip-flops and short shorts that revealed long, giraffe-like legs. She practically tumbled onto Ethan's lap. "God, it smells like my grandpa in here," she said.

Sophia's eyes flicked to her in the rear-view mirror.

"Hey Morg, we're hunting cars that we can fix up with some magic," Dylan said.

"Yeah, check out this car," Ethan said, showing her his phone.

"That hunka shit?" Morgan scoffed and looked out the window. "Whatever. I just need to get outta the house." She popped her gum. "Can you believe my mom is already planning a graduation party? It's like, 'You're done. Get out.'"

Morgan leaned forward to put her blonde head between the two front seats. "Your hair looks good, Soph. I still can't believe Eva copied you." She sat back in the seat. "So unoriginal."

Sophia touched the tips of her long hair and considered how Eva had even drawn a fake tattoo on her arm with pen, mimicking Sophia's own temporary tattoos.

"Map says to go left up here." Ethan pointed. "It's kinda far, but I stole granola bars from my dad's emergency suitcase, so let's do this." He chuckled, handing out the bars to his friends.

The ensuing conversation was sporadic and hard to follow.

Morgan leaned back on the seat. "You guys started that Spanish thing?"

"What color's the car, Ethan?" Dylan asked.

"Do you have to always talk about school?" Sophia asked.

"Calc, chem, that's all on—" Ethan said.

"No, I don't. But grades do matter," Morgan said, looking out the window.

"Matter in second semester senior year? *Right*," Ethan said, sarcastically.

The stereo had switched to an old country song that Sophia loved, and Morgan hated country. "Change the music, Grandma, 'kay?"

Dylan reached back and slapped her knee. "Morgan... Maybe we should play Bob Marley." He and Morgan had a unique kind of bond. Mostly it was about frogs. Dylan's favorite pastime was talking about or thinking about his Wax Monkey frog, Ted. Morgan was equally passionate about her African bullfrog named Bogart, and she would make dumb TikTok videos of her frog, where she'd hold up its arms and stand him on countertops to dance to Marley songs. She was actually pretty popular on the frog side of TikTok.

"Turn right on the highway," Ethan said.

"We're going out of town?" Dylan asked, a flash of stress wrinkling his wide brow.

"Do you think this car's gonna be any good?" Ethan asked.

"The assumption goes that if it's four hundred bucks, then it's gotta be crap." Sophia eyed him in the rear-view mirror. "But that's the point. Looks can be deceiving."

They drove for another ten minutes, bantering about The Wheel and social media memes and arguing about what song they should play next.

"This is taking forever. We should've gotten Subway," Ethan said.

Sophia thought he should've just strapped a feedbag onto his face; he was always eating.

Her stomach growled, too, but the thought of buying food elicited a tightening of her chest. She needed to pick up more shifts at The Wheel and eat less.

She pulled up to a stop sign and prepared to turn right onto the highway to find this hunk of metal. It would take way too much time to fix up any car for Ethan. But he wanted a way to escape his dad's sinkhole of fear. And this, she thought, gave him some hope.

Her phone lit up and, at the stop sign, she glanced and replied to a text message from her mom.

Mom:
Come home. Lots happening with the house. I'll fill you in.

Sophia:
whats up?

Mom:
We might have to move.

The sun dipped behind a cloud, and Sophia's heart dropped into her stomach.

5

Sophia

THE PURCHASE

Then: April 2

"Go right, go right," Ethan tapped on Sophia's right shoulder.

What happened to the house? Was there some sort of mold problem? Sophia turned right, as instructed, while her brain slowly worked to comprehend the news. She glanced down, dialed her mom twice, but she didn't pick up. She tried to get Siri to send a text to her mom, but the chatter in the car delivered a garbled message. *The creek away what's house music I don't like this song what's going on*

"It's just twenty minutes away. Ahhhh ... looks like it's at Anthracite Creek," Ethan said, looking at his phone.

"Down at the end of Kebler Pass," Morgan said, leaning over to look at the map.

Sophia's nerves wound tight around her chest. She zipped past the cows, the trees, the grass. She should go home. Where would they move?

"Hey, listen to this." Ethan tapped on his phone. "Did you know that Anthracite Creek was a mining settlement? Before that, a bunch of Indians lived there."

"Native Americans." Morgan kicked him.

"They were booted from the land," he said.

"They all were, dummy," Morgan said. "Our country calls it *relocation*. Which, of course, is bullshit."

"When's that?" Dylan asked.

"Late eighteen hundreds. But listen to this! This site says it's haunted."

Sophia's brain floated back to her mom. What did her mom mean? Why could they not stay in the house?

"Oooooh," said Dylan.

"Why would the car be *there*? There's nothing there," Morgan asked.

"No … there's that one caretaker's house and that new lodge they rent out for parties and weddings."

The car bounced and Ethan braced himself with a hand on the car ceiling.

Sophia thought of her mom, sitting on the bar stool with mascara lines on her cheek. She had no job. Would the rent jump? Maybe her dad could help? Where was he?

"Get this. Says a bunch of people have seen paranormal activity there," he said.

"Awesome. Let's check it out!" Dylan shouted.

"Like what?" Morgan asked. Her voice sounded tight.

"Ghosts, apparitions, voices…" Ethan said, reading from his phone.

Sophia shook her head slightly and gazed at the road. Her mind had finally sped back up to normal speed, and it was as if she had swallowed a gallon of caffeine.

Abruptly, she pulled over to the side of the road. "Don't have time, guys."

"What?" Ethan asked.

She flipped a U-turn right there on the highway.

"What're you doing?" Ethan asked.

"Yeah, what's going on?" Dylan asked. "I wanna see the car."

"Can't," Sophia said.

"What? Wait. No," Ethan said. "Why?"

"Soph, seriously?" Morgan bounced in her seat. "This is the most fun I've had in forever."

"More fun than frog videos?" Dylan asked.

"Never, Dyl. Frogs are cool."

"Why're you... What's so... It's just twenty minutes away." Ethan pointed over his shoulder.

"Something's going on with our house."

"Our house?" Dylan asked, a rumple of concern flashing on his face. "What?"

Sophia couldn't let him get worried.

"No big deal. Mom just wants to talk," she said, flashing an encouraging smile. "We're good."

"Okay," he said softly, looking out the window.

The car grew quiet. Sophia dropped off Morgan and then Ethan, who was subdued and sulky. When she and Dylan pulled up to their house, Sophia spotted her mom drinking a glass of red wine in a lawn chair in the tall grass. Her long dark hair blew in the breeze and a pair of round sunglasses covered most of her tiny face.

Sophia climbed out of the car and grabbed leftover trash from her car. Across the street sat a white Range Rover. There was only one of those in town, and when she saw blue hair in the driver's seat, her heartbeat spiked.

Sophia pretended not to see her, instead walking across the lawn towards her mother.

"Hey!" Eva's voice was unmistakable. Always louder than everyone else. Always kind of cringe. It was amazing to Sophia that she was somehow popular on social media and popular at school. She had a flock of people always following her around like little ducks. Sophia didn't get it.

"Good news!" Eva continued, as she waved and tumbled out of her car. "That lady Mrs. Ratno..."

"Mrs. Ratner?" Sophia corrected Eva before stopping and turning around to glare at her. The girl wore Toms shoes, ripped short jeans, and a simple black tank top. Beaded necklaces jangled across her breasts as she trotted closer. Why the hell was she there?

"Yeah, this is the weirdest thing," Eva said. "Mrs. Ranteno-whatever was put into some nursing home? Her kids came from Kansas and put her there because she got all senile." She rolled her eyes. "She's no longer in the universe if you get what I mean."

Sophia gazed at her, confused about why Eva would know Mrs. Ratner or her situation. And the crass way she spoke about her landlady irritated Sophia. Mrs. Ratner had always been so generous to her. Not just with money, but with time. She had shown Sophia and Dylan how to plant spring bulbs and let them earn money painting the house. She told them stories over cookies and hot chocolate about falling in love at age twenty with her husband, Bill, about traveling to Argentina, raising children, training for the New York Marathon, and more. Sometimes people forgot that old people were once young, too.

"She's gone?" Sophia asked. "Where?" The idea of not seeing her again felt crushing. She saw her at the house at least once a week.

"Some old person's home in, like, Carbondale?"

"Oh," she said. "Why are *you* here?"

"Because…," Eva said in a sing-song voice. "We bought your house!" She threw her hands out wide, as if Sophia had just arrived at a surprise party.

"We?" Sophia glanced at her brother, who leaned against the patio door, and at her mom, who sat stony-faced in her chair.

"My family. We're … we're buying it."

Eva owned her house. The news made Sophia feel as if she were falling down a dark well. She couldn't see straight, and blood rushed to her head. A weird feeling of impotence blanketed her insides. She gazed at Eva with heavy eyelids.

"Isn't that, like, so cool?" Eva looked at the clapboard house. "It has good bones. Told you."

So many more things flew into Sophia's head. *Well, if you couldn't buy Boulder, then come here and buy up Paonia. You're a regular old teenage tycoon. You stupid bitch.* Instead she just looked at Eva blankly and said, "Oh."

"There's good and bad news," she said with a fake pout.

Eva's parents should have been there to talk to Sophia's family, not *Eva*, their kid. *Why is she the one going around making these pronouncements like she's the newly appointed queen of Paonia?*

"Where's your dad?" Sophia asked. "Why are *you* delivering this information?"

"Manny? Home. He said I could tell you. Because you're my friend." She flipped her hair over her shoulder.

"No, I'm not," Sophia said.

"We *were* friends," she said, more hesitantly.

It was then that Sophia noticed yet another ink-drawn image on the soft side of Eva's forearm—same spot as Sophia's. And almost the same gargoyle design. "Remember? We hung out…"

"Until you decided to go spread lies," Sophia said. In October, Eva had just glommed onto Sophia, perhaps because she wasn't interested in her. And Eva needed everyone to love her.

Sophia began walking away from her, then turned back. "So what's your other news?" Her voice was flat, but her whole body felt like it was on fire.

"We're going to fix up your house and the place next door," Eva said.

Dylan did a fist pump and delight crossed her mom's face.

"But the bad news for *you*," Eva said, "is that my parents want to turn this place into a bed-and-breakfast."

The Flores File: Screenshot of Snap sent to Morgan from Ethan

April 9

[Photo showing the bottom half of Ethan's face—red hair, full lips, scruff on his chin. In the background, the back of the heads of three girls—Lydia, Eva, and Holly—can be seen standing in a line at The Wheel. Holly is shoving a muffin inside her mouth.]

Across the bottom of the photo Ethan wrote:

what if eva just disappeared

6

Eva

THE PRODUCT

Then: April 3

The bass drop thumped. Eva rolled her hips. Stepped forward. Backward. Right arm folded across her abdomen. Left hand extended toward the camera. She moved slowly, methodically, memorizing all the steps and counting out loud.

She stopped and replayed the thirty-second clip of "Don't Say Yes" at a slower speed to determine if each move hit the right beats. She had spent hours studying Jennifer Lopez dance videos, analyzing the best breakdowns to get ideas for moves. Three chest pumps. Two three-step turns. A bit of cha cha cha. Eva was out of ideas and couldn't move fast enough at tempo. Frustrated, she flopped back onto her white canopy bed, letting out a deep, disgusted sigh.

Closing her eyes, she tried to imagine what her old instructor Mrs. Whitcomb would have told her. It had been six years since she was forced to quit the modern dance competition team with Mrs. Whitcomb as her teacher, because her mom ran out of Grandpa's money. But Mrs. Whitcomb's stiff, high-heeled march, the one-two-three count, and the sound of terse hand claps stayed clear in Eva's mind. It was as if the woman continued to instruct Eva years later, like an imaginary friend. She'd wisp through the air, unseen, in a brown flowing chiffon cardigan and black leotard, and she'd push Eva to her edge, until she was breathless. She'd encourage her to be more refined, to smile, to have *fun*. Her invisible hand would touch Eva's shoulder blade now, remind her to keep her shoulders down, to emote with the music. She'd nod and remind her that she'd worked hard. She would gently push strands of hair out of Eva's face.

Eva slid off the bed onto the floor and banged her head gently on the wall—white with painted gold leaves and swirls —next to her. Then, she exhaled and imagined Mrs. Whitcomb's hand sweeping across her forehead, soothing her.

After a minute, she climbed off the floor and crept down the stairs to get a granola bar. She quietly opened the kitchen pantry door, removed one from a plastic storage basket, and hid it beneath her hoodie sweatshirt. Upon passing the master bedroom, she caught a glimpse of her mom standing in purple lacy underwear, flicking her straight dark hair over one shoulder and squeezing a bit of skin along her waist. She was gazing down at the skin, frowning, when she noticed Eva pass. She looked up.

"Look at this," her mom said. Eva stopped moving at the edge of the doorframe. Her mom frowned and wiggled the thin bit of skin between her fingers.

This was the moment where Eva was supposed to tell her that she wasn't fat. She had to tell her mom she was beautiful. If she didn't, her mom would pout, then ... the tsunami. The rage and the despair and the violence—the chase. "*What the hell did that mean?*" she would demand. "*You know you aren't so goddamn perfect yourself, you little bitch. Just wait for age to get you.*"

"It's just skin, Mom," she said. Appropriate response. True, her mom wasn't fat. She'd become so bony that her cheekbones protruded beneath the Botox and collagen injections. There was nothing fat about her.

"It's fat."

Eva flashed a fake smile. "Come on, Mom. You're perfect." She scurried past the doorway through the living room, eager to avoid a lecture about weight and beauty and anything else her mom believed would obstruct a girl from ever finding—and keeping—love.

"You better not be stuffing your fat face," her mother called to her. "Otherwise, you'll end up alone." She sang the last few words to her.

Eva paused. *You were never alone, Mom. You had me and my love before him.* Eva stopped mid-stride and gazed at the hardwood floor for a moment before responding cheerfully. "I'm not … eating, Mom," she sang. She touched her cheek with the tips of her fingers, trying to feel if her skin's softness came from youth or if she really was fat.

"And for god's sake, fix your hair."

With momentary hesitation, Eva removed the granola bar from inside her sweatshirt and held it up to read the nutritional label: 132 calories. Her stomach growled. She sighed and stuffed the bar into the back cushion of the green velvet chair.

She swallowed before tiptoeing past Manny's office to return to her room—one more challenge in the gauntlet of constant daily pressure. In her peripheral vision, she saw him pacing back and forth with white AirPods in his ears. "Hang on, Jeff," he said to the caller. He removed the AirPods and took a hurried step toward Eva.

"Hey babe." He tried for soft and gentle but sounded like a car salesman.

"Yeah, um … *Dad?*" He always wanted her to call him Dad. But it never felt right. He had come into her life two years earlier and never felt like a dad. Just a boss running her life behind what seemed to be a plexiglass wall. When he emerged from the other side of it, she always felt weirdly uneasy.

"Tonight." He pointed a finger at her. His face was only sharp eyes and thick, dark brows. "We need a collab session."

Her stomach clenched, and an invisible band squeezed her head. "Mom too?"

He shook his head. "One of those trunk party things. Oh. And you gotta get that next post out."

She pressed her lips together and nodded faintly before slipping away down the hall.

"I'm back," he said, resuming his conversation. He paused. "Listen, I gotta get a bigger number here. The girl has big influence."

As Eva climbed the stairs to her room, the pressure mounted. She needed to get her third video of the day finished and loaded. It had never been this hard when she started doing the dances just for fun, a year and a half earlier. She had maybe twenty followers back then.

She returned to her room, decorated straight from the pages of Pottery Barn Teen by her mom for "better video backgrounds." Eva flopped on her bed again and picked up her iPhone. She clicked on her TikTok account. In just a half hour, she had a hundred comments on her morning video.

She read the top one.

@babynative:
OMG get me a tutorial on this dance!

The video already had two hundred thousand likes.

She bit her lip and clicked over to her text messaging app, where she saw a series of new messages from Holly, Lydia, and at least twenty other faceless people she didn't really remember. She smiled. Dopamine tickled her head, and she rolled onto her back to read the first message.

Holly:
should i wear this h&m shirt?

Below, a photo of Holly, her silky white-blond hair falling over her tiny body in a navy blue crop top. She looked good. But Eva couldn't let her know that entirely. She replied.

Eva:
i love it
fits so much better than your other stuff

She clicked to the next message.

Lydia:
saw your post 🔥🔥🔥🖤🖤🖤🖤

While her mom feasted on perfection and her stepdad on money, Eva survived on adoration.

The Flores File: Video
Interviews
NOW

Rick Thomas (12th grade English teacher at Paonia High School): Every year, I try to make it interesting for my students. [Folds hands.] I vary the assignments based on who is in my class. And as time goes on, the demographics of our town … have shifted. And so, as a result, I have altered my assignments.

Morgan: Mr. Thomas thinks a lot of himself. But everyone knows his class was one step from a coma. He's like a walking Ambien. [Pauses, leans forward, and grimaces.] You *do* know what Ambien is. Right? Sleeping pill? [Satisfied, she smiles and leans back in the chair.] Yeah.

Madeline Hooper (former Paonia mayor and owner of Best Jams R Us): You want to know more about Paonia? We're tucked in here. Oh, so green. The pick-your-own peach farms. The wineries. The oh-so-lovely Mount Lamborn. It's just … well, let's say we're special.

Morgan: You talked to Mrs. Hooper, too? Oh, god. So yeah, she's, like, what? Plucked out of Maybury? We laughed that she thinks our town is, like, made by architects with angel wings. The reality,

though? [Clears her throat.] Okay. So, one side of the town is a bunch of hicks. I'm talking pickup trucks and gun racks. The other half of town are the rich kids whose parents are all woo-woo. You know, the Gwyneth Paltrow *Goop* types. No. Seriously. Nothing against them. But they've got those spacey looks on their faces all the time. Like someone sucked their brains out before they got here. [Makes her eyes big and tilts her head.]
They hold all these events in the old bookstore talking about past lives and sacred healing. [She lets out a loud guffaw.] The rest of us? Just normal. We're sandwiched in between.

Mrs. Hooper: Oh, some of those people like to talk about how they're drawn here because of the energy vortex. [Shakes her head. Pauses.] Silliness. Of course, yes, our historical records *have* mentioned that the Ute Tribes *supposedly* placed a curse on the white men who homesteaded here. But that's just hearsay. Why are you asking?

Holly Stephenson: First time I've heard that. About the curse. But it would totally make sense.

Mrs. Hooper: Of course, that's just hearsay. The curse and all.

Mr. Thomas: I recognized that not every single one of my students are college bound, so I give an option for the spring project. You could … do a variety of things. You could write any sort of literary project you wanted. Complete freedom, right? Some wrote newspaper stories about the school and so on and so forth. Sophia's project? Well. That did stir something up, didn't it?

Morgan: Told you, right? So fitting. We called him Mr. Ambien for a reason.

Ethan: Hated that class. Like half the time I never went. I picked to write a story. So did Soph.

Sophia: I don't really like to write. [Shrugs, looks out the window.] We were just trying to survive high school.

Ethan: Sophia? Her nose is behind a camera, covered in paint, or under the hood of that car. And the rest of the time, she was pretty much thinking about how to torture Eva Flores. [Waves his hands in the air.] I shouldn't have said that. It doesn't mean she killed her.

Sophia: Sitting in Ambien's class, the three of us, we were all just talking about what we could write about. Then Aidan Voinovich started saying all kinds of weird shit.

Morgan: He's the guy who might kill you at night. Totally. And after everything that happened, I *do* mean that.

Ethan: He just has that face. Like, eyebrows all drawn into his nose. Unibrow, really. The hunched shoulders. No words. Wore the same T-shirt with a cartoon of a dead, bloody cat with its head cut off. [Pauses and his eyes shift back and forth.] Is this on camera?

Morgan: And Mr. Thomas said we were a team. [Leans forward] Can you believe that? As if you need a team to write a story. I mean, we were supposed to do our own thing. And we did ... for a while. But thanks to Mr. Ambien, we got our very own Velcro Assassin sitting next to us every single day.

Aidan Voinovich (senior at Paonia High School): What'd they say about me? [He slumps in chair and crosses his arms.] It was all Sophia's deal. She got the ball rolling with that assignment, and I just ... finished it. I just saw what she was doing. They hate me 'cuz I'm smarter than they think. They thought they knew me... But... [Scoffs and looks away.] Sophia, Morgan, and Ethan? They were just three jerks who thought they were all better than the rest of us.

7

Sophia

IMAGINATION

Then: April 4

The afternoon sun shone through the window, warming Sophia's hair, and she rested her head on folded arms. Mr. Ambien paced in front of the class. She started to daydream again, imagining herself as Donna in the last *That '70s Show* episode she'd watched the night before.

"You'll need to be creative in how you present your project," he said.

Sophia wondered briefly: if she actually copied a storyline of a *That '70s Show* episode for this assignment, would Mr. Ambien even realize it?

The smell of watermelon Bath & Body Works spray filled her nose. That would be Lydia who dipped herself in that scent every morning. It didn't improve her personality, which was about as interesting as one of Morgan's frogs.

"You could write a comic book? You could present your story in video form? You could self-publish your own work online?" He smiled to himself, the whiff of moldy cheese floating as he passed. A couple of his stray nose hairs waved at Sophia as if they were arms extending from a dark cave.

"Shall we do some surprising things this semester when it comes to storytelling?"

His teaching style was filled with question marks. Ethan and Morgan used to mimic him when they hung out. *"You could steal me a six-pack of beer? Or make me a ham sandwich?"*

Sophia looked at Ambien, wondering how this project would ever make her a better person. How it would make her life easier.

"Can I do some art pieces?" she asked.

"Unfortunately, this isn't art class, Ms. Palmer. This is English."

Sophia rolled her eyes. She could've knocked out the project in a half hour if she could take photos and make a painting. This seemed like a project too easy for high school seniors, but that's the only reason why any of them took Ambien's class. Easy A.

"Divide into groups according to the list on the handout," he said, nodding to each of them with a prideful smile that said, *Am I not a genius?*

In their little circle, Ethan folded paper airplanes and Sophia drew cartoon gargoyles with big boobs on her notebook. Then Sophia smelled the familiar scent of Aidan Voinovich—sweat and feet.

Aidan was always weird. Ethan had said that in kindergarten, Aidan did things like eat plastic forks. He'd only grown more bizarre in middle school. Morgan said she once saw him holding a cat by the tail outside the pharmacy, and everyone knew that he now had a whole stack of empty prescription drug bottles in his locker for decoration.

"I'm going to tell a story with a cartoon," Aidan said.

Sophia didn't answer, focusing on her notebook paper, trying to think of how to start a story. "There's no way I can do this. I have no idea what to write," she said.

"I'll do a whole horror strip," Aidan said.

She didn't look up at him. But she could feel his gaze

heavy on her. He had a way of making you feel unsettled. Not necessarily in what he said or how he moved. It was his mere presence. Sophia had only known one other person like that in her life. And that was her dad's friend Ricky, who turned out to be a serious pedo and wound up in prison.

"Profound," Morgan said. Her voice was flat.

Sophia didn't even have to see it. She could feel Morgan's eyes roll. She could feel Aidan's scowl, though he didn't say anything more for a while. He was looking at his phone, then leaned back in his chair. "Yeah, and then…"

After a couple seconds of quiet, Sophia looked up. His dark hair fell in greasy chunks across his forehead. Two strands covered his eyes. The pause was so dramatic that everyone had stopped to look at him.

Aidan bared his top teeth. "I'll hang them comic strips on the front doors of all the people I hate."

Morgan grimaced with amusement. Sophia just gazed at him blankly, an expression she blamed on her mom: she'd do that without thinking. Not hating you. Not thinking much of anything. Just comprehension. But people always thought Sophia was going to beat them up.

"That's weird." Ethan said what was on all their minds.

"The best part? It'll be pictures of body parts," Aidan said. "Bloody body parts. That's *my* project."

The Flores File: Video Interviews
NOW

Ethan: Aidan. Did ya meet him?

Aidan: Hey, I didn't do nothing wrong. Sophia watched Eva. I watched her too, then I decided to watch Sophia.

Kayla Godfrey (sophomore at Paonia High School): The sheriff apparently talked to him and Riley. You want to find Eva? Get inside Aidan Voinovich's mind.

Aidan: The police got freaked out when Sophia told that story. About what I said that day in class. But I never said nothing about no body parts. I said I'd write a comic and then put the strip on peoples' lockers. She don't know what she's talking 'bout.

Morgan: We figured that was just Aidan trying to get attention. He's the guy who would brag about looking at porn in fifth grade. Every year, he'd try to say something more outrageous.

Sophia: That was some weird shit.

8

Ethan

THE JOURNAL

Then: April 5

Ethan could feel Morgan's anxiety as she stood next to him blowing her bangs away from her eyelashes.

"Why is Soph always late?" she asked, jiggling her knee. She huffed out a big puff of air again, but her hair landed back in her eyes.

"Why don't you just cut your hair?" Ethan asked, glancing up at her from his phone.

"*Glamour* said bangs are in. Very cosmopolitan."

Morgan stood on tiptoes and strained to find Sophia amid the snaking crowd of students who poured into school from the parking lot.

Ethan stared at his phone. "Did you finish *American Vandal?*"

Morgan ignored him. "I don't want to be late, but she's going to love what I have for her."

"Why are you always giving her stuff?" Ethan asked, glancing up. She was Santa all year. He leaned against the brick wall.

"Maybe it'll inspire her."

"I heard they were canceling it."

"What?" she asked.

"*American Vandal.*" He swiped through photos of the mock-umentary streaming series.

Morgan squatted on the ground and struggled with the zipper on her backpack before retrieving a large leather journal whose pages looked like they had torn edges.

Ethan looked at it, flicking his finger in its direction. "Why exactly are you giving her *that?*"

A quote was embossed on the book's leather cover: *If you want to change the world, pick up your pen and write.*

"She's so unmotivated for this project. Maybe she'll see she's a great writer."

"She likes cars. So you bought her a journal." Morgan always seemed to forget that Sophia knew what she liked and what she didn't—and that she didn't want anyone nudging her.

"No, it's handed down from my grandmother."

"Right." Ethan stuck a piece of gum in his mouth and squinted into the sun. The shrill sound of a bell blared over-head. Ethan shrugged one shoulder, as if he could wipe away the sound.

"There she is." Morgan pointed and Sophia strolled from her little car, the roof of which came up to her breasts. She wore jean cutoffs, an unbuttoned red-and-black plaid flannel over a black T-shirt, and black combat boots. The blue ends of her dark hair blew in the breeze. Her eyes hung half-mast. Her jaw set hard.

When she saw her friends, though, the hard veneer melted and she grinned, showing imperfect teeth. "'Sup?"

"I got you something," Morgan said, holding out the leather book. "Sorry I didn't wrap it."

"It's not my birthday." She gazed at Morgan blankly and didn't reach out to take it.

Morgan shrugged. "You need motivation if you're going

to get into MICA. It's not too late to apply for spring semester."

Ethan knew Sophia didn't want to go to Maryland Institute College of Art, one of the oldest art schools in the country. The tuition was out of reach. But Morgan had a laser focus on college and thought everyone needed to follow suit. She assumed that if they didn't go to college, then of course they'd get swallowed by the hole of ordinary, crap-paying jobs.

Ethan had been in The Wheel when the two girls had this conversation before.

"Why go to college for art, and run up debt, just to spend my life as a starving artist?"

"You need to go to college," Morgan had said.

"I can be a starving artist without the debt."

They all did that to each other. Morgan tried to nudge Sophia. Sophia tried to thwart Ethan's dad and his weird habits. Ethan nudged Morgan to be just a bit more irresponsible.

Clearly, by the look on her face, Sophia wasn't in the mood to be nudged. "Okay, thanks," she said, taking it and reading the inscription. "Cool."

"It was my grandma's."

"I saw that same book in a store in Carbondale," Ethan said, turning to walk inside. *"Grandma's" my ass.*

Morgan frowned at him. "I swear."

Morgan was known to stretch the truth, a characteristic that baffled her friends.

I literally break out in hives if I eat tomatoes. Ethan had made tomato sauce on pasta for her the next week, fed her red-sauce pizza, and then fresh mozzarella and tomatoes a few days later. No hives.

There was this taco place in Carbondale that literally had cockroaches running around the floor. Not true. No taco place. Ethan actually got Sophia to drive there just to see. They found out Morgan lied, but they didn't say anything to her about it.

This girl randomly gave me a hundred-dollar bill. For no reason. The girl had given her five bucks because she owed her money. Ethan was there.

My mom wins the local pie-baking contest every year. There was no local pie competition, and her mother was majorly allergic to the kitchen.

Morgan, however, wasn't as bad as her older brother, who was a true compulsive liar. If you told him you could ride a skateboard, he'd tell you he'd almost gone pro. *Oh, yeah. But then I hurt my wrist and I can't do it anymore.*

Morgan had good intentions. Ethan knew that. Sophia held the book out to look at it, flipping the pages.

Morgan was kind of stupid for giving them random stuff. Ethan wouldn't have done that if he had cash. But he didn't have a problem taking gifts from her. She had plenty of money, and he and Sophia didn't. Morgan once gave Ethan a really nice Patagonia down coat because it was too small for her dad. He loved it. But Sophia once told him it made her feel small when she couldn't return the favor.

"That's super nice of you," Sophia said, bobbing her head. "Thanks."

"I thought you could use motivation. You know. In Ambien's class."

Ethan rolled his eyes.

"Yeah." Sophia's voice sounded tight, like an ice pick.

"I'm just…," Morgan said, trying to explain.

Ethan poked at the book, and Sophia pulled it away, shoving it into her backpack.

"Well, thanks," Sophia said, bumping Morgan with her hip.

"Cool," Morgan said, a smile releasing with an exhale.

"Cool," Sophia repeated. They nodded before laughing together. "Hey. You're late."

Morgan looked like she'd been prodded by an electrical

poker. "Ahhhh man!" She turned, yanked the heavy metal door, and took off at a dead run down the hallway.

"Dude," Ethan said. "Why does she care so much?"

"Because she'll rule the world someday," Sophia said. The two of them meandered to their lockers.

Ethan gestured to Sophia's backpack. "You *do* know that's not her grandma's."

"Of course," Sophia said.

The Flores File: A TikTok posted by Eva Flores

April 5

[A selfie video of Eva wearing ripped jeans, a blue crop top, and a yellow plaid flannel. She's standing in front of Sophia's beige clapboard house, just outside the chain link fence. She motions to the house.]

Guys, I'm super excited because my family just bought this place in Paonia that'll soon be a bed-and-breakfast! Crazy thing is ... maybe it's karma ... but this house is actually now home to my biggest stalker, Sophia Palmer.

I guess... Things come around, right?

So, yeah, if you want to come check out my hometown, get into my world, find out where I spend my days and get my inspiration...

Then you gotta put this little town in Colorado on your list. It's awesome.

9

Sophia
OBSESSION

Then: April 5

Sophia walked around her room, brushing her hair, yanking the knots tangled near her neck. She'd tried to dye dark brown over the blue a couple months earlier, after Eva had copied the color. Ethan had just texted her the video of Eva standing outside her house. She must've recorded it early in the morning. The sun only shone on the sidewalk like that early in the morning.

Eva had stood right there on the sidewalk in front of her bedroom window and once again slandered Sophia in that perky voice. It made Sophia want to throw something.

"A bed-and-breakfast." Sophia growled, yanking on her hair. "As if that wasn't brutal enough. She had to go broadcast more lies."

Randolph leapt off the bed and hissed in response, as usual.

Sophia's mind skipped back to October, when Eva had first arrived at school. Everyone was abuzz at the fact that she was TikTok-famous, or microfamous, for the dance videos she did, smiling with perfect teeth, flipping hair, shimmying liquid hips. Sophia had watched some of the videos out of curiosity, but dancing wasn't her thing. Nor was social media.

While everyone else mimicked the dances in Eva's videos or watched similar ones for hours, Sophia spent hours on Craigslist looking at old cars. She'd slow down on roadsides where rusted-out Chevy trucks sat amid weeds. Sometimes she took close-up photos of the parts so that they took on a different identity: a rusted door with bits of turquoise and red paint looked like a swirling map of the ocean. A headlight looked like an eyeball and a grill the mouth of a mythical creature.

Somehow Eva had squirmed her way into Sophia's circle, taking interest in her art, after walking past the white tent out back one Sunday afternoon. Sophia begrudgingly showed her how to use acrylics and glazes to achieve different textures and dimensions on a canvas, and then Eva just started showing up all the time. Uninvited. Sophia didn't turn her away but didn't particularly look forward to the company. Morgan and Ethan were enough friends for her.

"This house is killer," Eva had said one day, "My mom wants a place right in town like this."

Sophia hadn't really realized what she meant back then. Eva lived in that house up on the hill with views of the mountains. Why would she want their piece of crap house in town?

Too many people like Eva had invaded Paonia in recent years. Of course, it brought people with money to buy her art and do her mom's meditations. But it also brought people like Eva, who floated in on white puffy clouds and peered down their noses in pristine sparkly clothes and faux-cheerful demeanor.

For several days in October, Eva appeared in Sophia's mother's meditation tent, where Sophia did her art. She'd hover above Sophia as she kneeled to photograph a pencil or a smudge of lipstick, and she'd asked questions. Questions. Questions. Questions.

"Don't you think the color is off?"

"What if you put chewing gum on it?"

"What're you trying to say with that piece?"

Sophia seldom responded, reticent before a person like Eva, who was a cardboard cutout of a girl.

One afternoon, Sophia tried to hide from Eva, avoiding the tent, and instead crawled under the Datsun to change the oil. But Eva somehow came around the house and trudged through the mess of old tires, rusty tractor parts, and barbed wire to find Sophia and her car in the far corner of the grass. Soon, she slid in next to Sophia beneath the car, smelling of bubble gum.

"What're you doing here?" Sophia had asked.

"Curious to know what's under here."

"Oil and dirt," Sophia said.

Fifteen minutes later, Sophia and Eva sat on the ground, leaning against the rusted and pitted car, not yet painted. Eva showed her an Instagram filter that made their two faces turn into a toad and a llama, and they giggled. "You should make a photo-painting-thing like this," Eva said. Sophia chuckled.

Eventually, Eva lamented about how hard it was to be famous on social media and how hard it was to be so popular at school. "Everyone wants to be me," she said, rolling her eyes. "The pressure is just…"

Sophia scoffed and stood up, dusting her hands on her torn jeans.

"You don't ever talk, do you, Sophia?" Eva asked.

To you, no, Sophia thought. She shrugged. "We don't have a lot in common." She paused and then went out on a limb. "Why do you come here all the time?"

"I like you." Eva pulled out her phone and pointed it at Sophia, who put away the oil can in the garage. She turned around and strode toward Eva, passing her to go back to the house.

"You *like* me?" Sophia snorted. "Hang out here for too long, and I'll make you change your mind."

The next afternoon, Eva showed up again like a hungry puppy. After a good ten minutes, she began making suggestions about how Sophia should sell her paintings in Boulder, should wear different shoes that matched her top, how she should wash her paint brushes differently, maybe cut her hair and go to a party Eva was throwing that night.

"Why don't you paint it yellow instead?" Eva asked, pointing at the canvas, which was clearly moody and dark, dotted with gray paints and red and black tire marks.

The constant chatter started to annoy Sophia.

"Why don't you follow me on TikTok?" Eva finally asked. She couldn't handle that someone wasn't interested in her.

Sophia shrugged with one shoulder. For Sophia, following people like Eva was stupid. She'd had the conversation with Ethan when Eva moved into town. "You either want to be like them, thinking they have a fantastic life, or you feel bad about yourself," Sophia had said. "It's just stupid."

"I'm actually one of the top-ranked—"

"Will you cut it out?" Sophia snapped. Then she pointed to the chair on which she sat. "This here? This is the artist's chair."

She pointed to Eva. "Your chair? That's the shut-the-fuck-up chair."

Eva's expression shifted, as if someone had shut off the power to her face, and she became stony.

The following day, Sophia was eating cereal at the table when a text popped up from Ethan with a link to a TikTok video.

Sophia had hit play. On camera, Eva, looking like a delicate elf, leaned into the camera, two hands on her cheeks. "Omigod, guys. I'm sorry I haven't posted in a while. I've had a little bit of a thing to deal with. Should I say this?"

Eva grimaced and sighed then reached up to rub her neck,

as if the stress was too much for her. "There's a girl at school, my new school, who kind of became all about me. And she's been stalking me. Sending me photos of weird art that she made." The video showed pictures of Sophia's art, photoshopped to include Eva's name with strange ugly hearts.

Sophia's skin had felt hot, and a vacant space filled her chest. Eva had made Sophia look like she was obsessed with her. *Why?*

"I'm only posting this so that maybe she'll leave me alone finally. Just so y'all know, so if something bad happens to me...," Eva had said to the camera.

Sophia had raged inside, her heart thumping like a hammer and a pressure building in her head. She leaned back in the chair, and the morning sun glared directly into her eyes. *That bitch. Why would she do that?*

"I just think ... everyone needs to get educated about stalkers, because it's not just people like me. If you all have had a scary experience, please comment below, and we can support each other and come together to be strong," Eva said dramatically.

A clip came on the screen of a video of Sophia walking in slow motion with that *look* on her face. Resting bitch face. That's what her mom called it. A bit of skin showed from under her T-shirt, and her stomach jiggled as she approached Eva. *Damn, I really am intimidating,* she had thought.

The next several months were even more painful than usual. Everyone thought Sophia had been fixated on Eva, and that she really had threatened her. By spring, it was kind of true. She *hated* that girl. She was a liar—fake, rich, entitled, and everything that Sophia despised. Now, she owned Sophia's home. Eva was the type who'd convince "Daddy" to kick Sophia's family to the curb, homeless. All because she didn't buy into fawning over her like the other kids did.

Now, inside her bedroom, Sophia returned from the memory and her stomach coiled tight, knowing that Eva wielded even more control over her life as her landlord. A roiling red rage flooded her. Sophia angrily pointed her hairbrush at Randolph, who sat in the corner of the room watching her. "I want revenge. I want control. I want Eva gone," she said. He scowled and slipped past her, out of the room.

Her phone buzzed with a text from Ethan with the picture of the junker Mustang.

Ethan:
its calling my name

Sophia:
its far

Ethan:
your my wheels

Sophia:
you need different wheels

Ethan:
thats why you take me
who knows, maybe there's money hidden inside the junker 😆

Right. If only wishes came true. She looked at the map. It was thirty minutes away. It was 10:30 p.m. Too late. She had to open The Wheel in the morning. She put down the phone and returned to angrily brushing her hair.

Her phone buzzed again. She sighed and picked it up. He was seriously annoying.

Ethan:
now now now now now now now

She smiled, paused for a moment, and then grabbed her keys off the table. She walked to her brother's room. "Come on," she said, motioning with her head.

A wide-eyed Dylan responded by immediately putting down his comic book and marching with her to the car. She hadn't told him where they were going, but he tended to always be game for hanging out with her.

They climbed into her car, and she sent a text telling Ethan and Morgan that she was picking them up. She could use a distraction.

The Flores File: Text messages obtained from Sophia's phone

April 9

3:30 p.m.
Sophia:
sometimes i imagine eva melting
she is ruining everything

Ethan:
Lol me too

Morgan:
she's not that bad

Sophia:
she will destroy me

Ethan:
she'd prob stab u a thousand times then wash her hands then do a
tiktok vid

Sophia:
omg
i fantasize about evil things

Ethan:
but she's got dope hair

Morgan:
facts

Sophia:
she stole that hair
shes evil

10

Sophia

ANTHRACITE CREEK

Then: April 5

A breeze whipped through the moonlit valley, and Morgan rubbed her arms. "This place's got a weird vibe," she said.

Beyond the meadow, the stark rocky Anthracite Peak loomed large.

"Where's this car? At this guy's house or what?" Sophia asked, tucking her hands into the pockets of her sweatshirt and craning her neck to look.

The four of them strode through the tall grass toward the creek, which was gushing with spring runoff.

"Remember that website *did* say this place was haunted," Morgan said, rubbing her arms. Sophia was surprised Morgan even came with them—not only because her parents usually freaked if she was out late at night but because she hated ghost stories and horror movies.

"I don't see the car," Dylan said, scratching his head and scanning the terrain.

"What's the curse, again?" Morgan asked.

"That's just a story," Ethan said, waving his hand.

Sophia was glad they had come. She wanted to find the Mustang. It'd be good to get into another project to survive the rest of high school and forget about Eva.

"I think we paddle-boarded through there." Sophia pointed at the rushing river, revealing fingers with chipped black nail polish.

"Looks cold," Dylan said.

Ethan looked down at his phone. "Looks like we follow that curve down by the creek."

"Did he say that it was at someone's house? Or just a junker on the side of the road?" Sophia asked.

"This won't take long, right?" Morgan asked. "What's the curse say, Ethan?" She slowed her pace.

"Stop." Sophia's voice cut the air. She didn't want proof that her friend was a coward.

Morgan dropped the conversation, and they made their way through the tall, dead grass. Gray wispy clouds cast dark shadows on the ground.

"He said the car was *not* at the *Whiteman* lodge," Ethan said. "Whatever that is."

"That it?" Sophia asked, pointing to what looked like an enlarged Lincoln Logs house. It looked brand-new, and she'd heard that it was intended to be some resort for rich tourists who wanted to taste the "authentic, rustic West." Yet it sat empty, with dark windows.

Morgan shrugged. "Guess."

They passed it and walked into an open field, along the creek.

"God, we shoulda brought Doritos," Ethan said, lumbering behind. "I'm starving."

"You're such a gourmand," Morgan said.

"What?"

"Someone who is extremely fond of eating. Vocab word."

Sophia pointed at the water's edge. "Look!"

She climbed through the two wooden rails of a dilapidated split-rail fence and stumbled through an open space, past a rusted wagon wheel and patches of weeds. A wooden structure sat a hundred yards away. It looked like an old shed.

"Who's that?" Dylan pointed to the field, where a shadowy figure stood nearby. Sophia squinted to make out the person amid the dim light. Tall, lanky. Maybe something on its head?

"Mister!" Sophia yelled. She turned to Ethan. "What's his name?"

He shrugged and cupped his hands to yell. "Hey, you the guy selling this?"

They jogged toward him, but like a mirage, the man seemed to dissipate the closer they came. Breathless, they arrived at the shed.

"Okay, now I'm freaked out. Where'd he go?" Morgan asked.

"Hello?" Ethan asked, craning his neck to look for the man.

"Weird." Sophia searched the area but could see no one. There were no big trees or buildings besides the shed to hide behind. Ethan slowly circled the slanted shed, about the size of a one-car garage.

Sophia pointed at the shed and mouthed the words silently. "Did he go inside?"

Morgan and Dylan hung back, while Ethan knocked on the wide barn door of the shed. "Uh, sir? You said we could come by ... even though it's late..."

The wooden boards, blackened and rotted in some places, hung like loose teeth from the roof, leaving gaping holes in the walls. Ethan swung open the door, and it made a high-pitched creaking sound. He leaned into the dark opening. "Sir?"

He pushed the door open wider, revealing the Mustang, looking like an old boxer who had lost his last fight. Bruised, toothless, rusted, and broken. A dent the size of a bowling ball scarred the hood. Patches of orange rust covered the doors.

The windows were broken and the tires were flat. Sophia grimaced.

"There she is!" Ethan said cheerfully.

"*That's* why we came?" Morgan asked. "Puh-leeze."

"Is that guy in there?" Dylan asked, peeking over Sophia's shoulder. There was no more room for anything but the car in the shed.

"Sir?" Ethan asked.

No response.

Sophia didn't know if it was even worth saving. "Maybe…" She circled it slowly, touching chipped blue paint, peering carefully through the jagged glass.

A deep voice shouted and Sophia jumped, backing into the crumbling wooden wall. Ethan's laugh roared, and he bent over. "Dude, you shoulda seen your face."

Angry, she walked over to Ethan and punched him several times in the shoulder. Hard. "Don't. Ever. Do. That. Again." He continued to chuckle.

"Yeah, sis, you looked so funny," Dylan said, laughing along with Ethan.

"Sorry," Ethan said through the last bits of laughter. "I couldn't resist. I half expected the dude to be lying down in the back seat with a chainsaw."

"That was super lame, E," Morgan said. She still stood outside the shed with arms across her chest. "Can we go yet?"

Sophia poked her head inside the car. It had no steering wheel, no back seat, and the dash looked like someone had ripped it apart with a crowbar.

"Needs a lot of work. A lot," she said, standing up straight. "I'm not sure it's worth…"

Ethan waved his hands. "Let's do it."

"It'll cost a ton in parts, and I don't even know if I'm capable—"

"It'll be so cool, Soph," Dylan whined.

"We're getting it. It's calling my name," Ethan said. He smiled and nodded at the car.

"Guys, it's late, and I'm getting nervous," Morgan said.

Ethan stood up straight and the four of them ducked out of the shed. Above, the moon shone brightly, revealing the anxiety that blanketed Morgan's face. When he closed the door, the walls and roof rattled.

"We can't get it. There's no buyer here," Morgan said, walking with stiff legs a few yards back toward the car.

"Did you even bring cash?" Sophia asked. "We'd have to figure out how to get it outta here. A tow truck and that could cost a lot—"

"Cash is in your car. Let's go get it."

The four of them ran across the open field, partly to hurry, partly in a playful race.

When Sophia came to the broken wooden fence, she climbed through the two rails and stumbled through an open space, angling to take a shortcut. Giddy, although not entirely sure why, Sophia briefly turned around to taunt them—and caught her foot on a root. Surprised, she pitched forward, and from knee to hip to breasts to cheek, she fell flat into a patch of cattails and thick, boggy black mud.

She let out a yelp, and as she did, clouds swept across the full moon, casting a dark shadow across the space. Cool air washed across the field.

The three of them gasped, and Ethan let out a bellowing laugh and leaned onto the fence to watch Sophia thrash in the mud and cattails, scrambling to get up.

"Nice one." He grinned and rested a foot on the bottom rung of the rotted fence. The board creaked and then snapped, and Ethan lurched forward.

Sophia climbed to her knees, covered in black stinky mud. "What the hell?" She got to her feet, standing with her fingers splayed and mouth wide open.

Any other girl would have squealed with whiny disgust.

But Sophia just laughed. She laughed so hard, a low-pitched *huhhhh-hhh-hhhuuuhhh,* that she almost peed her pants.

She doubled over and mumbled, "What the hell." She repeated the words over and over, dumbfounded by what just happened.

Ethan and Morgan chuckled as Sophia waddled back to them. They backed away from her. "Takes skill to fall on such flat ground," he said.

"Yeah…," Dylan said in a low laugh.

"So. Gross," Morgan said.

"Dude, I can smell you from here. What is *in* that mud?" Ethan asked.

"I'm gonna beat your ass, E!" She stumbled after him, arms outstretched like a zombie. He ran backwards away from her, laughing and pointing.

The three others made their way back to the car, keeping their distance from Sophia.

"I need a bath," Sophia said.

"After I buy this Mustang," he said, marching past her toward the car.

"E… dude. I can't stay like this." She gestured to her face, one side of which was covered in mud.

"Yeah, we should probably go home," Morgan said.

"Soph… Maybe if we wait, he'll show up?" Ethan asked.

"E… come on," Sophia said, gesturing to herself. Ethan tilted his head, annoyed.

After a long exhale, his shoulders dropped. "Fine," he said, defeated.

"Promise, we'll come back later," she said.

"You get in the hatchback. I'll drive," he said, stepping further away from her.

"You'd have to drown me in mud before you drive that car! Morgan, you drive." He didn't even know how to drive even though he was old enough. Another one of his father's fears: *what if* his son got killed in a car accident.

Sophia cackled, and a chunk of muddy hair flung across her face. She flicked it back over her shoulder and ran awkwardly after him. A breeze whipped past as she stumbled down the dirt path.

When she stopped to catch her breath, she thought she caught movement near the swollen river, and she felt the heavy gaze of someone—or something. The feeling unzipped something in her chest, that unsteady feeling of stepping off a tilting ride.

"Hurry!" Ethan yelled.

Unsettled, she unsuccessfully tried to wipe off her hands on her mud-soaked jeans. A shiver drew up her spine, and she sprinted to catch up.

The Flores File: Video
Interviews
NOW

Madeline Hooper: Well, I really would prefer to talk about Paonia. Because our economic development is quite impressive. We've got the wineries. The orchards. All this, with twenty-seven churches. Oh, and you've got the hemp people, the crystal people, and that reflexology stuff.

[Sighs. Pinches her lips together.] Well, I suppose I can tell you there is one area around here that the kids have been chatting about since the whole Eva case. It's an area right where the North Fork of the Gunnison River meets Anthracite Creek. It was the base for a mining operation a long time ago. Well, apparently there is more paranormal activity there than any place else in Colorado. Or so I've read. That's all I know.

Rick Griffith (local historian): White people like to honor the white people who settled these lands. But they basically came in and stole land from indigenous people. In this case, it was the Ute Tribe that spanned Southern Colorado up to Wyoming.
The white man came in, planted their towns here, established mining operations, and started farming land. The Utes lived in this valley for two thousand years, and they were peaceful.

Then the white man came along and tricked them, got them to sign a treaty that they thought meant they would share profits from their land. But instead, the white man stole their land and sent them to reservations in southern Colorado.

Madeline Hooper: Paonia is a terrific town. I don't think any of the stories are real.

Rick Griffith: The story goes that Chief Colorow was so angry that the tribe set fire to the entire valley and set a curse that the white man would never have success here. Any success would be met by a downfall. Mines in nearby Redstone went bankrupt. The people who bought the land along Anthracite Creek died in strange ways. They went off cliffs on the rocky pass. They just dropped dead inside their homes.

Star Caperson (a psychic medium): The spirits of the Ute chiefs still stand atop the cliffs, looking down on the valley, and oh let me tell you, they're mad. I see them sometimes up there. Their spirits. We need to make it right for them. People who stay in the new lodge down there say doors slam at night, lights flicker. But I have seen those spirits with my own eyes.

Madeline Hooper: Oh, those psychics in town will tell you stories. That Star Caperson? Oh, she's a character. Big curly hair. The bracelets.

Rick Griffith: Would you blame them? Of course the spirits—if they're really there—are angry. The whole history of Paonia talks about the settlers and refers to the ousting of native Americans simply as "the government relocating" them to reservations. There was bloodshed there. Lots of it.

Riley Neuman: Yeah, I heard Sophia and Ethan talking about Anthracite Creek at The Wheel. [Pauses.] But she never said anything about a curse. All I know was that she was *so mad* that Eva was buying her house. Just wouldn't shut up. They for sure went there one night. Probably to plan where they'd kill Eva.

Ethan: Riley? Yeah, she probably heard us. She's got ears as big as a rat.

Madeline Hooper: The kids apparently started going up to that spot in the valley after this whole Eva thing. They would go drink and have raucous parties. It was just a terrible, terrible thing.

Star Caperson: I am sure the curse was passed on somewhere. Until we rectify things.

Riley: I think that's just where Sophia buried the body.

Aidan: Police checked my phone to see if I went to Anthracite Creek. Of course I did. They knew that, and all. Sure, I got in the middle of that stuff, but I had nothing to do with no body getting buried there.

Ethan: There was no body buried there. Period.

11

Sophia
YOUR NAME IS MUD

Then: April 5 11:45 p.m.

Sophia's sneakers squished as she tiptoed along the linoleum floor of the dark entryway of her house. She hoped her mom had already gone to bed, because she'd been wound since she'd lost her job. While other people might mope around in pajamas all day looking for jobs on the computer, she was not that kind of unemployed woman.

Her mom woke every morning at six, went for a five-mile run, showered, and then dressed, putting on a full face of makeup and one of her best dresses. She would go to the park to look for jobs online and make phone calls from a sunny bench. "I'm not hiding away like some nobody," she'd told her daughter. "That jerk isn't gonna keep me down."

Sophia knew, though, that money was tighter than normal. They didn't have Internet or cable anymore. Her mom had a little bald patch on the bottom back of her head —which meant she'd been stressed out and tugging again.

"You stink!" Her brother said, scooting away from her. Scooting away from her, the outline of his hulky frame barely visible in the dark. She imagined his face was scrunched and his fingers plugged his nose.

"Still?" She looked down at herself before chuckling low. She looked like something out of *The Walking Dead*.

"It's bad," he said in a nasal voice, plugging his nose. "Better when the car window was rolled down." Then her brother sat on the sofa across the room, watching her. "I hope Ethan gets the car." His voice was still nasal.

"Maybe," she said.

Then he just stared at her with his mouth gaping.

"You getting me a towel or something?" She slipped off her shoe, and Dylan dashed to the bathroom. He returned with a tattered beach towel imprinted with a giant cartoon SpongeBob.

She grabbed it from him and sopped up the mud from her foot. She slowly stripped, and Dylan turned away and returned to his room. "Thanks for the fun, sis."

With her jeans around her ankles, Sophia lost her balance and slipped to the floor, landing on a pile of books, papers, and a wadded-up T-shirt.

She cried out, scrambling to her knees to stand, and eventually she stripped to her underwear and walked to the bathroom to shower.

It wasn't until the next morning that she noticed the streaks of mud across the open leather journal that Morgan's grandmother had or had not given her. She stood at the door with her backpack slung over one shoulder, and with a granola bar hanging out of her mouth, she let out a frustrated groan. She had tossed her wet muddy clothes on the open journal the night before, and now she leaned down and picked it up, cleaning off the streaks that scarred the embossed leather.

Squatting, she flipped through the pages. Mud stains marked many of them.

12

Sophia

INSPIRATION

Then: April 6

Ambien's face melted in front of Sophia's eyes. Or at least that's what she imagined as he paced through dust particles visible in a streak of sunlight.

First, his face would melt, so the drone of his voice would stop, then he'd dissolve into a paste that would sit in the corner of the room for the rest of the school year. She hated the way he spoke, the way he tried so hard, the way he wanted so badly to be liked. She didn't care if anyone liked her.

One time Sophia's mom had asked her if the girls at school liked her.

"The question is, do *I* like *them*?" Sophia had replied.

"We, as humans, think in metaphors," Ambien said, pacing back and forth. Eva and her twins, Holly and Lydia, sat in front of the room, diligently taking notes.

"We learn through stories," he said. "As Tahir Shah, author of *Arabian Nights* said, 'Stories are the communal currency of humanity.'"

Ethan leaned into Sophia. "Or a stupid assignment just to graduate."

She smirked.

"Perhaps this class, this assignment, offers you the most freedom you'll ever have in high school? Perhaps it gives you the chance to create your own reality?"

Ambien paced again into the light, his hands in his pockets, a wannabe professor gazing thoughtfully outside at the sunburnt lawn.

"After all, we all tell stories in our heads about ourselves and the world. Do you tell yourself stories about me? Why am I the way I am? What it's like to be inside my head? Maybe, you tell stories about how other people perceive you? Or why they do what they do?"

Yes, Sophia thought. *You were born talking about nothing. And I'm constantly jealous of all the people who haven't met you.*

While Morgan took notes, Ethan sat next to her, drawing on his notebook. He scrawled the words, *the questions! questions!* And then he drew a really bad cartoon of a guy tearing out his hair.

Ambien walked down the aisle, passing first Eva and her twins. Catching a glimpse of the girls made Sophia's ears burn hot. *She bought my house.*

Eva had swiveled in her seat to follow Ambien with her gaze when she caught Sophia's eye. Eva flashed a smug smile and twirled her pen.

The memory of Eva's cheerful words in her recent video rang in Sophia's head. The saccharine smile and fake pout. The lies that spun so easily from her lips. Her joy in stabbing Sophia one more time. *"Crazy thing is ... maybe it's karma ... but this house is actually now home to my biggest stalker, Sophia Palmer. I guess ... things come around, right?"*

Hatred seethed inside Sophia. *Things sure will come around, Eva.*

She let her imagination go. *They're back at The Wheel when Eva's blue hair catches on fire and she runs around the cafe, screaming. Sophia stands behind the counter, next to a sink with a long sprayer hose.*

Sophia picks up a glass, turns on the sink … and pours herself a glass of water. She takes a long refreshing gulp and watches Eva burn.

As Ambien approached, Ethan slowly slid his hand across the page to cover his drawing. Ambien was so close to their desks that Sophia could practically feel the rumpled fabric of his khaki pants, could smell the scent of his coffee breath, could hear his nose whistle when he paused.

Ambien turned on his heel, strode to the white board, and scrawled out the word *Einstein.*

"Einstein, the greatest thinker of all time, once said that imagination encircles the world," he said. "The great composer Richard Wagner said, 'Imagination creates reality.'"

For a moment, she let herself forget about the house, Eva, people like Hendy. She wouldn't ever admit this to Ethan—because if she found an ounce of anything worthwhile in Ambien's class, he would basically consider her as big a loser as their teacher was—but something Ambien said did inspire her.

She thought about the sense of power she felt with her car, in taking a rusted hunk of metal and making it new again. She thought about the satisfaction she'd felt in making art when things felt overwhelming, when her dark anger swirled between her ears and she wanted to break things. Instead, she picked up items that other people might toss in the trash—a ribbon, a bottle cap, an old Vietnam patch—and arranged the random chaos to her liking. The mouth-watering click of the camera shutter. She took the chaos of her mind and made it into something visually appealing in art. Maybe that's how she'd get through this project. She'd take it seriously. She'd write a brilliant story that let all of her emotion and distrust, her anger and hate, pour onto the pages. She would not write for the reader but rather for *her,* the writer.

She took her pen and, in the middle of the first page, still streaked with mud, she copied the quote: "*Imagination creates reality.*" And then underlined it three times.

Wicked Games

BY SOPHIA PALMER

The leaves swirled around Elsa Flotas' feet, as she pulled up the fur collar on her long trench coat. Her dazzling blonde hair hung down her back, and it swished in the blustery wind. The hair had partly made Elsa a star in this town. Parisian hairdressers had flown in from overseas to shoot her in photos, and girls across the city began to mimic her style. She'd been cast in advertisements and selected to star in the latest online movie.

Elsa came from a long line of creatures called The Invasors, who would travel to new lands and build their castles and enrich themselves at the expense of the ordinary people, called the Domestici, who lived there first. The Invasors would steal their land, steal their identities, lie to them and convince them to bow down and worship them. As an Invasor, Elsa's life was charmed.

As she ducked in the wind, swirls of leaves swept up her legs and body, and crowds of Domesticis passed her, stopping to revel in the glow around her. She seemed magical to them. And a handful of them, clad in meager clothes with thin, worn coats, bowed down on one knee. Their pant legs wet from the damp leaves and city trash.

Elsa would leap high and dance for them, generating a silvery stream of dust, and they knew if they could capture bits and pieces of those starry dust particles, it would make them glow too, just for a moment.

As she walked up to her home, a brownstone building that looked almost golden in the dim sunset, there were only three passersby who did not stop and revel in her beauty. They didn't bow down either. They stood cracking their knuckles, wielding clubs and scissors. They had been scorned by her, they knew what she really was, and they were determined to reveal the true essence of the queen to the people of the streets. One of them went by the simple name of Jane.

Elsa was too focused on her own glory to notice them, to remember them. They were invisible as she walked past. Elsa never dared wear a crown, for it would be too ostentatious. Instead, she sought to look like the commoners. Months before, she had set her sights on an artist in the crowd, the girl named Jane. She watched Jane day in and day out. She began dressing like her, asked her to come to her brownstone, where in the attic, she commanded Jane to paint Elsa's portrait, promising her she could pay her well if she liked it.

Jane wasn't sure why Elsa had picked her in particular because she wasn't the most talented artist in the land. She wasn't the most beautiful or interesting either. She was simply disinterested in Elsa. She painted the portrait but it wasn't to Elsa's liking.

Elsa said the nose was too big and the colors were wrong. Jane refused to fix it because it was a genuine depiction of Elsa's true nature, not just what everyone else saw on the outside. Elsa screamed at her, and was cutting and ruthless.

In the pouring rain, Jane now sat on the sidewalk outside with her two friends, baffled by the turn of events. She had only been honest with this queen.

Later, her bafflement turned to anger, and Jane cast a wicked spell on Elsa before trudging down the street to her home, which was but a small box tucked in by the trees. She knew that Elsa would have her due. Karma would come to her in Jane fashion.

The Flores File: Video Interviews
NOW

Sheriff Rawlings: Senior Bust is illegal. Period. We look for all the signs of when the party is going to happen. Where, when, all the details. We try to get on it. But it's different every year. This, apparently, was where the whole Eva case stems back to.

Ethan: I don't know who organizes it. But every year, word comes down about where the campout will be. My freshman year, I guess they all drove to Utah for the night. So it just depends.

Lydia: Biggest night of senior year. *Biggest.* My older sister? She said her Senior Bust was lit. Like, they jumped off of a forty-two-foot cliff into this lake. They were all on molly, jumping over the bonfire. She told me all about it. After that, I counted the days until spring for our Senior Bust.

Morgan: That stuff honestly scares me.

Lydia: Everyone figured that Eva put it together. But if she hadn't, it would have been way cooler than what it was. It was kinda lame.

Holly: Uh, can you say drama?

Ethan: Lydia's sister's class? Crazy into drugs.

Lydia: Actually. Ours sucked.

Holly: I honestly don't even remember what happened with Eva that night. I was pretty out of it.

Lydia: Holly messed up that night. That's all there is to it. I don't even talk to her anymore because of Senior Bust.

Sheriff Rawlings: Underage drinking, as we always suspect. We gathered that there was some sort of altercation with Ms. Palmer.

13

Sophia

SENIOR BUST

Then: April 7

M organ shook the tent like it was a bedsheet over a slanted piece of earth. "I can't believe we finally get our own Senior Bust."

"Geez, Morg," Ethan said. "Look at you—you don't even know how to put up a tent. How'll you ever put a drone on Mars?"

"It's got to have directions in the bag-thingy," she said slowly, frowning at the blue fabric blowing in the breeze.

"You're telling me that after all those times we went camping, you still don't know how to put up a tent?" Sophia asked, taking it from her hands. She ran aluminum tubing through the eye hooks of the tent.

"I never put it up."

"You never put it up," Ethan deadpanned.

A gust of wind swept through the small clearing among the tall waving pine trees, sounding more like a highway than nature. They'd found a spot high up in the hills, far outside of town, so that the cops couldn't find them and break it up like last year.

"No, you guys always put it up."

"That's not true," Sophia said. Her voice was quiet, distracted, as she focused on managing the flapping nylon material. A handful of other kids shouted to each other, walking through their tent space.

"This is a good one," said Phillip Hackett, pointing to an area just ten yards away. He wore a backwards red baseball cap, and a rifle stuck out of his backpack.

"Too flat," his friend Cam Houge responded. He steamrolled through the forest, carrying a backpack and cooler. From the back, he was only a hooded camo rain jacket and knobby legs.

"No, I did other stuff. Like, usually I stack the firewood," Morgan continued. "That's my job."

"She does stack firewood really well." Sophia nodded and swiftly put together the rest of the metal frame.

"Seriously good," Ethan said, putting up his own tent next to her. "Isn't it in the official American Camping Rulebook that each log can only take up four-point-six inches of space?"

"With a centimeter gap—"

"Shut up. This is Senior Bust. My last time," Morgan said. She put her hands on her hips. "You can't make fun of me. 'Cuz it doesn't even matter."

She sounded genuinely hurt. And if she were anyone else, Sophia would be ruthless. But she loved skinny Morgan and honestly appreciated her attention to detail, even if she never expressed that endearment. While Sophia wanted rough edges and mismatching chaos, Morgan needed clean lines and direction. Sometimes Sophia wanted that too, but she couldn't bend herself into someone else to get there, to be that. Plus, she didn't have the high-strung parents hovering over her shoulder, pushing her to go somewhere in life. She had her complicated mom, who was awesome and flawed, but as Morgan said, *easy.* She expected Sophia to find her way, and she gave her room to do whatever. That probably gave her the kind of confidence that Morgan didn't really have but needed.

"Where's the marshmallows?" Ethan asked, looking around.

"I don't get it," Sophia said. "Why would it not matter, Morg? Is this the last time you're *ever* going to camp?"

"Yeah, for sure."

"Please tell me you brought them. I swear I saw them…"

"What?" Sophia asked Morgan, ignoring Ethan.

"The marshmallows," he persisted. "They were in the car."

Again, Sophia ignored him and focused on Morgan. "What'd you mean?"

"Never ever, ever again," Morgan said, sitting on a rock to watch as Sophia attached the final piece of the tubing and then hammered in the stakes.

"That's gotta be a lie." Not enjoying camping was sacrilegious to Sophia. The mountains were part of her soul.

"I'll be in the city. Some big city. I'll wear, like, high heels and Gucci. I won't have to do this stuff."

"You'll never have excitement like tonight," Ethan said. "'Cuz tonight's gonna rock."

"Please tell me you didn't bring drugs," Morgan said, rolling her eyes.

"Naw, but those guys probably did," Sophia said, nodding to Chris Piirto and Amanda Toch. They were sitting on a rock digging into their backpacks and counting out loud.

"I thought this was supposed to be bonding," Morgan said. "But everyone's all grouped up." She waved her hand, irritated. "Just like normal. We're supposed to … you know. Have all of us. It's in the rules."

"There are no rules. Just tradition," Sophia said, finishing up the tent and wiping her hands on her pants. She still had mud beneath her fingernails from the other night.

Eva and her twins trudged up the hill. It was about a mile or two in from the cars, and Sophia had secretly hoped that Eva wouldn't have made it. Begrudgingly, Sophia wondered if maybe Eva was stronger than she thought.

"We're heeeeere!" Eva shouted. "Let's get this party started."

She dropped her backpack on the ground and turned on a speaker that played an irritating pop song that was overplayed everywhere, then began doing one of her favorite dances. Her hips moved like Jell-O, rolling, followed by swift shoulder rolls and hand claps. Holly and Lydia jumped in, followed by six more girls who were cheerleaders. Eva pouted her lips, then smiled, making wide surprised eyes as she moved—a true entertainer.

Sophia rolled her eyes and turned away. She was so over it. Wherever Eva went, it was a show. Riley had once mentioned that Eva made something like twelve thousand dollars per video, especially sponsored posts. A cosmetics brand had paid her to *drive to Target and pick out makeup for back to school this year.* The video blew up, and Sophia didn't get why.

"I don't know how she moves like that," Morgan said, tilting her head and frowning. "It doesn't make sense. From a physics point of view."

"Don't even think you could move like that," Ethan said.

"Neither could you," Morgan growled, glancing at him.

"I could, but I don't want to."

"Will you two stop bickering?" Sophia said. The bite of her tone shut them up.

Eva continued to dance while two boys set up her tent and sleeping bag right next to the fire.

"Maybe I really should learn how to dance," Morgan said, still watching. "I mean, then I'd have boys around to carry my stuff and put up my tent."

"You've got Sophia. No dancing necessary," Ethan said, sitting down on a rock.

Cam came back from the trees, carrying a twenty-four pack of beer. "A buck if you want one," he said. He was a toothpick with braces.

Ethan raised his hand and handed him a ten-dollar bill.

"You're going to drink ten?" Morgan asked.

He took his beer, reached across Morgan, and handed one to Sophia. She cracked it open and relaxed in a red camp chair.

"Is this what we're doing all night?" Sophia asked, pointing. "Watching the dance show?"

"Watch 'em or join 'em," Ethan said, before standing up and joining the crowd with his own moves. Morgan shrugged and got up too.

Sophia stayed put, staring at Eva. First the girl had ruined her life; now she was ruining a senior tradition.

The molly came out that night, and so did a wide range of alcoholic drinks, and after several hours, the senior bonding began in full force among most everyone—except Sophia, Ethan, and Morgan. They stood back and observed the traditional contest of jumping over the campfire—Phillip Hackett nearly tipped over backwards onto the flames. His red and brown flannel and his long ponytailed hair looked singed, but he didn't seem to notice.

Chris and Amanda, who'd been together since seventh grade, spent hours on the ground, attached at the mouth. Holly and Lydia constantly smushed together, squealing, for gooey group hugs and selfies with Eva, while Sophia and Ethan relaxed in camp chairs and talked about cars and coffee farming. Morgan milled about, looking for some sort of connection with anyone else sober enough to talk about life goals and the world. Only a couple humored her for a few minutes before finding other conversations or zoning out.

After a few hours, the campsite became a scene of twenty-five drunken seniors, stumbling, slurring, and laughing. Morgan and Sophia sat sober on the periphery, watching the show. Late into the night, Lydia and Holly whispered about Eva as their friend lay on the ground, seemingly comfortable in a down jacket, snuggled in the dirt and pine needles.

Sophia watched with keen and sober eyes as the girls sang a song together and giggled. Then Lydia held up her hands and shook her head. "No, no, no, we can't…"

"But it's a calling. She said she was sick of it."

"She's a sister…" Lydia said, slurring her words, before laughing and letting her lips flutter into a raspberry. "I can't … talk … my lips."

"You don't need those," Holly said. "You don't need to talk anyway … or say what you think… Eva doesn't like it when you think." Her words sounded chewy and lost, floating around the dying campfire.

The rest of the crowd had fallen into their tents, but Sophia watched from her chair as Eva lay motionless on the ground.

"You guysssss," Eva said. Sophia could only make out the bend of her nose in the dark. "You can do whatever… I don't care…"

"I have to pee." Lydia stood up and stumbled into the woods.

"Hold still," Holly said, pulling a knife from her backpack.

Sophia frowned. *Why a knife?* She watched calmly from across the fire, saying nothing. Just observing.

The blade glimmered off the firelight. Then Holly squatted over Eva for a long while. Her body moved as if she was tugging on something, and she tipped over to the left, losing her balance.

Sophia eventually crawled into her tent, snuggling into her sleeping bag next to a snoring Morgan.

Sophia continued to watch through the plastic window in the tent, until Holly finally stood up. The fire was only coals, and the night was dark like oil. Holly was only a darkened shape. "There! All better," she said in a sing-song voice. She climbed into the tent and left her friend on the ground.

Inside her own tent, Sophia laid there, eyes open, gazing at the dark roof of her tent, wondering what just happened between those three girls.

～

The next morning, just as the sky turned a milky yellow, a piercing scream erupted. Ethan rose first, stumbling out of his tent wearing boxers with a print depicting tiny bananas.

Sophia was next. "What?" she asked, breathless, worried for an instant that a bear might have been crawling around the leftover hotdogs.

Instead, they saw Eva sitting up outside the tent. Dew dotted her down jacket, and her hands locked onto her hair. Her long blue hair was gone: hacked off in jagged edges. The shortest piece came to her earlobe. The longest piece reached her shoulder.

"What the hell?" Ethan said, his eyes huge. "Why'd you do that?"

"I didn't, you ass," Eva answered. Her face grew stony, and she glared at Sophia. "*You!* You're my stalker!" She pointed. "*You* did this to me."

Sophia barely flinched, and her lips twitched in a stifled smile. "Right," she said, turning away to put on her shoes.

The accusation drew the attention of the rest of the camp. A couple people poked their heads out of their tents, and Chris shouted from within his. "Shut the hell up!"

Lydia stumbled out of the tent. "What?" She saw Eva's hair and gasped, covering her mouth. "*She* did *that* to you?" Lydia's gaze slowly turned to Sophia. "Ohmigosh."

Eva, covering her head, scowled and ducked inside her tent, whimpering.

Ethan and Sophia looked at each other with surprise. Ethan stifled laughter, while Sophia stared into the firepit. Consternation swept through her, and her nerves felt as if they were on fire.

Ethan moved to pick up some logs to start a new fire. "You hungry?" he asked.

Sophia barely heard him. Seeing Eva's jagged hair and the tortured look on her face felt so freaking good. It was exactly what she had wanted to do to Eva herself. It was *exactly* what she had written. And that in itself felt dizzying, like the ground was uneven. *It had to be a coincidence.* But then, what if it wasn't? The possibility that it wasn't a fluke delivered a rush to her head, as if she'd fallen into cold water.

"What?" Ethan asked.

"I'm having a moment. Weird. Tell you later."

When they arrived at Sophia's house later that morning, smelling of campfire and beer, she invited Morgan and Ethan inside.

"Soph," Ethan whined. "I'm hung over. I gotta go back to sleep."

"It'll just take a second."

"Just tell us, Soph," said Morgan. "I'm hungry."

"Yeah, starving," Ethan said. "You got any eggs?"

"You won't believe me otherwise," Sophia said. She led them down the dark hallway to her room, which was decorated with nothing but thrift-store pillows and three funky, artsy magazine pages taped to the walls. Her own hodgepodge homemade wallpaper. She picked up the leather journal off the bed and held it open.

"What?" Ethan asked, glancing at it and then rubbing his stomach. "Seriously. I need some food."

Morgan snatched the leather book. "You wrote in it…" She sang the words, glancing up, delighted for a moment, before opening it. Then she noticed the mud and water streaks on the pages and leather and frowned. "What happened?"

"Read," Sophia said.

Wicked Games

BY SOPHIA PALMER

Elsa woke to find locks of her glorious hair had been lopped off in her sleep. She couldn't understand it. She was surrounded by people who truly adored her. So they were as baffled as she that her hair was a crooked mess. She looked like a man, which Jane didn't think was all bad, but Elsa thought it was horrid. She cried for days, creating a torrent of river that flooded the streets.

But on the fifth day, Elsa reemerged from her brownstone, dressed in designer clothing and her short, cropped hair styled in a chic new look, and once again, people wanted to be her. Parisian designers ogled and began cutting other villagers' hair in this same manner. Soon, people around the country were calling their haircuts the Elsa, and she became even more popular.

The Flores File: Video
Interviews
NOW

Morgan: I read Soph's story and thought, *Wow, that's pretty spot on*. And for a second, I thought maybe she was the one who cut Eva's hair.

Ethan: Of course, that's what we all thought.

Becky Flores (Eva's mother): This was the start of it all. My baby girl. She came home in tears. In *tears*.

Manny Flores (Eva's father): She was always doing something with that hair, the clothes. I figured it was another one of her ... things.

Becky Flores: Horrid. It was *that Sophia*. All a big game. And now... [sobs] Eva's missing. [Purses her lips.] Coincidence? You tell me.

Manny Flores: I told her to own the hair. That's what we Floreses do. Own it.

Sophia: I thought it was all a big coincidence, that I wrote that stuff in the book. I did. [Swallows, rubs her eyes with her fingertips.] I did. Really. But...

Ethan: It was *just* hair. So someone cut her hair. So what? She flipped that blue hair around like she was... And she copied Sophia with the color too... She just ... I don't know. She deserved something ... and I'm not saying... But she deserved something way worse than having her hair cut off. The way everyone freaked out, you would have thought that something big happened. Now, because of that night, everyone looks at Sophia—and me too. But it wasn't us. The journal. *That's* what it was.

Morgan: Sophia wanted to test things after that night. But yeah. [Runs her hand through her hair.] After Senior Bust, we took things a little too far, though. Yeah. Big time. Or at least Sophia did.

14

Sophia
PROJECTILE VOMIT

Then: April 8

"Try something else," Ethan said, leaning on the bar of The Wheel.

Riley lurked in the background somewhere, endlessly wiping down tables.

"Like what?" Sophia asked, sitting up on the bar next to him. The cafe was empty, and the sun dipped down over the hillside. The town was like a group of bears, withdrawing for winter before emerging slowly come spring. They still weren't entirely out of their caves.

"Make her get a weird rash?" Morgan suggested. She sat at the bar a few feet away, not drinking or eating but doing her physics homework.

Sophia looked at her and smirked. She wasn't used to seeing a devious side in Morgan. She was a color-in-the-lines girl.

"No ... make *all* of her hair fall out," Ethan said.

"Redundant, dude." Sophia swung her legs.

"Projectile vomiting," Ethan said. "In class."

Sophia frowned. "Gross." She hopped off the counter. "It's so weird that I wrote that."

"What will her fans think of the butchered hair?" Ethan opened his phone. After a few taps, he clicked on a video.

In it, Eva spoke to the camera, her short hair dyed a brighter blue—waves of light beneath darker richer tones. Someone had transformed her hair into a wavy style with long curling strands that hung by her face.

"Someone cut my hair on Senior Bust," she said, retelling her version of the story. Her voice somehow balanced bravery, vulnerability, and confidence.

She should be an actress, thought Sophia.

The video had two million likes, and she was flooded by comments at the bottom of the video.

"Eva that hair is fire!"

"Why r u in that shitty town anyway?"

They went on and on. Ethan read them out loud, and Morgan rolled her eyes. "She's drama," she said.

"Why does she even live here?" Ethan asked.

"Because her parents wanted to get out of the city," Sophia said. She reveled in the fact that her friends disliked Eva as much as she did, but the gossip could often make her feel uncomfortable, as if she were standing on hot coals. She tried to change the subject.

"You guys want to borrow the Bowmans' SUPs and get on the water later?" Sophia wiped down the countertop, though it didn't need it. "The water'll be rolling."

Riley stood at the far end of the room, organizing the condiments and wiping down the face of the oven. It was clear she was busy, but her shifting eyes indicated to Sophia that she was listening—like a rat with ears perked.

"I bet Eva has never even been paddling on the river, never hiked, never biked," Morgan said, not looking up from her paper. "She doesn't fit here in her three-inch heels."

"You don't do any of that shit," Ethan said, reading Sophia's mind. "*Bike?* Do you even own—"

"I *know* how to ride. I'm a mountain girl—a Paonian."

"That's not a word," Sophia said, glancing at the clock. "You just got done telling us you weren't gonna camp again. The Gucci and stuff?"

"That's later. When I move."

"It's four, by the way."

"Crap!" Morgan said, gathering her things. "Chinese! Omigod, my mom'll freak. She just hired this tutor."

"Can I get a ride?" Ethan asked. "Tell Zeb that I just checked out early?" He looked at Sophia, who shrugged. Zeb was on another road trip.

"Hurry, E," Morgan said, shoving her books into her bag.

"Check it," Ethan said, pointing to a line of videos of girls with haircuts *just like Eva's*, doing her signature TikTok dances. "What the...?"

Sophia thought of her story again, and how the fans loved Elsa so much they cut their hair like hers. She got chills up her arms, and a lump formed in her throat. "Too weird," she said under her breath.

"Just like your story," Ethan said, dumbfounded.

"E!" Morgan stood at the door. "You coming or what?"

He shoved his phone into his pocket, took off his apron, and ran out the door.

"Later," he said before holding up a finger. "Don't forget. Next chapter is projectile vomit."

Sophia watched Ethan as he left the building, wondering if she really had written the future. If she indeed had some power of story, what would she write next? Would she really write more revenge on Eva? Would she change her own future? A combination of fear and giddy power flooded her, and her scalp tingled. Maybe she would close The Wheel early and get home to write.

"Your friends are really catty." Riley's voice cut the air, and

Sophia turned to see her coworker standing just a foot away. She could sneak up on you like a mountain lion.

Sophia, startled at first, recovered her coolness and simply glanced at her before stepping around the counter. She began placing chairs upside-down atop of the high-top tables.

"You know, friends—"

"As if you have friends, Riley," Sophia snapped. "Like you're the authority."

"They're mean-spirited," Riley said. "Eva doesn't deserve—"

"Has she even looked at you? Acknowledged you as a human?" Sophia placed another chair onto the table.

"Why're you doing that?"

"Closing early," Sophia said.

"On whose direction?" Riley's eyes were beady, and her crooked nose looked bigger in the overhead light.

The jingle of the door interrupted the conversation, and Eva strode into the cafe with her short hair looking just as good as it had in the videos. *Can't Eva ever just go away?*

Eva's voice rippled through the room. "We wanted to buy something with good bones."

Her confidence almost made the young woman following her invisible. The woman, mousy with big glasses, carried a yellow notebook and trailed Eva's long strides.

"This," Eva said, gesturing to the brick wall to the right. "This is cool. But we need better art in here."

Sophia and Riley stopped and watched them as they paraded through the shop. Eva pointed as if she were a teacher, and the woman scribbled notes as if she were a student.

After a moment, Eva looked up and acknowledged them. "Hey guys," she said, cheerful. "I'm helping my dad..."

Sophia's face was blank and Eva squirmed, only slightly, under her gaze.

"Oh, wait, Zeb hasn't told you," Eva said.

"Told us what?" Riley asked, her whiny voice like a nail on metal.

"Zeb sold the place ... to my family!" Eva grinned and did a little shoulder shake again—the thing that said, *Fuck you very much, Sophia Palmer.*

Sophia kept her face neutral, but inside fire raged again beneath the surface of her skin.

"What?" Riley asked. "When?"

"Last week. So yeah, we're in charge."

We're in charge. This felt targeted. This felt as if there truly was a malicious intent. Eva wanted to destroy Sophia; she wanted to ruin her.

"Um ... what're you doing?" Eva pointed at Sophia, who still held a chair in her hands.

"Closing," Sophia said defiantly.

"It's only four," she said.

"Yeah, place is empty," Sophia said.

Riley flashed a smug smile beneath stringy hair.

The jingle of the bell on the front door broke the tension, and a man walked in. Wearing a stubble beard and hip square black glasses, he strode toward Eva and placed a hand on her shoulder. It was subtle, but it was almost as if she shrank beneath his grip.

He whispered something to Eva, which made her lean away from him. He strode up to the counter.

"Manny Flores," he said. His voice sounded like a crisp white shirt. "Eva's dad. And ... I'm the new owner of The Wheel."

He didn't look like a dad.

Riley took a step forward, introducing herself. "I'm Riley, and I've worked here forever."

"And you are?" Manny asked, looking to Sophia.

"Sophia." Her voice sounded like ice. She knew she didn't exude the kind of kiss-ass needed to secure her job—a job her family desperately needed. She didn't bow down to people like the Flores family.

His steely hazel eyes locked onto Sophia's. She felt something stir inside her stomach. She knew he was old and someone's *dad*, and she'd be loath to admit it, but he was hot.

"There are going to be some changes around here," he said.

15

Sophia

SPAM ISN'T ENOUGH

Then: April 8

"And then he fired me," Sophia spat. She wasn't going to cry. Instead her frustration swirled into a feverish anger.

"We'll figure it out, baby." Her mom took a sip of red wine from a small glass jar. She used a spatula to poke some gelatinous light-pink meat sizzling in a pan.

Her mom could always shove down any anxiety, always determined to believe that everything would be okay. That they'd land on their feet soon enough. She almost wore it like a badge of honor, Sophia thought. But it wasn't honor. It was stupid. Sophia wasn't an adult yet, but even she knew that they could be homeless in a matter of weeks.

All because of Eva.

Eva was poison ivy. Beautiful, soft, shiny. But she was toxic, and Sophia felt as if she were drowning in piles of it. Soon she'd be clawing off her own skin.

"I mean, why me?" Sophia whined, but she knew the answer. Customers had complained that she'd been slow to make their sandwiches, that she wasn't buckets of warmth.

She didn't deserve the job, and she knew it, but still, things had been good before Eva's family showed up. Zeb was the kind of owner who had been born into money and didn't care if Sophia and Ethan were lax.

"Well, you'll find another job," her mom said.

"In this town? Not likely," Sophia said, leaning on the refrigerator. She knew her reputation was that of an ice queen, but it had never mattered.

Until now.

Sophia sat at the kitchen table, the salty smell of the sizzling meat making her slightly nauseated.

A plate of Spam, white rice, and soupy canned corn slid in front of Sophia. She'd wanted to lose a few pounds, and so maybe this dual joblessness would do the trick. Nothing like cheap canned meat for dinner twice a week to turn your stomach.

"Thanks," Sophia said, pushing a fork into the meat.

Dylan strode into the kitchen and plopped down across from Sophia. Without a word, their mom slid an identical plate in front of him. He dug into the food and began chewing loudly.

Sophia glanced over her shoulder to see her mom downing the rest of the wine in three big gulps.

"You're not eating?" Sophia asked.

"Naw, big lunch." Her mom refilled her glass of wine.

Her mom was always thin, but she looked skinnier that day. Her cotton pants hung on her protruding hip bones.

Worry and fear blossomed again in Sophia's chest, and she pushed away the plate, unable to eat.

The next day, Dylan joined Sophia to look for a job. She filled out applications at eight places, including the bakery, the diner, the barber shop, the Paradise Theater. Everywhere.

As they rounded the corner of Mervin's flower shop, she felt something heavy weighing on her. It wasn't anything she felt inside, but rather that feeling of walking down a dark alleyway and feeling like someone was watching you. A chill ran up her spine. She turned and looked over her shoulder, assuming she'd see someone watching her from, say, a bench or a window. She saw no one.

Just as she pulled open the heavy glass door, though, she caught something out of the corner of her eye. A figure sitting in a parked car, about two hundred feet away. He was facing her in the driver's seat. *Is that Hendy?*

"If you worked here, do you think you get to spray paint the carnations?" Dylan asked.

"Huh?" She barely heard him, and she couldn't help but gaze at the car as she stepped inside the shop.

A dark feeling swept through her that someone had seen her slash Hendy's tires. Now he was readying to get even. She swallowed and entered the shop. Dylan sniffed some pink daisies in a jar.

"I betcha you can be a bagger at Don's, Soph," he said. "Let's go there next."

"Sure," she said. "It'd be cool to work with you."

While she waited at the counter for a tiny stick-drawing of a woman to notice them, she noticed some really crap art on the walls. A horrible sunflower that looked like it had been painted by someone who was drunk at the time.

Sophia asked the stick lady if the shop was hiring, and the woman pulled out an application from beneath the counter without a word. She handed it to her hesitantly, eying Sophia's henna drawings on her arms and reading her purple T-shirt that said *Suicide Squad* across the bust.

"We don't really need help now. But we'll keep it on file," she said. That was standard for, *Go ahead, please waste your time filling it out, and we'll put it in a drawer to make you feel better about your job hunt.*

Sophia took it and nodded. "Sure. Yeah."

"These real?" Dylan asked, as he pulled a petal from a pink tiger lily.

She yanked his arm. "Yes."

As they were leaving, she stopped at the door and turned around to look at the woman behind the counter. "Hey, do you hang stuff from local artists here?"

She looked up, peering over rimless glasses. "Um, yes, often."

"Can I bring in some pictures then?"

"Ummmm…" She pursed her lips.

"I have some pictures I made."

"Oh." She blinked several times with a blank expression. "I'd have to see the work before I could let you do that. Don't you go to high school here? You're just a ki—"

"I'm an artist."

The Flores File: Comic strip obtained from and drawn by Aidan Voinovich

April 7

[A series of images featuring sketches of what appears to be Eva Flores and Aidan kissing.]
Speech bubbles include the following:

Aidan: *i luv you alot Eva*
Eva: *me too. Mwah!*
Aidan: *stay down here with me were its dark and warm. plese? forver?*
Eva: *yes yes yes! you matter more then tiktok*

16

Eva
BARBIE'S REVENGE

Then: April 10

Eva's mom leaned on the doorframe to her daughter's room. "I found a place in Denver that will do hair extensions."

Wearing matching rose-colored yoga pants and a crop top, she took a long sip of a green smoothie.

Eva pressed a tack into the wall, hanging another line of dangling LED vine lights—a new look for her videos. She looked over to her mother. "Do you think it looks bad? My hair?"

Her mom tilted her head and pressed her lips together before sighing. "It's not your best look. I just don't want it to affect your numbers."

Eva's face felt hot.

Her mom turned and left Eva alone in her room.

Eva had grown to kind of like the new haircut. She'd seen movie stars brave enough to cut their long locks off—Jennifer Lawrence, Emma Watson—and people still thought they were beautiful. *I am not my hair. Or my TikTok numbers, Mother.*

She'd spent so many years wanting her mother's attention;

meanwhile her mom sought the perfect man to "complete her." Eva'd spent countless nights at sleepovers with neighbors because her mom was out on dates with rich men she met on some high-end dating app. Eventually, Eva grew used to getting only snippets of attention from her, usually critiques of her appearance.

As she hung the last string of dangling lights, Holly and Lydia showed up. Eva put on her mask—unattached, upbeat, positive, confident—which typically prompted them to worship at her feet. It was the only way she knew how to be with people, and it felt good when they did kneel down.

"Omigod," Lydia sang, her voice low like a viola.

The adoring rush of dopamine made Eva feel better already.

"Love the vines … and the lights. It's like…"

"A fairy room. I know," Eva said confidently. She'd put a link in her bio to order them and she'd get commissions from any purchases.

Holly's white-blond hair looked shiny like a Barbie's, and Eva felt a twang of jealousy and irritation. She touched her short hair.

Eva thought Holly was too quiet—she knew she was in trouble. Lydia had already told Eva about what Holly had said to her at Senior Bust. How Holly hated the way Eva "controlled" them, the way she never let Holly think for herself, how Eva wasn't being authentic, the way she didn't care about anyone but herself. *Holly should have known that Lydia would tell.*

"God, I can't get over how dope your hair is, Eva. Makes me want to whack mine off," Lydia said, pulling on her dark brown locks. "You still pissed?"

Eva ignored her and sank into a white fur papasan chair. She looked up at Holly with a stony stare. "By the way, don't you have some apologizing to do?"

"What?" Holly asked, leaning her back against the closed door.

"Lydia told me all the shit you talked about me." She picked pieces of lint off her pink tie-dye tank top. Through her peripheral vision, she could see Holly cast an accusatory glare at Lydia.

"I didn't say anything," Holly said.

To make her uneasy, Eva changed the subject. "Did you guys see that video of that guy? Posted by that Chris guy…"

"Chris Piirto," Holly said. Her voice was laced with irritation.

Holly needed to get down on her knees and beg for forgiveness. She wasn't, and that pissed Eva off even more. But she didn't let it show.

"Yeah…," Eva said absently as she searched for the video on her phone. Making fun of people always pumped her up with something, gave her a superior feeling that wasn't easy for her to get anywhere else. "From Senior Bust, that guy … you know … he has the gun rack on his truck… He fell over this … you gotta see…" She laughed. "Wait, here. Omigod."

"*Phillip Hackett,*" Holly said, a sneer spreading over her face. "He sits behind us in Spanish. And he comes here all the time to shovel the snow." She threw her arms up. "Jesus."

Stunned, Eva shot her a withering look. Holly needed to be making amends, not critiquing her memory of stupid guys in their class. She was no longer the timid little doll Eva would dress, arrange, and play with. It was as if her skin had cracked and a new hidden part of her shined through. And it made Eva feel smaller.

"What's with you?" Eva asked.

"Do you know *anyone's* name?" Holly asked, pulling away from the door. "You've lived here all year. And it's a small town." Her voice petered out in typical disdainful Holly fashion.

Eva gazed at her with a tilted head. Her voice was ice. "Do their names really matter?" She looked back at her phone. "Lydia, you gotta see. You'll die. He looks so stupid—"

"Yeah, names do matter. And you know what?" Holly stood there for a couple breaths. Then she straightened herself and her voice strained as she spoke, nervous. "You see everyone as faceless followers. We're real people with our own real minds."

Eva's blood was glacial. Holly didn't know her.

"What the hell—" Lydia said. *Loyal Lydia.*

"I'm not buying into this ... this ... fake ... this ... bullshit."

"Bullshit?" Eva turned to look at Lydia with raised brows and a humoring, open-mouth grin. Inside, humiliation burned at her eyes.

"Yeah." Holly jutted her chin, and her face flushed red.

"Get out of my room." Eva's voice ripped through the air, sharp as knives.

"Happy to," Holly said, flashing an angry smile. She opened the door, pausing for a second. "And your hair? You look ... you look ... like a genetically engineered person ... gone wrong. You should've never copied Sophia Palmer."

"Out." Eva pointed. "Get. The. Fuck. Out."

Holly slammed the door behind her. Eva's head burned. Her instinct was to self-consciously touch her hair, but she couldn't show weakness in front of Lydia.

"What the hell?" Lydia said. "I think Sophia Palmer got into her head."

Eva sat in her chair, unmoving, until Lydia reached out and rubbed her back. "Forget about her."

Irritated, Eva pushed Lydia's hand off her. She didn't need her.

She just needed everyone else in the world.

17

Sophia
IOU

Then: April 11

T he scent of an overly sweet cinnamon candle flooded the inside of the flower shop, and Sophia grew hot, wearing a sweatshirt and standing with an armful of canvases that she had carefully separated with old towels. It had been three days since her last visit, and she was determined to prove to this woman that her art was good enough.

Hopefully, this lady hadn't heard about what Eva Flores said about her last fall. *That's stupid. Why would she care about high school bullshit?* The fact remained, however, that this was a small town. Hendy was clearly thwarting her mother's efforts to get a job, and now Sophia was worried Eva's libelous behavior would crush Sophia's chances of making money, too.

The stick-like woman was still on the phone, and Sophia eventually leaned her canvases against the wall.

She leaned an elbow on the countertop and watched her sit as still as a statue, listening to the caller. She wondered if the woman had perhaps not even blinked. She studied the lady's super-smooth skin and full lips. Maybe she was one of those ladies who had "work done" on their face.

"Yes, yes, yes," the woman replied before glancing up at Sophia, scowling at her, and turning away.

Sophia let her cheek fall onto the counter, and she briefly considered whether this woman had seen her slash Hendy's tires, if she'd heard bad rumors about her mom, and if she'd ever gotten decaf from Sophia at The Wheel. She flipped through memories in her head. Did she ever serve a stick woman at The Wheel? Had she been rude to this lady? She hoped she hadn't blown her chances of selling art here.

She sensed something, or someone, behind her and turned her head to see Manny Flores—Eva's dad, her former boss, her new landlord—standing just a couple feet away. Startled, she jumped and stood up straight.

"Hey…," Manny said with an easy smile. "Didn't mean to scare you."

"Oh," Sophia said, flustered. Her body felt wound, and she felt herself brace tight, like an animal expecting prey to pounce. He and Eva were destroying her.

"What's this?" He pointed to the canvases leaning against the wall. Sophia considered ignoring him. She considered just pretending he wasn't there. But something about him— charming, engaging, gentle—made her turn to him. The expression on his face made her think he was genuinely interested. "My art. I … wanna sell it here."

"Here?" He looked at the tiny space and scoffed.

"Yeah," she said. "It's better than this junk." She nodded her head to the ugly flower picture.

They both ignored the entire herd of elephants in the room: the fact that she was at war with his daughter. That he'd just fired her from her job. That he owned her house.

"Anything is," he agreed, offering a dazzling smile. How could she be so flustered by this guy? No one flustered her. No one had ever been so distracting.

He fired you. He is your landlord. He's Eva's dad.

He hesitated for a moment. "Can I … see your…?"

"My…?"

He pointed to the canvases and looked back at Sophia over his shoulder. His eye contact was enough to deliver that weird flip-flop to her stomach again.

"Uh, sure." She stepped forward quickly to pull the canvases back and show him the images. She had brought just three, all of which had a floral theme, to better fit with the shop. He stopped and studied a large blown-up photo of a bee hovering over a yellow sunflower. The edges of the image were blown out and painted with a thick white oil paint.

"Wow," Manny said, picking it up and holding it in front of him. "Impressive."

Sophia looked at the stick woman, who was finishing up her phone call.

"Sorry about the other day … at The Wheel," he said.

Sophia scoffed. "Yeah." She didn't look at him.

Manny smiled gently. "Well, looks like I have to make it up to you."

"Finally, I'm done! Sorry about that," the shop owner said with a flabbergasted sigh.

Sophia turned her attention to the woman and explained how she hoped she could hang her art there for sale. "It's free decoration for you, really." Sophia knew she was a terrible salesperson. Especially if she really had given this woman decaf a time or two.

The woman studied the art with the light edges of a frown hovering on her face. Sophia's face felt hot. *No one understands my art,* she thought. *She thinks it's weird, just like everyone else.* The woman finally retreated a couple steps. "Well, they're … interesting."

Sophia, unsure of what to say, stood quietly, gazing at the woman. *Interesting is good, right?*

"Well, I think they're remarkable," Manny said before taking a step toward the woman with a hand extended. "I'm Manny Flores. I collect art."

Collects art?

"Oh," the woman said, unsettled. "I'm Pamela Bennett." She brushed her hair with her hand, suddenly self-conscious. "I... Can I help you?"

Manny shoved his hands into his pockets. "I just saw this lovely young woman come into the shop and had to ... um ... see what was up."

Sophia frowned. He came in to see her?

"But, to make it worth your time..." He reached inside the refrigerated cooler and removed a single red rose. He handed it to Sophia with a downturned head and bow. She took it, baffled.

He tossed a twenty-dollar bill onto the counter, and out of view of the shop owner, he gave Sophia a slight two-finger salute and a wink. "Here's to me finding a way to make things up to you."

Sophia didn't want to be charmed by him. And she didn't want to *like* the attention. In reality, he was ruining her life. He was the dad of her enemy. He was a freaking adult. But she was charmed.

The door clicked shut and he disappeared, leaving the Stick Woman and Sophia both speechless. A tiny smile crawled up one side of Sophia's face.

The woman still didn't want Sophia's paintings.

The Flores File: Screenshot of Snap sent to Eva from Lydia

April 11

[A photo taken through the window of the flower shop, showing Sophia and Manny Flores talking closely. Sophia is holding a rose and looking at Manny with a flirtatious smile.]

Caption:
"we got to talk"

Eva's reply:
"she is obsessed with me"

18

Sophia

STALKER

Then: April 13

T he banging of lockers slamming seemed slower than
normal. The people moving through the hallway
almost felt as if they were in slow motion; eyes
lingered longer on Sophia. A funny feeling swept over her as
Morgan approached with fast scissor steps. Ethan lumbered
behind her.

"What the heck are you thinking, Soph?" Morgan asked.

"Yeah, I thought you were done with social," Ethan said.

Sophia gazed at the two of them blankly. It was as if she
were inserted there, mid-conversation, but she had no idea
what had been said previously or what they were talking
about.

The lock unlatched and she swung open the locker. On
the bottom shelf sat a pile of blue hair.

Blue hair. She reached down and picked up a few strands,
confused.

Two sophomore girls, Kayla Godfrey and Dakota Rawlings, passed her as she held the hair. "Whaaaaat... She *did* do

4444444

it," Dakota said quietly, gasping. They put their heads together and hurried down the hallway.

"Eva thinks you cut her hair, which, in a way, you did," Morgan said, who held a stack of books. She blew her bangs out of her eyes.

"I watched Holly do it," Sophia said, rolling her eyes. But that didn't explain why the hair was in her locker. "Who did this?" Her friends gazed at her with wide eyes and shrugged, just as baffled as she was.

"What's the deal with your Instagram?" Ethan said. "You've got your journal. Why go so—"

"*Ordinary.*" Morgan interjected.

"Yeah, where's my projectile vomiting?" Ethan asked.

Sophia dropped the hair back in her locker and took a long exhale with hands on her hips. "What the hell are you guys talking about?"

"Your Instagram ... Um ... please tell me you weren't really sitting outside of Eva's house," Morgan said.

"Those super close-up photos of your face... Like, why would you post *that?*" Ethan asked. "I think you're pretty but ... no one should..."

Sophia shook her head and began walking to first period. "I don't have Instagram."

"Yeah you do. At least as of yesterday," said Ethan.

"See," Morgan said, opening her phone. A few clicks later, and Sophia was staring at an account with her name, her face, photos of herself, her house, her cat. It was as if she had been in a coma and woken up to find an imposter had lived her life while she was asleep. "Those aren't mine. I didn't take those."

She scrolled up, and the top three photos made her whole body go still. One was an awful closeup of her face, so close that you could see the smeared eye makeup beneath her bottom lashes, the bumpy and red imperfections of her cheek, the cracked line by her mouth. *Who took this? Where? When?* A feeling curled inside her—as if eyes bore down at her from the walls.

The last shot was of Eva, taken from outside her house, looking into Eva's bedroom window. Eva looked to be dancing, a hip out to one side, and through the gauze-like drapes, she looked beautiful, almost ethereal. Below the photo there was no caption. Just a purple smiling devil emoji.

"That is *not* me. It's not. I didn't do this," Sophia said, shaking her head. She pushed away the phone and strode down the hall. People passed her with wide eyes, a few of them whispering. She had shed her usual aloofness momentarily, and as a result, she felt dizzy, as if she were dangling from a thousand threads and spinning wildly out of control.

"Soph, you don't need to take pictures of her. That's kinda creepy—" Ethan said, catching up to her and zig-zagging around oncoming students in the hallway.

"It's an imposter?" Morgan asked, trying to keep pace with Sophia's brisk stride. "I read about this. People making fake accounts. That's *so* illegal."

"Of course it's fake," Sophia said. "You guys *know* me. I hate that shit."

"Ohhh," Ethan said slowly. "Do you think Eva hates Holly too?"

"Why would I know?" Sophia asked, dodging shoulders, trying to keep her pace brisk, to outrun the conversation.

"'Cuz, she had, like, embarrassing pictures of herself on her Insta. One was her on the toilet."

Passing students' gazes lingered on her before flicking away quickly. Now they *really* thought she was obsessed with Eva. It was like those dreams of showing up naked to class, and there's no place to cover up. No way to wake up.

"But the hair in your locker…," Morgan said tentatively.

"Eva," Sophia said. "It's gotta be Eva. Jesus." She scoffed and picked up the pace.

It was as if she only had to utter her name or, rather, think of her, because around the next corner, she nearly ran into her blue-haired nemesis. Dressed in a short red-and-black plaid skirt and black Rolling Stones T-shirt, *just like Sophia's.* Eva gasped and jumped out of the way. Her wide doe eyes looked up at Sophia with fake timidity.

Sophia shared her stony blank face, wishing it worked like Darth Vader's invisible grip, making people drop to their knees.

Right as they passed, Eva hissed a single word beneath her breath. *"Stalker."*

19

Ethan

MISSING PARTS

Then: April 13

Ethan clutched the door handle as Sophia zipped around tight corners like a NASCAR driver. He'd been in her car enough to know that he should subtly grasp the handle, so as not to piss her off and make her go faster. He glanced at Morgan in the back seat. By the expression on her face, she clearly felt the same way.

But the very fact that Sophia could even make her little Datsun get up to seventy on this little two-lane highway gave him confidence. If he was really going to get a ticket out of town, he needed wheels. And when your dad won't invest in a car, it's best to buy a junker, fix it up with your car-savvy friend, and then have wheels when you need to escape. He hoped they could fix up this Mustang in half the time it took her to do her Datsun. He had already been stashing away money, taped to the inside of his sock drawer, to ensure his dad didn't blow his plans like last time. He had even taken free online programming classes online; he'd do freelance coding once he found his own place.

"How much you think it'll cost to fix up?" Ethan asked.

Sophia glanced at Ethan. "Dunno."

"So I don't get it. Is Eva that psycho that she'd create a fake account?" Morgan asked.

"Maybe that's how she gets more followers. Fake accounts," Ethan said with a chuckle.

"Did you call them to take it down?" Morgan asked, looking at Sophia and leaning up to the front seat.

Sophia nodded, staring straight ahead. She gripped the steering wheel tight, a sure sign of irritation, Ethan noted.

"What'd they say?"

"I had to file a report."

"And…."

Sophia shrugged. "We wait."

"So she can just keep posting things," Morgan said. "That can't be legal. Can't we call the sheriff?"

Sophia was quiet, and Ethan could tell that Morgan's analysis of the topic was grating on her nerves.

"There's gotta be a way to prove it's not her."

"So let's listen to some tunes," Ethan said, turning on a Cage the Elephant song. He still was curious to know more about the Instagram account, but he figured Sophia might just explode if the conversation continued. Lately it was like she had a ticking clock on her forehead that only Ethan could read. Morgan never seemed to see it or hear it. She didn't even consider looking for those subtle clues.

As they approached Anthracite Creek, Ethan spotted the shed where they had found the Mustang before. He hoped the car was still there.

"The guy knows we're coming, right?" Sophia asked.

Ethan's head felt tight. He hadn't been able to get a hold of the seller since that first night Sophia fell in the mud. He prayed he wasn't wasting Sophia's gas money or time by driving out there. But if he had told her, she wouldn't have gone to check. And he *needed* to check.

"Yeah, yeah," he said, looking out the window. After they

turned off Kebler Pass, he saw the dirt road, marked only by a boulder spray-painted orange, which led to the cabin.

"You … uh … wanna see a cool place?" he asked.

She frowned and looked at him. "No. The shed's just up there." She pointed ahead to the right. Her hand hid inside the oversized sweatshirt she'd made herself. She had dyed the main white sweatshirt a gray-purple with black handprint stencils, cutting off the sleeves and replacing them with black sleeves from another old sweatshirt. It was the weird kind of stuff that Sophia wasn't afraid to do.

"My dad. He's building a cabin. I wanna see it." The day prior, his dad had given him a hand-drawn map of how to get there. He'd been building it over the past four months. Normally, a guy might be excited that his dad was building a cabin in the woods. It would mean fishing, hunting, cozy nights reading by a fire. But for Ethan, this was pure anxiety, a cabin designed not for lazy days and unwinding but rather, for the end of the world. He feared his dad would make him go with him to this cabin to live off-grid. He'd sure go nuts if Ethan ever tried to leave.

He'd once asked if he could go live with his mom in Tulsa, and his dad freaked out and went and bought a Ring security camera. He'd also go into Ethan's room and repeatedly check on him in the middle of the night to ensure he wouldn't leave. And he installed spyware on his son's phone.

Sophia didn't speak, which at times made Ethan feel uneasy. "Yeah, well, it's cool if you don't want to," he said.

"Where?" Sophia asked.

"Turn left up there."

She yanked hard on the steering wheel without applying the brakes and roared up a dirt road.

"Okay, so we're not going to look at the car as planned?" Morgan asked. "Um, I have homework…"

"Maybe stop up there," Ethan said, pointing to a cluster of trees off to the left. Sophia stopped the car, and the three of them climbed out of the car. The air felt still and smelled fresh like pine. It eased an ounce of his anxiety.

"Why exactly does your dad want a cabin? It's, like, in the middle of nowhere up here," Morgan said.

"Why does he do anything?" Ethan pointed to the trees. "This way." His dad had spray-painted a rock orange on the side of the road as a guide to get there, and he left small rock cairns to show the path through the woods. Together the three of them walked up the road and around a bend.

Sophia was quiet again, picking up a long stick as they walked.

Morgan chattered, taking up the rear as they made their way through bushes and trees. "I didn't even know this place existed," she said.

"Think that's why my dad likes it," he said. Curiosity propelled him—maybe because he worried he'd have to go find his dad up there someday. Yet he couldn't shake the nervous need to turn around, run back to Sophia's car, and immediately buy that junker car—all so he could just escape this craziness.

Morgan crossed her arms over her chest. "Is that guy gonna be there very long? Isn't he expecting you to buy the car, E?"

Around the bend, they saw it. A little lean-to cabin. Two windows. Light wood planks. A door with four locks. "Did your dad build this thing himself?" Sophia asked with a scoff.

"Yeah, think he did." Ethan stopped flat-footed.

"Wow, it's pretty good," Morgan said.

Ethan didn't want to go any farther, didn't want to check it out and dive into his dad's tangled world. It looked like it was big enough to fit maybe two people.

Just staring at it for those few seconds made him want to throw up. He *needed* that car. He *needed* sanity.

"Cool. We better hurry." Ethan swiftly turned on his heel

and began briskly walking away. He headed back toward the road.

"Yay!" Morgan clapped silently and jogged on tiptoes to follow. "'Cuz I feel like someone could just chop us up in these woods and no one would know."

"Wait. Guys," Sophia said. She didn't leave the cabin. "Don't you want to check it out more?"

"No. Let's go," he said.

When they arrived at the spot along the creek where Sophia had fallen in the mud, Ethan didn't really expect to find the guy selling the car nearby. The seller hadn't responded to any of his messages on TikTok, and his account had been disabled. But still, Ethan hoped that if they went back, they'd find him, chat him up, and get Sophia's eyes on the car in daylight. And if the guy was MIA, then maybe Ethan would borrow a favor from Phillip Hackett to haul it with his uncle's tow truck. He'd just *take* the car.

They walked through the tall weeds by the river, and Ethan's nerves wound tight. He wanted that car, and it took everything in him not to just sprint to the shed where the car had been earlier. The shed looked far more decrepit in daylight.

"You *did* call the guy." Sophia had a bullshit detector that was far more precise than anyone else he knew.

"Yeah."

She looked at him.

"Well … no."

Morgan let out a loud guffaw.

"He wasn't responding!" Ethan said. His voice became squeaky, as it often did when he got defensive. "But dude. I wanted to see it again. In daylight."

Sophia stopped in the field—not far from the mud where

she fell that other night—and she suddenly went eerily still. Ethan watched as she slowly turned her head, as if watching an invisible movie.

"I'm sorry, I just—" he said.

She held up a hand to stop him, and a hot flash of anger zinged through him. Her eyes darted and scanned the area, and she looked far away, as if she'd just pressed pause on her life.

"What's she looking at?" Morgan whispered.

Ethan shrugged. He was getting the damn car. He strode toward the shed and kept talking to Sophia. "I want you to see, because I think I can get vinyl seats cheap on eBay." Sophia didn't respond and he turned around to look at her again.

She was still standing in that spot, looking dazed.

Morgan's brow furrowed. "Soph?"

"Dude, you coming?"

"I've got homework, guys, so…" Morgan's overused go-to excuse when she was uncomfortable, bored, anxious, hungry, or in this case, freaked out.

Sophia popped out of the stupor after a moment and soon trailed them over to the shed. Ethan pulled hard at the door, and the familiar creaking sound felt less creepy than it had the other night.

Ethan's heart dropped into his stomach, and disbelief washed over him. The shed was empty.

"Nooooooooo," he whined, throwing his head and hands back in disappointment.

Sophia mirrored his disappointment, putting two hands on her head. "Shit."

He scanned the empty landscape around them. A field. That empty lodge way down the way. River. Forest. Nothing else.

"Dude. Did he just sell it without giving me a chance to counter?" Ethan asked.

The three of them stood there in the empty space for another thirty seconds or so, while Ethan kicked at the ground, cussing his frustrations.

"That sucks so bad, E," Morgan said. After a few seconds, she tried to lighten it up with sarcasm. "Seemed like a real heap of gold you guys found."

Ethan barely acknowledged her. He was swimming in defeat. This was more than a car.

Sophia put a gentle hand on his shoulder. She was the only one he'd ever told about his dad's story—about how he'd learned from his uncle that his dad's mom had left him when he was little, and he was molested and then abused by a middle-school basketball coach. Sophia and Morgan knew how Ethan's older sister died of a drug overdose a few years earlier, and after his dad began to get fatalistic, his mom left town.

"I'm never gonna be able to leave." He considered his dad's volatility. If he tried to sneak out after graduation, would his dad track him down under the guise of saving his life?

"Where?" Morgan asked. "Leave where?"

"There are buses, planes, trains…," Sophia said.

He rolled his eyes. "What were you looking at over there?"

"Where?" Sophia asked.

"In the field, you were just staring at nothing," Morgan said.

Sophia gazed at them blankly. "I don't know what you mean."

20

Sophia

DEADLY VIBES

Then: April 14

Dylan ran over to a tall, skinny headstone and patted it with two hands. "What about this one?"

Sophia strode through the tall grass in the cemetery with her camera in hand and stopped before the headstone. It read:

A limb has fallen from the Robinson family tree
"Art is not always about pretty things. It's about who we are, what
happened to us, how our lives are affected." —Elizabeth Broun
In loving memory
Sharon Robinson
Artist, wife, mother, grandmother
2/12/47–4/1/06

Sophia gazed at the stone for a number of seconds, considering what Sharon Robinson might have been like when she was alive. *What happened to her? What was her story?*

She lay on her stomach in the grass to get a ground-level shot of the headstone. She'd read about graveyard art online, and she was inspired by the idea that art surrounded her in the cemetery. In fact, some cemeteries were becoming destinations for art. Maybe people would like to buy artsy graveyard pictures.

"Get your feet out of the shot," she snapped at Dylan. He jumped back with his worn black sneakers.

She felt his heavy gaze as she took a couple more pictures.

"What?" she asked, looking up at him.

"You're just ... crabby."

"Yeah, well, there's a lot going on." She still couldn't get over the fake account Eva had made in her name.

Sophia had never been one to go to war with girls and dive into catty fights, but Eva felt different. This was not some tit-for-tat about boys or rumors. It was about her family. Eva wanted to be queen, and Sophia wasn't about to serve her.

She glanced up at Dylan, who stood with one hand in his pocket, the other holding up a blow pop that he gnawed. He was always literally game for anything that Sophia wanted to do. He was a child in a man's body, and she couldn't go around snapping at him.

"Sorry. I'm glad you're here, Dyl." Sophia tossed her head toward the rows of headstones enclosed by a tall wrought iron fence, as if the bodies might somehow run away from death. "You're the perfect grave scout."

"Really?" He swallowed a bite of candy and his shoulders straightened. He pointed to the right. "I bet we'll find good dead people over there."

She followed him a few paces before spotting a black spider crawling across one gravestone, so she stopped, knelt, and focused. The camera captured a sliver of one side of the bulbous body, the tiny, sculpted hairs on its legs.

When she stood, she noticed someone—a man—approaching from some forty yards away. Her nerves tingled, and she jogged to catch up to Dylan across the empty graveyard.

"That guy's following us," Dylan said, nodding.

Instead of fear, Sophia felt a burst of adrenaline. She'd kick the shit out of anyone who tried to mess with them. She'd wail on the guy with her camera if necessary.

She glanced over her shoulder, and her breath caught. It was Manny Flores. He wore a blue Patagonia fleece and jeans, and his hands were in his pockets. *Why would he be in the graveyard?* She frowned and continued to walk in the other direction.

"Hey! It's Sophia, right?" he asked, smiling and jogging to catch up.

She slowed her pace and turned to look at him. "You always hang out at cemeteries?"

He chuckled and stopped just ten feet away. "I could ask the same about you."

She squinted at him. He was so … out of place.

Her brother approached them, standing near, protective— unusual, because Sophia usually was the one to protect him.

"Saw you from the road back there. I was … uh … driving to check out a property for sale, and thought I'd say hi," he said.

She didn't respond.

"Why're you photographing *here?*" He grimaced and scanned the rows of headstones.

She looked at him for a long moment, taken by the sharp angle of his jaw and the easy smile, and then turned away. She pretended to look for a good shot of a headstone in front of her. "I like to think of all these people and their stories. I guess I just… I don't know. Maybe I'm curious to know how they died."

"You've probably been imagining how *I'll* die, right?" he asked.

No, just imagining all the ways Eva might die.

After a moment, she spoke up. "Burning in a forest fire might be a good one," she said. "Maybe a steak knife through the eye."

She walked away, flanked by her brother.

Dylan pretended that Manny wasn't there. "What about that one? It's a husband and wife."

She nodded and took a photo.

"Pretty annoyed at me, huh?" Manny asked, following slowly behind.

"Yup." *You fired me, sicced your daughter on me.*

"Can I make it up to you?" He leaned forward, attempting to get into her peripheral vision, smiling, his hands still in his pockets.

"And how exactly would you do that?" she asked, not looking at him. *And why would you care to make it up to me?*

He casually strode up beside her. She slowed her pace and stopped to look at him. She gazed at him directly in the eye. He was probably five inches taller than her, and he was so close that she could smell him—a hint of sandalwood. His smile and confident ease clashed against her jagged resentment.

"Use your imagination." A crooked smile spread across his face, and it ignited her nerves. She gazed at him with *the look* but he didn't shrink the way everyone else always did. It was as if he took it as a challenge.

"Well, when I live in a cardboard box, maybe you can hand me a fucking flower. That makes it all better, right?"

"You can do better than that," he said. "I *am* an art collector with a wide network. Maybe I can introduce you to … an artist? Someone who can tell you how to make it in the industry someday."

"Right," she said. That's all she needed. Some pretentious artist who was oh-so-generous enough to brag about themselves and tell her how maybe someday she'd be someone. Maybe.

"Like I said, use your imagination," he said with that damn wink.

"I'll do that," she said casually before turning away to snap a photo of him next to a tall headstone with fake pink flowers jutting from the top.

"I can't wait to see what you come up with, then."

She glanced up as he strode away. Curiosity and a strange tickle of maleficence flickered in her chest, and it left her uneasy. He was a grown man; it was completely inappropriate for her to be attracted to him.

Dylan approached and stood next to her, squinting at Manny as he left the cemetery. "I saw that guy with Eva and her mom."

Sophia watched Manny, curious, without responding. A white car passed in the distance, and she wondered for a moment if it was Eva's white Range Rover. But the road twisted around the cemetery, and she couldn't see clearly.

"Isn't he married to Eva's mom?" Dylan asked.

"Yeah, I think so."

"I think he likes you."

"I think so, too."

21

Sophia

GET OUT

Then: April 15

On Sunday, jackhammers growled on the back patio of the house next door—the fallout of the Flores purchase—and they gave Sophia a wicked headache. The noise had reverberated through the walls all morning: as she showered, as she brushed her teeth, as she fixed her hair and dressed.

Her brother's room remained dark, and Dylan lay still in his bed. He could always sleep through anything. When Sophia passed two empty wine bottles on the counter, she was surprised that her mom was already up and out of the house. Both of them needed to start looking for new jobs. She'd try the bread company, the orchards, the weird gem store. She had about as good of a shot as her mother did, except surely Hendy's lies were blowing most of her mom's chances.

Angry with the noise, she flung open the front door and saw a green piece of paper tacked to the warped plywood. It flapped in the breeze as if it were alive. She pulled it off the door and read it.

· · ·

Eviction Notice

Flores Inc. hereby gives Jennifer Palmer and ALL OTHER OCCU-PANTS HOLDING UNDER THEM, thirty (30) days' notice to vacate the rental unit located at 317 Third Street.

Reasons for Eviction:

1. New owner

2. Renovation

3. Zoning change

Sophia stared at the note as anger boiled in her chest. She had no idea where her family would go. Prices in town had climbed dramatically, and Mrs. Ratner had given them more than a deal.

Sophia crumpled the eviction notice. She wasn't going to be forced to move again. She wouldn't.

She turned and looked at Manny's stupid rose in a single vase on the kitchen table. "Make it up to you, my ass," she snarled before marching over and yanking the rose out of the vase. She carried it outside, threw it on the ground, and stomped on the flower.

Thoughts swirled in her mind: Eva's cheerful grin, her copycat blue hair, her poor-me victim videos, her obsession with selfies. Eva's joy over her family's decision to buy the house. Sophia getting fired from The Wheel. Manny's false charm. *What the hell was up with that?*

Sophia returned to the living room, sunk into the couch, picked up her pen, and with a trembling hand, she leaned over the dirt-streaked journal, preparing to write something new. Something *better* than a boring story about some girl who had her hair cut off.

She was going to rewrite the future. Rewrite her own story and Eva's too.

Denver Post

MAY 9

Local TikTok Star Still Missing

PAONIA—Police are investigating the whereabouts of a teen who has been missing for four days from her home in Paonia since Saturday.

The girl, Eva Flores, 17, was apparently involved in a game played out at Paonia High School that involved a writing project at school. Flores was a popular TikTok personality with 4 million followers and started a number of dance trends on the social media app popular among young people. Flores is apparently worth an estimated $2 million, according to the site, TikTokFamousNet-Worth.com. The Delta County Sheriff is investigating her disappearance, as well as a forest fire that spread over two acres in the area in which the teen was last seen.

"We're asking anyone with any information about Ms. Flores and the fire to come forward with information," said Sheriff Geoffrey Rawlings.

The teen's parents, Becky and Manny Flores, looked distraught during a press conference with reporters and said their daughter had been the target of bullies at school for months after she moved to Paonia from Boulder. They said one teen cut her hair off, and that things took a dangerous turn soon after. They pointed the finger to a group of teens they said were bullying her, but police have found no firm evidence to make formal charges.

One of the suspected teens, unnamed because she is a minor, told police that a journal gave them a unique power over Flores, although no further details were provided.

"Something happened to my girl," said Manny Flores, a former Boulder real-estate developer who managed his daughter's social media career. His wife, Becky, wept behind him as he spoke. "She had everything, and those kids took it away."

Police said they will continue the investigation into Flores' whereabouts. But oddly, Manny Flores called off search teams for his daughter after just eight hours of volunteers scouring the mountains and hillside surrounding the Western Colorado town.

22

Sophia

MOUNTAIN GIRL

Then: April 16

When Sophia pulled up to school, Ethan and Morgan ran to the car. Sophia slowly rolled the crank to lower the window.

Ethan placed his hands on the top of the car and stuck his head into the window opening. "Did you hear about—"

"What, that I was evicted?" Sophia responded.

"Dude, what?" Ethan recoiled.

"What?" Morgan asked from behind.

"She got evicted," he said over his shoulder.

"Dude," Morgan said, throwing her hands up. "When?"

"This weekend."

"You didn't tell me!" Morgan said. "You should've texted."

Sophia shrugged and climbed out of the car.

"You know ... um ... you can always stay with me," Morgan said.

"Or me?" Ethan said.

Sophia glanced at him and rolled her eyes before reaching for her backpack on the back seat.

"I mean," Ethan said, "my dad's still mad that you poured out all that water from our hallway."

"Yeah, because we all need buckets of water in our hallway," Sophia said.

"True," Morgan said. "Maybe I should write about buckets of water in the hallway for Ambien's class. A fire. Maybe a story about a fire..." Her voice trailed off as she considered it.

"What if *your* story comes true too, Morg?" Ethan asked.

"You don't think...," Morgan said.

Sophia stood quietly beside them, leaning against the car, as Morgan became more animated, running her fingers through her hair as she worried about her own story. "I just *have* to get a good grade, guys," she said.

"I'll just write my own story, where I won't be homeless," Sophia said. "Right?"

The three of them walked through the parking lot and, when Sophia's gaze landed on the red brick school building, she stopped, flat-footed. Someone had spray-painted the brick wall with pink and purple flowers and a silver heart ... and the word *Eva*.

The words of the story she'd written Sunday flashed in her mind.

Elsa asked them to surprise her. To display their love in the most grandiose ways. To gift her their most precious belongings and children. To strip naked. To sacrifice each other to show their love...

Sophia stared at the graffiti with a gaping mouth. Inside her own mind, she was screaming, shock and delight and terror colliding together like electrical charges.

"Crazy, isn't it?" Ethan asked.

Sophia chuckled and walked past the pink wall to the front door. Ethan and Morgan followed her inside.

"They love her," Morgan said, dumbfounded. "It's the same floral design that's on her TikTok and Instagram page.

Like her ... brand. Of course she was just outside taking a video in front of it."

"Mrs. Evans is gonna lose it," Ethan said.

Sophia's head buzzed. She felt as if she were experiencing one giant déjà vu. She'd lived this before. She'd already seen it.

"Why is everyone being so nuts over her?" Morgan said, jogging to catch up to them. "I don't get it. It's not like she's curing cancer or sending people to Mars."

Sophia didn't respond. She was taken with the boisterous energy in the hallway. Voices rang with excitement, and at a louder din than normal. People ran through the halls, clustering in a ball of bodies near the cafeteria. It took a moment before Sophia realized they were gathered around Eva. Like bees swarming their queen.

Eva passed by two frumpy younger girls. One of them handed the other a piece of some sort of breakfast bread.

Eva strode up to them with her throng of ten or twelve people following. A couple of kids held cell phones up, taking videos.

"Did you make that yourself?" Eva asked the girls.

The taller one nodded.

"Oooh, looks so good," she said. "I didn't really eat today."

"Give her your banana bread, Dakota," said Grayson Dyer, a skinny junior with acne-pitted cheeks.

"Yeah," a couple kids cheered from behind.

The taller girl held tight to her bread. "I was trying to keep it for later," she said quietly.

"Kayla, don't be a ho," one of the girls shouted.

"Yeah, not cool," said another.

After a moment the girl and her friend hesitantly handed Eva their bread.

"Really? For me?" Eva squealed as if it were a surprise.

Sophia watched with still more awe, knowing she'd written

the part about the kids in the candy shop. This was playing out in real life. But instead of candy, it was breakfast treats. She watched as Eva ceremoniously gave the kids who advocated for her pieces of her bread.

"Hey!" Aidan Voinovich approached Eva from behind. She turned away from the kids, stared at him warily as he lumbered toward her, flipping greasy hair out of his eyes.

"Yeah, so uhh ... what's your name again?"

"Aidan. I texted you. I comment on all your stuff?"

She gazed at him, not registering recognition. She simply blinked, waiting.

"I, uh, I know you're doing that wilderness thing. And so here." He thrust a closed hunting knife out, offering it to her.

She grimaced and looked at the knife.

"You could get kicked out of school for that, you idiot."

She turned away and strode down the hall. Aidan's face blossomed red, highlighting splotches of dark purple acne, and he put the knife back in his pocket. He watched her leave with the walk of a runway model. Quickly, he sniffed and wiped his nose with the back of his hand, his jaw set.

"Eva!" a small girl called from the crowd. Eva smiled, showing off perfectly white teeth, and waved.

"You're gonna be mine," Aidan said slowly under his breath, and his eyes narrowed as he watched Eva.

Sophia watched him a moment longer, wondering what was going on in his head. She hadn't written that part into her story.

"What happened?" Morgan asked, turning to Holly. Everyone had heard how Eva had scorned Holly for something that apparently happened at the camping trip.

Holly leaned against a yellow locker. "She posted some video announcing a weekend event that she'd pay for and said it would give everyone the chance to join her in being TikTok-famous," she said, nostrils flared. "And she wanted people to show their love or something ... and that she needed a bunch of outdoor gear to be a true Coloradan." She scoffed. "Basically, a lame way to get people to buy shit for her."

"Who's going on the trip?" Morgan asked.

"She organized a random lottery. Ten *lucky* people get to go." Holly rolled her eyes.

Sophia turned to watch the scene as if it were on a movie screen, amazed by the bizarre show of adulation. Eva had always been popular and fawned over, but never like this.

"When is this event?" Morgan asked.

"In three weeks." Holly rolled her eyes. "This is going to be the most nauseating three weeks of my life." She turned and walked away.

Eva's fake squeal echoed above the hubbub, and through the thicket of people, Sophia spotted her holding a stand-up paddle board.

Phillip Hackett squeezed through the crowd, shouting, "This is what you need, girl." He presented her with a green camping tent.

"It's from REI!" he shouted.

"Like that matters," whispered Morgan.

"You guys are amazing!" Eva said. "This is going to be a blast."

A group of girls screamed near Mr. Pitt's chemistry room, and Morgan and Ethan flipped their heads to see what the commotion was about. Sophia followed their gaze, feeling somewhat overwhelmed by the chaos of the scene. *Did I make this happen?* She'd written a basic shell of a story, and she never really knew what to expect, how it would play out.

"What the...?" Ethan whispered.

Andrew Rogers, a sophomore soccer player, ran down the hallway, arms splayed open, yelling. He wore only a G-string and striped black and blue socks pulled up to his calves.

"What the hell is going on?" Morgan whispered in awe. "It's like someone flipped the crazy switch."

Sophia smiled, feeling a twinge of excitement inside her

stomach. She should have really written something more horrific for Eva. She should have had her fall through the linoleum floor of the school. If she had written that, would it have happened? There was so much she hadn't understood about this weird power, but just touching it, the mere outline of what was possible, made her whole body tingle.

Andrew zigged and zagged through the crowd.

"Did you see his ass?" Ethan asked, craning his head to watch Andrew as he skittered around a couple girls.

"I love you, Eva!" Andrew yelled, before shaking his butt in a mimic of one her famous dance moves.

Principal Evans came racing after him in high heels, yelling at him to stop.

"Did you write this in your story too?" Morgan asked.

Sophia nodded slowly, a look of pure awe flooding her face.

"Holy shit," Morgan said. They both turned to watch Andrew slide in his socks on the linoleum, dodging people.

"But why did you write *this* shit?" Ethan asked.

Sophia couldn't look away from the melee around her. The squeals. The teachers running after Andrew and eventually tackling him. Someone threw a purple raincoat over his lower half. Eva hugged Lydia, who stood with a thrilled, open-mouth grin.

"Just testing stuff," Sophia said eventually.

"Is there projectile vomit coming?" Ethan asked. "I want to be out of the way if—"

"It's better," Sophia said, a wry smile climbing up her cheek. "Just wait."

Wicked Games

BY SOPHIA PALMER

Elsa grew emboldened by the knowledge of the power she held in her hands. The Domesticis would follow her and love her no matter what. She began choosing whom to imprison and whom to invite to elaborate galas.

Elsa paraded through the city, as if the streets were a giant Monopoly game, buying up things as she pleased. A cottonwood tree looked sparkly like diamonds in the light, so she ordered her minions to chop it down. She saw a lovely ornate candy store with candy canes in the windows. When she strode into the business, her velvet coat flapping in the wind, she saw two children counting pennies at the counter to buy their gumdrops. "This is our allowance," they said.

Elsa demanded they give her their allowance, and then she laughed and pointed to the door. "Get out. No candy for you."

Her guards came into the store, pushing out the shop owner and the children. "This is my candy store, and only I will eat this candy," Elsa said, tossing her head back with a cackle.

When she looked out the window, she saw her onlookers mimic her body language. They, too, tossed their heads back in laughter. She reached into a box of gumdrops from the window display and tossed ten of the gumdrops into the crowd. They fought over the gumdrops, pushing each other out of the way, kicking and biting.

On her return to her brownstone, Elsa passed Jane, hiding in her box on the street. Elsa decided she wanted the box, too. She decided Jane should be thrown into a prison, and called in burly guards to haul off the disheveled and dirty girl. Jane screamed and clawed, but she had no voice. Elsa had taken that too, tucking it away into her Gucci purse.

Inside her home, Elsa would occasionally walk past the window of the second floor to see her adoring fans. She spotted a young girl in short blue hair dancing on the sidewalk below, mirroring the steps that Elsa had created and performed on stage a week before. She liked it, and so she invited the girl inside her home. She kept her in the living room, and would feed her a steak dinner at night. Soon, Elsa began collecting people who performed and amused her most. Commenting on their skills in what they saw as an authentic and endearing voice. Her feedback made them love her more, and soon, people began camping outside her brownstone in the cold.

The snow spun around their heads, and the night sky offered no warmth, yet they were there. They sat inside REI tents and snuggled deep into sleeping bags at night. They cooked their food over little camp stoves, just to witness a glimpse of Elsa. After all, she could do anything and her fans adored her more. She stood at the window, just staring with a blank face for a mere five seconds. When she turned away, they cheered and placed piles of gold at her doorstep.

Elsa wanted to see what else she could get them to do. Maybe she could get them to strip naked in the cold. Maybe she could make them kill each other. Hurt each other.

One morning, feeling especially spry, she yanked open the window and yelled to her fans. They cheered and finally silenced waiting for her to speak. Elsa asked them to surprise her. To display their love in the most grandiose ways. To gift her their most precious belongings and children. To strip naked. To sacrifice each other to show their love....

Elsa didn't know what that would entail, but she hoped it would be good.

The next morning, her spies told her that some people did not see her in all the glory she deserved. A small handful of critics had argued that she could only survive on a stage, as a pampered queen, and that if her followers had seen her in the wilderness, they would see her true colors.

"The wilderness will eat her alive," a critic had said.

To prove them wrong and win them over, she organized an outing in the magical forest to the East. She'd never been there before, but she knew with the proper equipment, she'd show she could rule on any ground.

But the wilderness had other plans for her.

The Flores File: Video Interviews
NOW

Morgan: I couldn't believe that everything happened—all because of Sophia's story. I mean, it took me a long time to digest it. It scared me, because you never really knew what Sophia was thinking. So I wanted to be on her good side and be, like, a good friend. I begged her to write things for me.

Ethan: The craziness at school was fun. But the other stuff she wrote? That was ... over the top. Was I afraid, though? Yeah, kinda. I mean, eventually. Later.

Sheriff Rawlings: No, we didn't find the perpetrator of the vandalism of the school. But yes, Andrew received a proper consequence... He's a minor, so I'm not at liberty to discuss.

Mr. Thomas (AKA Ambien): Yes, the rumors are that this all started with the school project in my class. Of course I'm flattered.

Aidan Voinovich: I loved Eva first. So no, I didn't like all that attention she ended up getting.

Mr. Thomas: Aidan did appear to have an infatuation, yes. [Folds his hands in his lap.] We learned that later, of course.

Sheriff Rawlings: Aidan's family fully cooperated with our investigation. And we did learn things. [Pauses. Lips pursed.] What did we learn? [Pauses. Crosses his arms, indicating he's finished.] I am not at liberty to say more.

23

Sophia
ART TRAP

Then: April 19

Sophia wrote another chapter, and two nights later, she ducked into the tent outside her house.

She slipped through the white canvas before gluing the photos onto a silver-painted canvas and polishing them with a lacquer glaze. She planned to ditch school for the next several days, because at least ten pieces needed to be finished fast to meet demand.

That is, if her story went as planned.

The twang of country music played in her earbuds as her mind wandered. She imagined Eva packing up her house and moving back to Boulder. But first, Sophia had to make her pay. She thought about the next chapters of her story, and how she'd pull the thread on the invisible clothing that Eva wore until she stood bare before the world. She imagined the crowds of kids at school, pointing and laughing, and a wicked feeling of power flooded Sophia.

The feeling surprised her, much like that thrill of realizing you could fly in a dream. The thought also elicited another feeling that slowly slid into view: a sliver of self-doubt. Was this normal? Enjoying the power of knowing Eva would suffer?

"Hello?" The man's voice was silky.

She turned around to see Manny Flores standing in the opening of the tent. Dark stubble dotted his chin, not in the hungover five o'clock shadow way, but in a *GQ* sort of way. It sent a flame through her stomach and tugged her out of her artistic tunnel.

"You again," she said.

"Yep, 'tis I," he said, stepping inside the tent. His presence shifted the energy of the space. Sophia felt her jaw tense, a twinge of excitement, of expectation. Now, she'd see if her magical story really worked.

The tent smelled of incense and fumes, and red and orange paint splattered her overalls. She stood up, wiping her hands on her pants.

"So this is where the magic happens." He nodded at the ten canvases lying on the ground in various stages of development.

"This is it."

"It's…" He frowned, and Sophia noticed how thick his eyebrows were. A flicker of panic flew through her: what if he hates it? He's not supposed to hate it.

"I'm particular about art," he said, walking slowly through the tent.

With hands in the pockets of his pants—made of a trendy gray wool—he took in each piece with the eye of an expert.

Sophia watched him, trying to read his expressions. Then she caught herself, her neediness. Her story would give her what she wanted.

She painted a coat of red lacquer onto a canvas, swirling the brush into small circles.

"I've seen a lot of great work over the years, and I've never seen anything quite like this," he said, pausing to study a finished piece of lace and gold glitter with photos of gravestones. He leaned over it, quiet for several moments, the only sound in the room the sound of Johnny Cash's low voice in her single earbud and the wet sound of her brush dipping into the paint.

"I love it. And this one…" He held up a simpler painting with a distant photo of Dylan in the graveyard surrounded by a sky of painted silver stars. She'd mimicked Jackson Pollock's style.

"I…" Her brush dropped onto the pallet. She knew this was what would happen, but it still flooded her with a heady thrill of satisfaction. *He said he loved it.*

She gathered her wits and regained the shrewdness that led him to the tent. "Yeah, the stars in that one makes me feel like—"

"Like you want to put your hand out to touch the stars … like falling rain," he said.

She was taken aback. She intended someone to feel when looking at the painting. "Exactly."

She calmed her breath, knowing it'd be a dead giveaway. She wasn't used to important people like him even glancing in her direction, let alone paying attention to her.

"You ever thought of having a gallery showing?" he said, standing up straight.

"Hmmm," she said, sounding unimpressed. She didn't look up. The red was becoming too thick, but she wasn't thinking about the picture anymore. The paint represented her mind, wrapping circles around the same thing, pulling him in, deeper and deeper until the paint dried and he was stuck. Until he was part of her painting. Part of her story. Another piece glued to a canvas.

"And this one. Is it for sale?" he said, holding up a large piece. It was a black-and-white photograph of early 1900s Paonia with Native American Utes in full headdress—one she had photocopied and blown up from the library—with red splattered paint, bright photos of Colorado wildflowers, gold glitter, and black painted tire-tread marks down the middle. It was a mishmash of the valley's history and beauty and pain and lies, and she hadn't even known why she made the piece.

It was something that had come to her in the middle of the night two days earlier, and she crawled out of bed with the express intention of making this picture.

"Not everything's for sale," she said.

"What's your price?"

She knew immediately the answer. "Land."

"Land?" he scoffed. "Come on. What, a thousand? Five hundred?"

"I want The Wheel and my house. And I'll give you the painting," she said.

He set the picture down and Sophia's chest clenched, worried that her story wouldn't be right. That she didn't have the control she expected. The stories followed things in surprising ways, never quite the same as the words on the page.

She imagined for a moment what it would be like to own The Wheel. What it would feel like to fire Riley, change the decor to be funky art, and get rid of that broken foreign coffee maker. She'd paint their house, knock down some walls to open up the kitchen and add a new window in the living area so her mom could drink coffee and see the sun rise.

"That's quite an ask." He chuckled.

"Your call," she said. "I know more people will be coming to town to see my work."

"More people."

"Yeah, maybe thirty," she said. *I wrote this. So it will be.*

"Did you organize a show?"

"No," she said. "They'll just come."

She stood up and turned to wash her brushes in the bowl behind her. The sun was dipping down behind the trees outside, casting dancing shadows on the tent's walls. "I gotta clean up now."

She closed her paint tubes and picked up the bowl and the brushes. She ducked beneath the flaps of the tent, leaving Eva's dad inside. She was making her way through the tall grass toward the back door when he called to her.

"You're only seventeen?"

"Yeah." She stopped and spun around slowly, throwing a hip out. Sophia wasn't used to feeling sexy—boys in town never did much for her. But this man, he was different. And something devious sprouted inside her. She could easily be the seduce-your-dad kind of girl. Anything to crush Eva.

"You're quite a handful for seventeen," he said slowly.

She could feel his eyes on the bare skin that showed between her sports bra and baggy jean overalls.

"So I'll see you around?" he asked. In his eagerness, she felt an enormous power shift occurring, transferring it all to her. Just as she planned.

"Sure," she said, slowly shrugging one shoulder. A few strands of hair fell across her face, and she bit her lip.

"Hey, uh…" he said. "Why don't you come to The Wheel?"

"Why?"

"I have a proposition."

She shrugged. "Sure."

"Monday night?"

She nodded.

"Brilliant."

Wicked Games

BY SOPHIA PALMER

Meanwhile, Jane was sitting in a jail cell when the guard came to her with good news. She had painted beautiful pictures in her cell, celebrating the Domesticis rather than the Invasors. She had also struck gold in the jail cell, digging slowly, methodically with a kitchen spoon.

Jane would get her cardboard box back where she'd happily live, she'd get out of jail and she would not only have a job, but an entire empire of her own. She bought a crown to wear in private, allowing no one else to see it, except her two friends.

"How did you know there was gold buried in that jail cell?" Jane's friend had asked.

"Because the spirits told me."

24

Sophia
THE GALLERY

Then: April 23

M onday night, Sophia rolled up to The Wheel for her appointment with Manny Flores. She imagined Riley's contemptuous look when she walked through the door. *You're fired,* Riley would say. Sophia didn't really care what Riley thought, but she didn't really want judgment. Certainly not *her* judgment.

As she climbed out of the Datsun and walked to the front door, she expected the cafe had probably already been remodeled. She expected life-size posters on the walls of Eva grinning in a half-shirt with the TikTok logo in the corner. Sophia chuckled at the thought as she yanked open the front door to the coffee shop.

When she stepped inside, she froze. Someone had removed all the tables, painted the walls a stark white. She stood flatfooted and gaped at the strangeness of the empty space.

"Hello?" she said.

"Sophia!" Manny's voice echoed from the back kitchen. He stepped into the room, wearing jeans and a Black Keys concert T-shirt. He looked handsome as usual, way younger and not like *someone's Dad*. He held his arms out wide, expectant. "Well?"

"What's this?" she asked.

"Your work," he said. "It's a gallery for your art."

"I'm..." She slowed her pace and took in the vacant room. The fact that he'd just shut down The Wheel meant Riley was out of a job, too, which gave Sophia some joy.

"I want to commission you to create huge ones. I want an entire gallery with just Sophia. Whatever moves you. I know an art dealer in Santa Fe, and he sent an email out to his clientele with a photo of your work."

"You're showing *my* stuff." She had written it, not exactly like this, but she had written this story. It was happening. *Everything* would happen just as she wanted.

"They love it."

A devilish thrill swept through her, and she turned to gaze at the stark white walls, the wonder of it all lifting her. Her chest expanded, as plans spun in her mind. She'd skip school and take her camera out to some place... Maybe... She didn't know what the pieces would look like, but she would just photograph whatever moved her.

"When?" she asked.

"Next Thursday," he said.

That wasn't much time, and Sophia worried her work would be rushed and not very good. Maybe she should have focused on the timing of her story better.

She turned to him. "And my offer? Selling my painting in exchange for The Wheel and my house?"

"I thought about it, and there's no way I could pass it up," he said quickly. "You know what? It's a deal."

It was an absurd deal. She knew it. His rational mind knew it. But she had written it.

"I knew you'd say that." Confident, she tossed her dark

hair over her shoulder. His eyes didn't leave her as he strode toward her slowly.

"I'm thinking, maybe, a large canvas, a thirty-three by forty?" Manny stood close to her, closer than necessary, and gestured at the wall, his arm just inches from her chest.

He was clearly interested in her, and she found she liked the attention a lot more than she'd expected. She'd pretty much blown off most interest from guys in town, because all the boys seemed to be douchebags, except for Ethan.

She'd use this to her advantage. She leaned into him, hoping he'd feel her breath on his neck.

"Perfect," she said quietly.

"One large one there would give it a polished..." He paused and turned slowly to look at her, his eyes trailing from her eyes to her mouth. She gazed at his mouth too and bit her lip. Toying with him would be fun. It would be a game. Another way to mess with Eva.

"Yeah?" she whispered.

He returned his gaze to the blank wall. "A classic look."

She nodded slowly and let the silence—and the sexual tension—between them linger. She took a few slow steps away from him, gesturing at another space along the wall.

"And here?" She tried her best to look up at him through wide, coy eyes, a play really on his desire for her. But there was something real to her own attraction, despite the weird nature of this new interaction. The dark eyebrows, the five o'clock shadow, the way he thoughtfully gazed at the blank wall, as if her art already hung there.

From what she'd seen, what she'd heard, this was a man who was stoic and business-like, with a hawk-like determination.

Here she held him in her hands, like putty. All she had to do was put pen to paper, flip her hair, lick her lips, and lean in close. She had trapped fire in a glass.

"You...," he said, waving a tan hand up and down, tracing

Sophia's body. She didn't think she looked sexy in short cutoff jeans, a retro Orange Crush T-shirt, rows of long beaded necklaces, and combat boots. Yet the way he looked at her, you would think she was standing in a negligee. The idea that he thought she was hot—wearing *this*—intrigued her even more, and she felt momentarily as if she were an observer watching the scene play out.

"I think," he said, "here you can add…"

"More," she said slowly, nodding at the wall.

"Yeah … more…" He turned to look at her with that dazzling crooked smile. "Pictures, I mean."

She liked this too much. She turned to look at the white wall again.

"You know … you're the most interesting person I've met in Paonia," he said, more relaxed. He put his hands in his pockets and smiled at her.

"Really? I'm pretty much the least interesting person here." She didn't smile back.

"Yeah, I was taken by…" He stopped, sniffed, and scratched his cheek. He became straight as an arrow, as if pulled out of a trance. "Okay, so I can swing by and see what you've got … in say … maybe two weeks?"

She nodded, doe-eyed again, attempting to lure him back in with invisible wire. *This is fun.*

"I'll let you know how many people I can get here for the event. And you? You get painting."

"No prob," she said, nodding. She stuck her hands into her pockets and moved slowly to the door. She exhaled. "Well, yeah, I need to head out."

"Oh!" he said, moving with a jerk. "I almost forgot…."

He pulled papers from his back pocket and then, grasping her arm, slowly placed them into her hands. "I signed the deeds over to you."

"What?" She looked down at the papers. She wasn't expecting it so fast.

"The Wheel and the house," he said. "All yours."

The papers crinkled between her fingers, feeding an electric power that thrummed inside her chest. In her hands, she held the keys to her freedom. Then she would have hundreds of big art collectors in town buying her pieces. *Her* art. In *her* gallery.

"I'm honored," he said softly, touching her arm.

Ownership in exchange for one stupid painting? This was too easy.

People had told her before that her pictures were cool. But she knew some people really just thought they were weird. Only the rich tourists who moved through town wanted them. Her classmates always nodded and said, *wow.* Her dad had really encouraged her art the most. He was the first to show her mixed media art—something he'd learned at a stint at a hippie commune where he had spent a few weeks. "You got something in you, girl," her dad had told her.

When life spun out of control, usually because of decisions he or her mom made, art gave her comfort. It became a centered point that wouldn't move while everything else whirled wildly around her.

Yet now, people *wanted* her art. And she was getting what *she* wanted. She was getting *everything* she wanted. She was writing her future, and the idea of it still felt as if she were being lifted off the ground by helium balloons. Thrilling. Exciting. But at the same time, a bit unnerving.

She stared at the deeds in her hand for a long moment, reading her name on the documents, before glancing up again.

"I'm gonna take care of you," he said before pointing at her. He winked. "Promise."

The Flores File: Video
Interviews
NOW

Sophia: Did I think he'd give me The Wheel? *And* the house? Hell no. Was I thrilled? Uh… *yeah.*

Becky Flores (Eva's mother): She destroyed us. Everything she did. Sophia Palmer put a spell on my husband.

Riley: I heard her talking to Ethan at school after she got fired. She said, *Eva's dad is so hot.* That is seriously messed up. He's so *old.* But there she was, going on and on about how she was going to write that down, or something.

25

Sophia
NO MORE SCRUBBING

Then: April 23

Inside the kitchen, her mother frantically scrubbed the perennially stained white sink.

Despite the fact they'd been evicted, she had continued to care for the house, hammering down the broken step on the porch and fixing the leaky faucet. Her energy around the house grew to almost a frantic pace, as if the busier she was, the greater the chance she'd be able to stay, the greater the chance she would find a job, that her life would be stable again.

At least she isn't clipping the grass with scissors, thought Sophia.

Sophia tapped her mom's arm, but she just continued to furiously scrub the sink. She tapped again. "Uh-huh," her mom said, not looking up.

Finally, Sophia pulled on her shoulder, forcing her to turn around. "What?" Her mom's tone bit the air.

"We own this place now, Ma," she said before she pulled out the deeds. She held them up by her face. "We own it."

"I don't..." Her mom frowned and squinted at the paper. "What's this?"

Sophia explained that Manny had given her The Wheel and their house. Her mother took the deeds from Sophia, put on her reading glasses, and slowly sunk into a kitchen chair. She flipped the paper around, examining it carefully. "These are real?"

"Yeah," Sophia said.

"Why?" She set the papers down on the scratched kitchen table. "Why'd he give these to you?"

"He traded them for a picture I made."

Her mom gazed at her, biting her lip. Sophia wanted to tell her about the story, about the journal, how her world was slowly unfolding as she wanted. But she knew her mother wouldn't believe it.

"What'd you promise this man?" Her tone cut the edges of Sophia's nerve.

She snatched the papers off the table. "Art. He liked my art, if that's so hard for you to believe."

"I'm not saying—but Sophia. A whole café? Our home?"

Sophia's chest contracted. Her mom had been her fan, encouraging her to take art classes in school and showing her online art videos. But now she didn't think her art was good enough for a grown man to like and pay for.

"Thanks for believing in me." Sophia stood and stormed out of the room, heading for the front door.

"Oh, come on," her mom called to her. "You're a good artist. We know that—but there's got to be more ... more to it than a single painting."

Sophia punched open the door and exited the house. Dylan sat on the front porch, his lanky body bent over the bench as he practiced a yo-yo.

"Hey sis," he said. "I can do Around the World. Watch."

Sophia knew how she'd gotten the deeds. In a way, her art *had* gotten them. In a way. Did it matter if it was her art or the fact that she could make Manny drool with one lick of her lips? *She* had done this.

"You know what?" she yelled to her mother through the screen porch. "There is more. He commissioned tons of art from me, and he's gonna have a gallery showing, and he's gonna help me sell a bunch of it to fancy big-time art collectors."

"But *why?*"

"Who?" Dylan asked.

"Because he says I'm talented," she said to her mom, before marching to her car. Her body felt rigid as insecurities and anger swirled through her chest. She wanted to lash out at everyone.

26

Sophia
WISHES

Then: April 25

E than walked down the jagged path from the A-frame house. Suddenly he tripped, lurched forward, and fell flat on his face.

"What is wrong with you?" Morgan climbed out of the car and sat on the hood with Sophia. Morgan pulled thick sandwiches out of a plastic bag. "You walk about as good as Sophia."

Sophia didn't think it was funny. She didn't want to be with anyone that afternoon, but after Morgan had called her a bazillion times, she finally stopped painting and agreed to meet them. Morgan had bought them lunch for a picnic at E's house. It sounded better than the jar of peanut butter and some eggs in her refrigerator.

"My dad buried rice in the yard, just in case," Ethan said.

"In case what?" Sophia asked. Her tone had a bite.

"You know." He shrugged. "He strapped the shovel to his car again too." He nodded to his dad's red Jeep parked five yards away.

Sophia hopped off the hood of her car, marched to his

dad's car, climbed up onto its tire, and yanked off the shovel that was strapped to the rooftop. The thing was heavier than she expected, but she tossed it into the bushes.

"Why'd you do that?" Ethan chuckled.

"Because he didn't need it." She marched back to her car, picked up her sub sandwich, and took an enormous bite of bread, cheese, and salami. She tore into it like an animal and aggressively chewed. Her whole body felt wired, on edge.

"He's gonna flip," Ethan said.

"Good," she said through a mouthful of sandwich.

"So how about instead of doing *that*, you write something in that magic journal that takes away this whole end-of-the-world stress? I can't take it anymore," Ethan asked, unwrapping his own sandwich. "Oh, and write down that I get a brand-new car?"

A swell of empathy filled Sophia's chest. He just wanted sanity, an ability to know the future would not be calamity and Armageddon.

"I want my dad to just stop. You know? Like, not be so worried." He looked off in the distance at the juniper and pine trees that flanked his house.

"Ah, E… It'll be okay," Morgan said through a mouthful of tuna salad.

"How you doing about your grandma, Morg?" Ethan asked, changing the subject like a pro.

Morgan's body deflated. "It's, like, not even real… She was so sick for so long. But I still can't believe it." She set her sandwich on her lap and looked out at the pine trees. Her face softened, and her eyes looked wet. "Until her, no one in my family has ever died—"

Morgan went on talking about her grandma, whom Sophia knew and liked, but her brain couldn't help but wander elsewhere. Her story consumed her. "I'm sorry Morg," Sophia said, but it felt half-hearted.

"How's your mom?" Ethan asked. *How will Eva respond when people hate her?*

"She's pretty devastated. She's still in her pajamas," Morgan said. *Would it be terrible to give Eva cancer? Yes, people would feel sorry for her.*

"So, you hear back from those schools yet?" Ethan asked, taking another bite. She imagined Eva, smelling and homeless, begging for money on the side of the street. A flurry of excitement flooded Sophia's head. She smiled.

"No," Morgan said, her shoulders slumping. She swiveled on the hood to look at Sophia. "Hey, that's what you can write, Soph. Maybe you could get me off the wait-list for University of Michigan and Harvard."

Sophia glanced at her friend and chuckled. Morgan was so greedy.

"I'm serious." Her words were muffled as she chewed.

"Yeah, yeah, okay, sure. I'll write it in," Sophia lied. For some reason, this seemed like too much. Morgan already had money, the best grades, already sought to be the best in everything. She didn't *need* that.

"What *have* you written?" Morgan asked. She swallowed and took a long drink of her Diet Dr Pepper.

"You'll see."

Morgan rolled her eyes. "But you'll write mine in there soon, right? Because I have to make a decision by May first."

"Can we at least see what you wrote?" Ethan asked.

"It's supposed to be a group project, right?" Morgan added quickly.

They were like the kids she saw in the cereal aisle of the grocery store, begging for Fruit Loops after being told no. It irritated Sophia. It was *her* journal. Her story. Eva wasn't targeting them; it was Sophia who had been victimized here. Sophia whose job, whose home, whose freaking identity had been taken from her. And here they were, bitching about Harvard and … okay, Ethan's complaint was legit. But still.

She had been through enough. Why couldn't she just enjoy this one thing for five minutes before her friends wanted her to break off pieces for them, too?

"Shut it, guys," Sophia said, inspecting her sandwich.

"Dude," Ethan said quietly and took a bite of his sandwich.

Morgan's face fell and she chewed slowly with a furrowed brow, not looking at Sophia.

Sophia didn't care if they were bent out of shape. She couldn't think about all the shit these two wanted to happen in their life. All she could think about was fixing her family's situation, about finally having people see her talent, and about Eva and how, hopefully, she'd ruin her.

Flores File: Text messages obtained from Sophia's phone

April 26

1:30 p.m.
Morgan: can u guys help with estate sale for my grandma the 29th?

1:40 p.m.
Ethan:
u bet
how u holding up?

1:45 p.m.
Morgan:
ok i get waves of anxiety sometimes i want to throw up

1:50 p.m.
Ethan:
im sure she was ur fav grandma
come get me and we can hang and talk?

1:55 p.m.

Morgan:
thx ok gimme 10 min

3 p.m.
Morgan:
soph, can u come too? ill buy pizza

April 29

9 a.m.
Morgan:
u coming today?
Soph?

10:20 a.m.
Ethan:
guess its just us

Wicked Games

BY SOPHIA PALMER

Jane began to make art that honored the spirits of people who gave her the new crown. They too had been punished by Elsa's ancestors, the Invasors.

Jane called on those spirits of the Domesticis for power, and she began to paint portraits of Domesticis who had died long before. She honored them with the art, and soon, many people fell in love with them. They wanted to buy and take those pictures and hang them in their homes. They paid with mounds of gold.

One member of the Invasor Royalty, in particular, enjoyed her work: Elsa's father. He took a keen interest in helping Jane earn her rightful position in the world. Elsa's father, who people called The Royal Man, decided he would do anything for her, fall at her feet, worship her, buy her art, sell her art, everything. He became entranced. He began to see Jane as the truth and wanted to do anything to follow her. Jane stole his attention from Elsa.

The new-found clarity that took hold of The Royal Man caused great heartache to Elsa. He began to throw money and fortune at Jane. She acquired valued property and, guided by the ancient spirits of the Domesticis, she dug deep into the ground to uncover gold that the Invasors had not yet found. Jane furiously painted, drawing on inspiration from the land around her. The broken homes made of cardboard, the words, graves, and memories from ancestors.

She also cast a spell on Elsa. It would break the trance the people had fallen under, and make them see her as truth, as Jane had painted her in the brownstone weeks earlier. Elsa would see that the portrait was an authentic version of herself, a person who stole and stomped and looked in the mirror all day. And she'd discover that the mirror only told her lies.

27

Sophia
BETTING BIG

Then: April 25

Everything that Sophia had written was starting to play out. Eva's family would fund the Paonia Wilderness Escape in two weeks. They'd stay at the haunted grand lodge at the base of Kebler Pass. As written, Eva had mooched items from adoring fans, and they had expressed their adoration. She was about to be humiliated in front of her biggest fans in a forest that had long been rumored to be cursed.

Everyone in school simply understood it as a great opportunity to create great social content, and it was the chance to be TikTok-famous alongside Eva. Sophia, Morgan, and Ethan put their names in the hat for the lottery, knowing they would be among the few picked for the weekend.

And ... of course, when Eva announced the winning names over the loudspeaker that morning at school, Ethan, Sophia, and Morgan traded sly smiles. While Eva felt like the queen, Sophia sat with the private knowledge that it was really she who wore the crown. And if Eva were smart, she wouldn't want to give an angry girl like Sophia such a sharp crown. But she didn't have a choice, did she?

After school, Sophia snuggled on the sunken couch and spent her time writing in her magic leather notebook. She leaned over it, scribbling so fast the words ran together. Her hand smudged some of the blue ink, and for a moment she panicked that it might ruin the magic of it all.

"Whatcha doing, sis?" Dylan asked as he passed through the living room.

"Writing a story for school," she said.

"You seem mad. Is it a bad story?" He stood with the posture of an eight-year-old.

She realized her brow was stitched together. "No," she said, pausing. "I don't think so. The bad guy loses."

"Well, that's good then," Dylan said. "Can I read it?"

"Not yet," she said, closing up the journal. She tucked it under her arm, feeling as if her story wouldn't come true if someone else touched her book, let alone read it.

"Will you write me into your story?" he asked.

She didn't answer and kept writing.

"Morgan said that book is magic."

She looked at him and frowned but still didn't answer. She didn't want to delude him into thinking the world was magic, but yet here she was, writing something that foretold the future. *That was magic.*

"She said you can make stuff happen."

"Not really," she said and then continued to write in the journal. "It's just all imagination."

"I like imaginary stuff. Can you make good stuff for me? I'd be a good character, I think," he said, tapping his foot on the end of the couch and scratching his ear.

"Sure, you'd be."

Normally, she'd tell him how he was a good character in her life already. Normally, she'd put down her journal and talk to him, tell him about what was going on in her life.

But at that moment, she just wanted him to go away. He wouldn't understand. Wouldn't understand that this *was* for him, for all of them, what she was doing. That he was tied to her future, and Sophia was going to make it all work out okay.

"That mean you'll put me in?"

"Sure." She stood up and stretched. "I'm gonna head over to see Mom at work."

Dylan clicked on the TV. "'Kay, I'm supposed to work at six," he said without looking at her.

"Yeah," she said, putting on her shoes and half listening. Her hair dropped across her face, and she couldn't see him.

"You're gonna take me, right?"

"Mmmm hmmm." Her mind wandered as she thought about never working a stupid job again. After graduation, she'd just paint and fix up cars forever. She'd make it all happen.

Sophia drove with purpose to the gas station. She yanked the stick shift, and she pressed the gas to the floor of the car when Ethan called her. She answered him on her headphones.

"So...," he said.

"So what?"

"You said you were gonna go home and write."

"Yeah," she said.

"What'd you write?" he asked.

"I can't say," she said.

"You could have just done projectile vomit and made her keel over and die the next day. Not this big elaborate weekend."

Sophia chuckled. "What's with the puke?"

"It's the ultimate."

"Isn't keeling over and dying the ultimate?" Sophia said, turning the corner to get onto the highway.

"Sure."

"You know if I wrote that, it really could happen," Sophia said, suddenly more aware of her power than ever.

"Right, right. And you'd also write that we got a new president, and we all didn't have to do any work at school to graduate."

"I gotta write that. And more," Sophia said.

"What'd you write?" he asked.

"I like surprising you. Gotta go."

Sophia ended the call, feeling annoyed by everyone's curiosity. She wanted them to be patient, to see how it all played out, and her shoulders and chest lifted from the power of finally being in charge. She smiled all the way to the gas station on the corner of the highway.

Inside the gas station, her mom stood behind the counter and a bulletproof Plexiglass wall.

"You came to visit me at work, baby," she said, throwing her arms out and spinning around. "Well, what do you think of my office?"

Sophia tried to smile, but seeing her smart and beautiful mom stuck in these dead-end jobs killed something inside her. Her mom acted like it was the best thing ever, as if she actually enjoyed work. It was all a game, trying to convince her everything was okay. Just like she used to do when her dad went comatose or decided he had to pursue some new idea.

She remembered clearly the time her dad ran to the thrift store and bought all the frying pans he saw because he decided they were going to pan for gold in Marble, Colorado. It wasn't even the kind of equipment you'd use to pan for gold. *Maybe we'll strike it rich,* her mom had said. *Who knows?*

The upside was that it got them to settle in Paonia. But long after her dad left, her mom still struggled to get by.

"So no one offered you a job at the bread store? Or the orchard?" Sophia asked.

"Hendy's got pull everywhere in this town," she said.

Sophia's stomach tightened. She should write some horrible future for Hendy in her journal next. He deserved worse than some slashed tires.

"Listen, I want you to buy a lottery ticket," Sophia said.

"This *is* my lottery ticket, babe," her mom said, taking a sip of Diet Pepsi and gesturing to the small store. She sniffed the air. "But I gotta figure out that smell."

Sophia thought her mom sounded delusional. "No, Ma, I wanna pay for the ticket, but you have to buy it," she said.

Her mom stared at her blankly.

"'Cuz … I'm not legal to buy?" Sophia said.

"Hon, your dad took me down the gambling path once, and I'm not going to go there again."

"Mom, this time it will pay off. Promise… Please. Just buy it?"

"Oh, this one time, I'll win, right?" Her mom laughed, a jaded cracked sound that Sophia seldom ever heard. "Never heard that one before."

"Please? It's just two dollars."

Her mom sighed and reached to take the two dollars that Sophia held out. She bought herself a ticket, waved it in the air, and smiled. "Lucky day!"

Sophia felt as if her mom was slowly cracking. That the facade of *everything is going to be alright* was starting to drive lunacy into her voice and eyes. For a moment, Sophia worried Ma'd been drinking wine before her shift.

She hadn't. She couldn't. That wasn't going to be her mom again.

"Hang onto that and watch the numbers, 'kay?" Sophia said. "And when you win, let me make just four buying decisions, okay? Only four. And you can have the rest of the money to do whatever you want."

"Right." Her mom just gazed back at her, baffled. "If you're so convinced, why don't you just take it then, hon."

Sophia snatched the lottery ticket and shoved it in her pocket.

"Thanks," Sophia said, pushing through the glass door.

"Hey!" her mom said, but Sophia simply got in her car and drove off.

184

28

Sophia

FRENZY

Then: April 26

Sophia pretended to go to school but instead drove her car around the corner and up the hill, parking it behind a bush. She then called the school, imitating her mom's voice to excuse herself, and after her mom and brother left the house, she'd sneak inside the tent to make more paintings. She spent much of her time driving to the cemetery, where she took more photos. A crooked tree. Plastic flowers on a grave. Words carved onto a bench. Dangling beaded necklaces.

She researched the names of people who had died and read their obituaries, then photographed what they loved. A dusty saddle in a nearby barn. A pile of mystery paperbacks at the thrift store. A close-up of a mother holding the hand of a child. The crooked line of a church steeple, a mountain bike tire, the bubbling cherries oozing from a fresh-baked pie.

While taking the pictures, she felt emotions sweep through her that were so strong she sat in her idling car and cried for thirty minutes. The beauty of their lives and sadness of their deaths.

On the second day, Sophia arrived home after taking pictures for twelve hours, the sun had long since set and her mom stood in the doorway to the kitchen, waiting with arms crossed over her chest. "Where the hell've you been?"

Sophia wasn't used to her mother paying any attention to where she went. She typically didn't blow off school. And she typically didn't leave home without telling anyone where she was headed.

Sophia simply looked at her mom, sighed, and dropped her purse and camera bag on the floor.

"You don't go to school, you don't answer your phone, you don't bother telling me where the hell you go."

Her mom took a sip of wine and placed a hand on her hip. The air smelled stale, as if the windows had been shut for weeks, and the house was dark. Only a small lamp lit the corner of the room where Dylan sat in a chair looking at his phone. He looked up and watched the scene between mother and daughter play out.

"I went driving around for some art."

"Some *art.*"

"Yeah, I promise it'll pay off. People are gonna pay a lot of money for this and—"

"Sophia Marie, you're in goddamn high school. You can't just go and do whatever the hell you want—"

"Mom, it's gonna sell. I promise." Sophia took off her camouflage jacket, squeezed past her mom, and went to the kitchen and opened the refrigerator.

Her mom swiveled to follow her, and Dylan popped up out of his chair too. He stopped a few paces away from her, curious, with raised brows.

Empty shelves glowed inside the refrigerator, outside of a single container of yogurt. She grabbed it, opened the lid, and dug in with a spoon.

Her mom's thin figure appeared as a shadow in the

kitchen doorway. "What makes you think you can just go off and not—"

"Mom, it's an investment. I'll catch up at school." She swatted a hand at her.

Her mom swallowed the rest of the wine in her glass. "You're grounded."

"Grounded." Sophia repeated with an incredulous laugh. Her mom hadn't thrown that out since she was eleven. "Right."

"When I call, you better answer your goddamn phone." Her mom turned away and walked to her room.

Sophia sat down to eat the yogurt. Dylan stood in the doorway, his dark hair sticking up like little horns, his shoulders drooping on his lanky frame. He gazed at her with an unfamiliar look on his face. He hadn't been used to seeing strife in their family since their dad left. Sophia felt suddenly as if she were the enemy, the problem. And the look on his face startled her.

"You'll see, Dyl—"

He turned away and went to his room.

An emptiness filled the room, making Sophia feel cold and stony. She sat quietly alone in the dim kitchen, studying the dents in the kitchen table while she ate her yogurt. She wished her family understood what drove her.

She could easily buy a million lottery tickets, but she needed somehow to feel like she earned this. Something inside her, a tiny voice, pushed her to create this art and sell it. She had to do it. It was as if the art had become more important than food and water. The world would see her and finally validate everything she was.

But they didn't understand. They couldn't.

When she finished eating, she slipped into the tent out back. In the dim light of a single lamp, she fell into a trance.

The curling flow of delicate brushes. The acrid smell of paint. The buzz of the printer. The ideas came to her like rows of steady ocean currents, one after another, crashing into her. She absorbed them completely and feverishly created her visions.

Hunger and exhaustion took hold of her, but she continued painting and printing images. After some time, her work became furious and she got a second wind, her fingers spinning fast, her heart racing as she created multiple canvases that night.

Inspired by the story of a woman who lived in her car as a child, saved her father from a burning building, and went on to become a teacher, she wrote the word hero in charcoal and glued pages of textbooks to the canvas.

Another girl loved beading and gardening, so Sophia scattered turquoise and red beads with a photo of spring blooms. For three days, the creativity flowed out, as if yielding to some other power working through her.

Some canvases were huge, the size of a coffee table. Others were as small as a five-by-seven photo.

The art honored dead people: their love, their sadness, their stories.

As she put together her collection, it felt good, a cathartic sort of fury and cleansing. She was painting the stories that needed to be told. As she worked, she heard their voices and their cries, and it felt as if a stream of consciousness moved through her.

Finally, she sat back with a deep sigh of satisfaction. She was done.

29

Morgan
BIG GULP

Then: April 29

Sophia strode across the lawn and plopped down on a gold vintage sofa, a slushie in one hand, the straw in her mouth.

Morgan turned around, startled to see her friend lounging on the furniture her family had set out for the estate sale.

A mixture of delight and irritation swam inside Morgan. In recent days, Sophia had been so consumed with her own story that she didn't seem to hear or see anyone else anymore. It chafed Morgan that Sophia barely acknowledged her grandma's death on text. The Old Sophia would have been on her doorstep the next minute. But Morgan wasn't about to say anything. No one, including Morgan, wanted to piss off someone like Sophia.

"I'm sending Eva down the river. It's gonna be awesome." Sophia kicked her feet up on the coffee table in front of her.

"Oh, I'm fine. And you?" Morgan said with hands on her hips. "Didn't think you'd show up."

"Saw you outside with all this stuff on the lawn, so I stopped." Sophia sucked the last bit of bright red slushie out

189

of the straw before pulling it out of the drink and holding it in the air above her tongue. It sparked prickly panic inside Morgan. Her mom wanted top dollar for these items and was uber-anal about any kind of food or drink on furniture. Morgan imagined Sophia accidentally dumping slushie onto the velvet cushion. "Careful," she whispered.

Sophia rolled her eyes.

People began to flood onto the lawn now. An old man with a cane. A lady with a fuzzy peach-colored sweater with a picture of a cat on the front. About ten yards away, Riley Neuman and Aidan Voinovich hovered over a table with old World War II memorabilia and coins. She'd have to watch those two. They'd probably put things in their pockets.

Sophia followed Morgan's gaze and then sighed. "God, we can't get away from them." She returned to sucking on the straw. "You wouldn't believe what I'm writing."

Ethan appeared behind Morgan, grabbing her shoulders and startling her. "Hey," he said, breathless. "Oh, Soph. You're alive. You helping us today?"

"Helping you do what?"

"Today. This," Morgan said, waving her hand at the furniture. "The estate sale."

"Oh, so that's why you got all this furniture out." Sophia turned to lie down on the sofa, putting her muddy shoes on the crushed velvet. Morgan's body tensed.

"Her grandma's stuff," Ethan said slowly.

Sophia knew Morgan was tight with her grandma, that she'd go to her house every day after school in middle school. Sophia *knew* her grandma. She spent a ton of time there too, eating her fresh-baked bread and learning how to make candles and do tie-dye.

"I texted you," Morgan said, not taking her eyes off Aidan, who bent over to study a steak knife. She thought maybe she could smell him several feet away. A whiff of manure. *He better not stick that knife in his pocket.*

Sophia peered inside her cup and started digging out more slushie. She briefly looked around at the lamps, rugs, books, knickknacks, and tables set out on the lawn. "Why's your grandma selling this stuff anyway? It's nice."

"Because … she's … *dead?*" Irritation threaded Morgan's words.

"Oh. Yeah. Sorry."

Morgan gazed at her, a hand on an oak dresser, not speaking, a simmering irritation with her friend brewing inside her. She waited for Sophia to acknowledge her grandmother's death. Ask how she could help. She waited for her to *be Sophia again.*

"Can't help. Had a couple minutes before I got to go meet Manny at The Wheel."

"Who?" Morgan asked.

"Eva's dad. Well, stepdad."

"Why're you meeting *him?* He's the guy who fired you, right?" Morgan frowned.

Ethan nodded. "Yup."

"You'll see."

That was Sophia's answer for everything. So secretive. So arrogant.

Ethan looked to Sophia, hopeful. "Hey, can I see that chapter about my dad?"

Worry spread inside Morgan. She'd seen his dad push further and further into a tornado of paranoia. She worried what would happen to Ethan if his dad forced him to join his Armageddon Manifesto.

"Yeah, so…" Sophia scratched her eyebrow with a finger. "I'm not done. I'm taking care of Eva. I'll do it, though."

Ethan's face fell.

Sophia raised her hands in the air. "But…," she sang. "I got huge news."

They stared at her blankly, mildly curious. Morgan still felt irritated and she crossed her arms over her chest.

"I own The Wheel."

"*Our* Wheel?" Ethan asked, his mouth gaping open.

"Yeah, it's *my* Wheel now." Sophia said with a smirk. Ethan tilted his head, the orange glint of his hair shining beneath the sunlight. He frowned.

"You own The Wheel now," Morgan said, repeating it slowly. "Did you write that?"

"Yeah, can you believe it? And my house, too. I don't have to move."

Ethan shook his head. "How did you—"

"Because I wrote it. Because he bought a painting I did. That's how he paid for it."

"He?"

"Manny."

Manny again. Morgan gazed at Sophia, wondering why she was even talking to Eva's stepdad. What exactly had she done to get The Wheel?

"Please tell me you aren't sleeping with him," Morgan said. That was not Sophia's style. She barely looked at boys, let alone men. But she was so *different* now.

Sophia's gaze was deadly. "You really think I'd do that."

"Where's the projectile vomiting?" Ethan smiled, flopping into a leather armchair and trying to lighten the mood.

"Oh, but guess what else? I'm going to sell a shit-ton of art. And … drum roll please…" She twirled her hands in the air, the cup tipping slightly.

Morgan's shoulders clenched with anxiety, anticipating the slushie to spill on the maple coffee table.

"I'm gonna break up Eva's parents."

"You … *what?*" Morgan couldn't erase the disbelief. Her friend was changing into someone she didn't even like. "What're you thinking—"

"You'll find out … later." She tipped the cup to her mouth and dumped a chunk of slushie in her mouth.

"Lemme see what you wrote," Ethan said, extending a hand.

Sophia ignored him and instead stood and stretched an arm overhead.

"Yeah, did you write about U of M yet?" Morgan asked. She'd been obsessively checking email from Harvard, Cornell, and the University of Michigan—all of which had wait-listed her. Not having a firm answer on where she'd go to school ate at her nerves. Even though some people, like her aunt, told her that no one cares where you go to college after your first job, *she* cared. She hadn't even considered if this was what she *wanted*, or if it was simply what was *expected* of her. This was what she needed, and she knew as soon as she asked that Sophia was going to let her down.

Sophia shrugged and put the straw in her mouth.

"You *did* write me a chapter though, right?" Morgan asked more urgently. She glanced around the lawn and noted how Aidan's eyes stayed trained on Sophia. It wasn't a natural stare. It was a hungry one, and it gave Morgan the creeps. She looked away.

Sophia pinched her lips together. "No," she said through a sigh. "Haven't gotten to it yet."

"I'm still wait-listed. I could go to CU but that's ... everyone in Colorado goes there. But also, my uncle, he's got pancreatic cancer. Oh, and I could probably use a car upgrade. E and I both wrote down a bunch of stuff. I can just text it to you."

Sophia rolled her eyes. "You've got a sweet Highlander. Practically new." Her voice was flat. "Listen, I'm not Santa."

The words stung Morgan, making her skin feel prickly. Morgan couldn't help it. She had to bring it up. "You know that journal I gave you? The one making all this stuff happen? Well, that's my grandma's."

Morgan raised her eyebrows, waiting for Old Sophia to emerge. Old Sophia who was thoughtful and paid attention.

Sure, Morgan knew it was a lie, but still, *she* had given Sophia the journal—and she had recently wondered what would have happened if she had kept it for herself and not been so generous to her friend. Would *she* have had some sort of supernatural storytelling ability instead of Sophia?

Sophia didn't respond.

"Dead Grandma Rose," Morgan said slowly, her cheeks burning with irritation. She looked at the recliner on the lawn, the place that her grandma used to sit every night. Her grandma's thin face peering over mystery novels. Grandma Rose would insist on shoveling her driveway every day, reading up on tech stocks, and hiking into the forest to cut down her own Christmas tree in the forest. She had been vibrant before the cancer.

And she had been important to Morgan, and clearly, Sophia couldn't care less that she was gone. She couldn't care less that this was so incredibly hard for Morgan. She had no idea that Morgan had cried herself to sleep every night, knowing that she'd lost the one adult who really understood her, who really loved her for who she was and not what she did. Her parents were parents. But they didn't slow down like her grandma did. Didn't *see her* like Grandma had.

"Yeah … right. That's what you said," Sophia said, half paying attention. Her eyelids were heavy with *that look.*

Sophia crunched the Styrofoam cup and tossed it into Morgan's clearly marked recycling can.

Where is Old Sophia?

"Hey, but seriously, what about my *sanity?*" Ethan asked, his body tense.

Sophia shrugged. "It's all good—just wait." An annoyed look flashed on her face.

"You're starting to get a little power hungry…" Morgan said suddenly, but her voice petered out when Sophia turned an icy glare on her.

"Yeah," Ethan agreed.

"Power hungry?" Sophia repeated, putting a hand on her hip.

"Yeah, I text you, like, all the time, and you don't respond," Ethan said.

"You won't *tell us* what you're writing," Morgan said.

"Whatever." Sophia waved her hand at them and took a couple steps to leave. "I gotta go."

"You know, this whole thing is kinda making you…" Morgan said.

"Making me what?" Sophia gazed at her with a hard look and cocked her head. "Huh?"

"Mean," Ethan said.

"Yeah." Morgan's cheeks burned, and she guided Ethan away from … whomever had taken over Sophia's body and replaced it with a cold, unfeeling bitch she didn't even recognize. "Maybe you should go. Have fun with Eva's dad."

30

Sophia

JEALOUSY

Then: May 2

Sophia sat in the driver's seat of her car with the windows down. She smelled of paint fumes, and the crisp spring air offered relief to the sweat that dotted her forehead. Exhaustion and silent accomplishment collided in her chest.

She had completed twenty pieces and found herself sitting in front of The Wheel—now the "gallery." She couldn't quite believe that this was really happening, and she sat quietly for a few moments to take it in. Her head felt dizzy and her eyes still felt blurry after days of painting and little sleep and food.

She strode confidently into The Wheel, tape measure and hammer in hand. For two hours, she mounted the art on the walls. Some pieces were clustered together, others staggered farther apart. She measured and climbed on a stool to ensure they looked just right, that the lighting was perfect. She had never been to a gallery before, but she assumed this was what it should be like.

As she hung the last painting, Manny walked through the glass door without saying hello. Dressed in jeans and a black

T-shirt, he moved silently through the room, hands in his pockets, admiring the work. Sophia had written this into the story, that he was going to love the art. He *had* to love it.

But still, her heart pounded with anticipation as she waited for his reaction.

"It's moving," he said, nodding. He walked past her, and she took in that faint smell of sandalwood. He gazed at an image of Chief Colorow, a Ute leader and warrior. "It's exactly what I wanted."

Her shoulders relaxed, and she exhaled quietly.

"How're we going to price these?" he asked.

Sophia shrugged. She leaned against the bar, put her hands in the pockets of her overall jeans. "How much you thinking?"

"Five to ten thousand for the big ones and at least nine hundred for the small ones."

She couldn't swallow and a heat filled her head. She couldn't believe that kind of money would ever be possible.

He turned to look at her thoughtfully. "You know, you remind me of my daughter."

That was not at all what she had expected him to say. Absolutely not. "What?" Her voice was sharp. She was *nothing* like Eva.

"Oh, I know you two aren't friends anymore," he said, striding closer to her. "But what I'm trying to say is … that I see something remarkable in you."

He stopped and looked at her with a soft expression, and it touched her. Her own dad had said he'd seen something in her, too. Now he wasn't the only one.

He pointed gently at her. "I think you can really become the next big thing."

Sophia exhaled and chuckled. "On TikTok? No, thanks."

"No, in the art world." He walked slowly past each piece, pointing out the lines, emotion, and movement he noticed in each picture, things she hadn't seen with her own eyes, things she never even intended. But art was like that. It became whatever each individual person felt when they viewed it, colored by their own experiences.

"I know some dealers in L.A. New York."

Sophia didn't respond.

"I'm sure they'd want to meet the beautiful artist herself," he said with a wink. "I'd take you with…" He rubbed his stubbled chin and lips before taking a step closer to her. "If you're game," he whispered. His small lopsided smile made something stir inside her.

She let him take her hand, let him kiss it, watched him hold it—as if she were outside her body. She would be a big artist. This man was enamored with *her*.

"So Thursday," he said slowly. "Your audience will want to mingle with you."

"You want *me* there?" She didn't expect to be there. "I don't have anything to wear."

"I bought you a black dress."

She swallowed and nodded before gazing at a painting on the wall. It was the sunflower piece he'd seen and loved in the flower shop. Seeing it hanging on the wall, like a real gallery piece, made her feel unsteady. Pride blossomed in her chest.

Manny left the room to retrieve the dress, and he was so quiet, she wasn't sure if he was coming back. She turned to look for him, see what he was doing and thinking.

In that swivel, her elbow and shoulder thumped directly into him.

Manny was holding the dress. He was there, so close, right next to her, surprising her, and before she could take a breath, he pulled her in for a kiss.

Stunned initially, she soon sank into the kiss, into his lips, into the earthy scent of his skin. His hand fell onto her hip, and her hand climbed to his shoulder. Her stomach quivered, and she found herself enjoying it. She placed her other hand at the base of his neck and sank further into the kiss.

"A-hem."

Startled, Sophia pulled away and turned to see Eva and her mother standing in the front doorway.

Sophia couldn't have planned it any better. A smile crept across her face, as she watched Eva's mother, a skinnier, older version of Eva—but without the Smurf hair. Her mouth gaped open before her shoulders crumpled into devastation. She turned on her heel and stormed outside.

Eva stood there longer, her hand on the doorknob, her cheeks pink, and her eyes darting between the two of them.

"You … slut!" Eva said, breathless. Her face contorted, mirroring her mother's, and she ran to catch up with her mother. Sophia watched through the window as Eva's mom, angry, shook her head and pushed Eva away.

Sophia's heart soared. It was exactly what she'd wanted. Exactly what she'd hoped for. Now for the biggest test: *How would Manny respond?*

Manny rubbed his face. "Well." He sighed. "*That* was…" He gazed at Sophia's mouth again. "Pretty spectacular."

The Flores File: Video Interviews
NOW

Ethan: Did she fall for him? Naw. But I'm sure she figured it was one more crack in the Eva thing.

Sophia: I didn't do anything with him. I just ... made him *feel* things, I guess.

Becky: All I know is that my husband sees that girl Sophia one day and falls in love with her art. Eva was crushed. And I, well, I just couldn't believe it.

Ethan: Eva was a walking zombie. I passed her at school, and she looked like hell. Couple people said hi, and she was a robot, responding to them without any kind of emotion.

Holly: Eva was different about that time. She was really down. Everyone chalked it up to the divorce, but I think more was going on. She never really shared, but I could tell. That girl's issues went way beyond her parents' split.

Lydia: She and I were *so close*. She really confided in me. More than anyone. Eva and I didn't know Sophia was the other woman until I saw all the art. But now that Eva's gone, it all makes sense. Right? Of course Sophia wanted her out of the way. Right?

Manny Flores: I'd been unhappily married for a long time. Sophia wasn't the reason. She's a child.

Riley: Sophia was into him. She's the type for sure. She's that kind of predator.

31

Sophia
FULL BLOWN WAR

Then: May 2

"What the hell are you doing?" Eva's voice cut the air.

Sophia, startled, searched the dark for the bodiless voice. Eva popped out of the trees and stood in the gravel driveway.

When she saw her nemesis, Sophia chuckled. Mascara smudged Eva's eyes, and her short hair looked disheveled.

"How long have you been there, hunkered down in my bushes?" Sophia asked. Eva must've been waiting for her for at least two hours to come home from The Wheel after the kiss. Sophia decided to stay awhile longer after Eva and her mom had walked in on them. She sat on the bar and made out with Manny for a bit. She let him run his hands over her body.

Then she'd gone to Subway and eaten a sandwich in the car, reliving the feeling, over and over, of this grown man fawning over her. He was so into her, and he was so breathless as they kissed. It was clear he wanted to have sex, but she wasn't ready for that. She'd just wanted to toy with him.

"You don't know what you're doing." Eva's chest heaved with emotion.

"Oh, I think I do." Sophia smiled and climbed the two steps up to her front door. Sleep-deprived and running on fumes, she needed to collapse on her bed. It'd been endless days and nights of painting. Eva was going down, and that would help her sleep.

"He's not what you think he is," Eva said.

"What ... *married*? To your *mom*?" Sophia heard the devil in her voice, and it pleased her. The slower the words came out, the more they would burn.

"You don't—"

"Didn't you say something about karma in your TikTok post? What comes around? Or something like that?" Sophia said in a gentle voice, her head tilted in pretend confusion.

"He probably tells you that you're a star," Eva said, breathless, swallowing hard.

True. And she was going to be.

"That's what he'll always say to get what he wants."

Sophia opened the door to her house and stepped inside.

"You're just a pathetic whore," Eva yelled the words, her chest leaning forward, desperation on her face.

"Jealous much?" Sophia asked, before slamming the door on Eva, who stood in a wide stance, her arms dangling.

"I'd watch my back if I were you!"

Inside the house, Sophia leaned her back against the door and threw her head back and let out an unfamiliar cackle. It was too perfect. Too freaking perfect.

"What's so funny, sis?" Dylan asked. He sat in the armchair watching SpongeBob.

"Nothing." She regained her composure and headed down the hallway toward her room.

"Who's outside?"

She didn't answer. Inside her bedroom, she tossed the black dress Manny gave her onto the unmade bed. She wondered if it would fit, if Manny had stolen it from Eva's closet. Better still.

"Who *was* that?" Dylan yelled from the other room. "Where were you anyway? Are you not getting my texts?"

She didn't answer. Instead she closed her bedroom door.

Flores File: Text messages obtained from Eva's phone

April 25

7:30 a.m.
Riley Neuman:
hi
u don't know me but i know sophia and ethan and they r talking about u
so u know

Eva:
u worked at the wheel

Riley:
yes! u remember me

Eva:
y

Riley:
sophia hates u and talks about getting back at u for your post

Eva:
so

Riley:
i would watch your back
she has some journal
can u get together to talk?

April 30

8:15 p.m.
Aidan Voinovich:
what r u doing

Eva:
nothing why

Aidan:
im doing a project and wanted ur help

Eva:
how

Aidan:
i think ud be a good model

Eva:
what?

Aidan:
your pretty

Eva:
thx

Aidan:
can we get together

Eva:
why

Aidan:
for my project

32

Sophia
FAME

Then: May 3

The overhead lights, the white walls, the lack of furniture, and the smell of rich and earthy hors d'oeuvres transformed The Wheel into a different place.

At least forty-five people were already mingling when Sophia arrived at six-thirty. She took in the clusters of gray suit jackets and crisp white shirts. Perfume and fat necklaces. Heels and manicured fingernails. They sipped red wine and munched on crackers with crab meat and pointed at the paintings as if they were really significant pieces.

Her heart pounded and her throat felt like a desert as she watched them—real-life art collectors—ogle over what she'd made. Her head was filled with helium.

Sophia stood by the door for a few minutes, just watching. Manny eventually came over to her, grabbing her hand—and not letting go. He whispered in her ear, "You look beautiful."

She smiled and shrank away, worried the people at the show would notice their relationship. His eyes felt more intense than the previous day.

"We gotta get a picture of the lovely artist on opening night," he said, pulling out his phone. He waved his hand toward Sophia. Butterflies swam in her stomach. She was nervous, and she rarely felt that way.

"Sophia, why don't you stand in front of that piece right there?"

She tottered over to the hanging canvas with a macro photo of a cemetery headstone. She smiled, proud, feeling a little like this was a dream, and he snapped the photo.

"I think my eyes were closed—"

"Oh, and Sophia, will you get a shot of me and Mr. Yanz here?" Manny pointed to a heavy-set man who looked like his face had been struck by a spatula.

"Oh. Sure." Sophia felt like a poser—so out of her element. She could barely walk in those shoes. She didn't fit with all these rich people. She held up the iPhone, and Mr. Yanz smiled and posed with Manny. Sophia took two pictures of them.

"Put that back behind the bar, will you?" Manny asked before returning his attention to Mr. Yanz, who went on about some private yacht.

Sophia took the phone to the bar and clicked on the photos they'd just taken. She swiped past the Mr. Yanz shots to see her picture—her eyes were indeed closed.

She accidentally swiped again, and her heart fell into her stomach. The previous photo was of her. A candid shot of her walking across the street downtown. She swiped right. This one was a photo of her outside her house, of her walking past the chain-link fence.

Swipe again. Sophia and Dylan shooting pictures in the cemetery. A shot of her through her bedroom window, stretching in front of the mirror.

Swipe. Looking at the car in Anthracite Creek. She swiped faster and then opened up the entire photo roll.

There were at least fifty shots of just Sophia. In her car.

Walking into school. Dropping Dylan off at the store. Walking up to Ethan's house. Leaving Morgan's. Washing paint brushes in a bowl inside her tent. Squatting low by Hendy's Volvo with the knife in her hand.

Her stomach clenched and she felt ill, dizzy. What the hell had she gotten herself into? She dropped the phone on the counter as if it had stung her. *Who is this guy?* Then she picked up the phone and deleted the photo of her slashing the tires before shutting it off.

Manny's chin suddenly rested on her shoulder, and her body went rigid. She put the phone on the counter. "People love you." He whispered the hot, breathy words into her hair. "I'm starting to feel the same."

She put on a phony smile. She didn't even know how to smile in a fake way, but she was figuring it out. She extricated herself from his pawing hands and slowly pulled away from him.

He stepped closer and put his mouth near her throat, eliciting a frosty chill down her back. "We're going to do great things together."

She spun away slowly and caught a glimpse of him gazing intently at her. The smile that once looked so charming now looked threatening.

"I…"

"There are some people I want you to meet." He took her hand and threw his head toward the crowd of people. As they strode between the people, he lost his grip on her hand. He headed toward a smiling gray-haired couple. Surely he expected Sophia to follow.

Instead, with her heart pounding and her skin crawling, she slunk behind a circle of laughing middle-aged people. A whiff of strong perfume flooded her as she yanked open the door and rushed outside.

On the sidewalk, fresh, cool air felt welcome, and in teeter-totter fashion, she ran in the heels to her car.

She drove several blocks away before pulling the car over, yanking off the dress, and throwing it out the window. She felt as if ants were crawling over her skin, and she shivered as she shrugged into jeans and a Johnny Marr T-shirt. *Shit. Shit. Shit.* Who was this guy, anyway?

She'd been fishing, playing, and she'd caught a piranha. She'd wanted him to be enamored. But now … not like this. Her story had spun out of control. She hadn't expected the guy she was playing head games with to be a complete psychopath.

Was that even a real deed he had given her for The Wheel? And her house? Or was that some sort of fake paperwork? Her fingers trembled as she opened the glove compartment to look for the deeds. Breathing heavily, she rifled through a bunch of papers before remembering she'd given the deeds to her mom. It was just as well, she didn't really know what you did with a deed, or how to even tell if it was real.

She was shoving the papers back into the compartment when the lottery ticket fell onto the floor. She picked up the smooth ticket she'd bought from her mom at the gas station.

It was already seven o'clock. The lottery drawing had been two hours earlier. Breathless, she opened the lottery website on her phone, feeling some sort of hope. If she won, she could wash psycho Manny off her skin.

This would be a trifecta if it all worked out according to plan. She wouldn't need Manny to sell her art. She'd open her own gallery. Elation, nerves, and anger crashed together in her chest. She found the winning numbers on the site and slowly checked the numbers on her ticket. Five. Twenty-six. Twenty-nine. Thirty-four. Six. Ten.

She read the numbers at least three times, holding her breath before exhaling heavily. "Holy crap," she whispered quietly. She scrolled down to the winning jackpot. Six million dollars. *We won.*

Of course they had won. Still, she couldn't breathe. Her throat seemed to be stitched together. Was this what happened to everyone who wins the lottery? She read the numbers a fourth time to ensure she wasn't fooling herself. She was right. She had won. She gazed out the window, feeling light-headed. She wrote it. She wrote the story.

The whole street was dead, outside of the distant parked cars and the light of the gallery a few blocks away. She didn't need anyone. All she needed was this little piece of paper with some number on it. She considered what she should do next. Scream and run around the car? Call her mom? Text her friends? No. This was an in-person visit for sure.

She put the car into gear, her mind moving at a frantic pace. She should probably play every lottery in every state. She considered all the other things she could make happen with her story: traveling the world, meeting glamorous people, making art for world leaders and movie stars, getting whatever she wanted.

She drove straight to Morgan's house and banged on the door, but no one answered. She jiggled the handle and yelled for her friend. The door was locked, the house empty. She sat in the driveway and texted her. Morgan didn't respond.

Ten minutes later, she pulled up to Ethan's house, heart pounding, turning up dust with the tires and blaring rap music on the car stereo. She jumped out of the car and sprinted through his back door, weaving past buckets of water in the hallway and nearly tripping over three five-gallon jugs of gasoline. That was new. Now his dad was collecting gas for the end of the world?

She burst into the bedroom to see Ethan, clad in boxers, standing in front of the mirror. Startled, he jumped and spun around to face her. "Dude!"

"Sorry," she said breathless, shutting the door behind her. "But it worked. My story worked. The gallery showing with Manny—"

"Manny?" Irritated, he sat on his bed and pulled on a pair of gym shorts. "Are you really fucking Eva's dad?"

"No," she said. "He's actually pretty messed up—"

"Where the hell have you been? You don't respond to text. Morgan and I are like, what, invisible to you?" His voice was sharp and his posture was stiff. She'd never seen him like that.

"Whatever." She wanted to tell him the good news. All of it. She inhaled to speak.

"You should hear what people are saying in town—"

"E..."

He scoffed and sat down on his twin bed and picked up his phone and began flipping through Instagram. Disinterested.

That irritated Sophia. This was huge news. She'd gotten control back of her life. *And he cared more about some random person's photo on social media than her?*

"E!"

He gazed at his phone, seemingly refusing to look at her. "People are calling you a home-wrecker and saying you threatened to beat up Eva outside your house."

"No ... that's not what happened."

He rolled his eyes. She didn't feel like going into the fact that Manny had been watching her. That Eva had been the one hiding in her bushes. That she had no intentions of carrying on with Manny. Sophia felt defensive, and she wasn't used to seeing Ethan aloof. *She* was the aloof one in the relationship. "I just got back from a *gallery showing.*"

"Big time!" He chuckled. "What'll you write next for yourself? That you'll go on a world tour?"

She rolled her eyes. She wasn't going to let Ethan bring her down. People had come *for her* work.

"I've got even bigger news. Big." She threw out her hands. Her giggle turned into a cackle, and a hint of something else crossed her face. Something, perhaps, more devilish.

He looked up, annoyed, all his signature warmth gone from his face. "What, already?"

"I won," she said.

"Great. Good." He looked back at his phone before glancing at his bedroom door. "Now I know."

Sophia knew he was pissed at her. But she had good reason for being unavailable. "I won the goddamn freaking lottery." She pulled the lottery ticket out of her back pocket and held it up between her hands in front of her face before squealing again.

"You...?" Ethan stood up slowly, leaning in to look at the ticket. "How much?"

"I won the lott-er-eeeeeey," she said again, dancing and twirling the ticket in her hand.

She repeated it over and over, until Ethan grimaced at her. "Dude," he said, shaking his head.

Breathless, after a moment she said, "Six million."

"Six million dollars?" Disbelief washed over his face.

"No, pesos, dumbass."

"Wow." He looked shocked. But then, after a moment, he shook his head again and looked back at his phone.

Okay, this was the final straw. Her beat-you-up-face appeared. "What the hell is wrong with you, E? You act like I'm telling you that I got my stupid period or something lame like that."

"My dad told me that I've got to go with him to that cabin," Ethan said, looking sullen. He took his eyes off the phone and stared directly at her with a hard-set jaw.

Slowly, the sentence registered in Sophia's mind. "What?" It was at that moment that she'd noticed the state of his room. She'd never seen his room messy before, but it was littered in dirty laundry and computer magazines.

"There's no way you can live in that little—"

"It's gotten worse. He goes down these rabbit holes on YouTube and Facebook, where they just feed him more conspiracy theories."

"Oh. Ethan...," she said quietly.

Ethan nodded. "He bought more stuff. More guns."

"You're going with ... him ... then?"

Defeated, he waved his hand at Sophia. "You know, you should really go. I want to be alone right now." He stood up, walked to the door, held it open for her. "At least one of us got lucky."

Aspen Times

May 10

Gas Station Attendant Hits Lucky Day in Paonia

By Jeffrey Slater

PAONIA—A Paonia gas station attendant won the Colorado Lottery last week, pocketing a $6 million prize.

Jennifer Palmer said her daughter encouraged her to buy the ticket where she worked at the Conoco Station off Highway 133 in Paonia. She had only been in the job for two days when she bought the winning ticket.

"I was shocked," she said. "The only thing I've ever won before is a cooler in a raffle at Walmart."

Palmer, 38, is a single mom who has lived in Paonia for five years. She said she has no current plans for how she will spend the winnings.

Palmer's family has received significant attention from tourists in recent weeks because her daughter, Sophia Palmer, 17, hosted a gallery showing of her artwork last week.

The mixed-media pieces depict haunted images of people who

once lived in the valley. Some of the artwork sold for $7,000, according to Manny Flores, a local businessman who is managing Palmer's work. He plans to show her artwork in Los Angeles and Santa Fe in the coming months.

"Sophia is the closest thing to Njideka Akunyili Crosby or Damien Valero," he said.

Crosby, a Nigerian artist, is known for her historical, political, and personal references and "figurative compositions that conjure the complexity of contemporary experience," according to critics. Valero is a French artist whose work is often shown in exhibits across Europe.

If the Palmer family's lucky streak stays alive, then maybe global stardom is next.

33

Sophia
OBSESSION

Then: May 3

Sophia's fingers felt as if they were vibrating. Lying on her bed, she stared at the ceiling. After being booted by Ethan from his house and ditching the art show earlier, her head was buzzing. Ethan was mad—but he'd get over it. And she'd won huge money. Fancy people with cocktails had ogled her artwork.

All of it was too much for her brain, and a slight twinge of a headache began to poke at her temples. Her body felt exhausted from the past several days, yet thoughts crashed inside her head, driven by the power she suddenly wielded. Throughout her life, she'd been hanging onto her father's kite tail, dragged wherever the wind took him.

In years past, even if Sophia's family had been rooted in a secure home, her dad's behavior was unpredictable. When they lived in Ohio, she came back one day to find he'd decided to take a sledgehammer to the kitchen wall, believing that it blocked the light and energy. It was a rental unit, and the landlord was furious. Another time, he had blown all of his paycheck on a Tony Robbins seminar and came home speaking in all caps and singing cheesy 1980s songs and talking about "unleashing the power within." Next, he got wrapped up in yoga and self-help seminars. Then he was gone.

Now Sophia held the key to her family's future, their stability, quite literally by putting pen and paper together. She considered what she'd written next in the story. She was anxious to see how her revenge against Eva would play out, and how it would compare with the story she'd written. She couldn't believe she had secretly orchestrated this entire wilderness event. *And* she had just won the freaking lottery.

Her phone buzzed, and she turned it over to look at it. Another text from Manny. Her stomach clenched tight with the sobering memory of him. The photos on his phone... He had been *following* her. He had been *watching* her. The knowledge of it sent spindly chills down her back.

11:15 p.m.
Manny:
I'll use my imagination. 🔥

It was the fifteenth text she'd gotten from him in two hours. They came in a flurry at first, and Sophia never answered them. She scrolled through them again.

7:45 p.m.
Manny:
Where'd you go?

7:46 p.m.
Manny:
Hello?

7:51 p.m.
Manny:

Why are you ignoring me?

8:00 p.m.
Manny:
Are you coming back? People are asking.

8:04 p.m.
Manny:
We had a deal.

8:07 p.m.
Manny:
Are you back at your house?

9:01 p.m.
Manny:
The show is about to end. I guess I'll clean up now.

9:45 p.m.
Manny:
You know, you really embarrassed me.

9:50 p.m.
Manny:
And still, you don't care to respond…

9:51 p.m.
Manny:
I know you read that.

9:52 p.m.
Manny:
I put myself out on a limb, and you bolt. You have no idea what's going on in the adult world.

10:30 p.m.
Manny:
I left my wife.

10:54 p.m.
Manny:
I'm driving around looking for you. Worried.

11:01 p.m.
Manny:
Did I do something to hurt your feelings?
Can I make it up to you? 😔 😢

She heard a tinkling sound at her window. It sounded light and scattered, like tiny pebbles hitting glass. She listened again. Rocks. Was he outside her window?

She crawled low on the floor, huddled beneath the window, and then waited, holding her breath. She couldn't bring herself to peek out the window, for fear that he'd see her. She wasn't really afraid of him hurting her. *Or was she?* She just didn't want to deal with him anymore. She'd had her fun.

Manny had clearly already been interested in her when he shouldn't have been, and she had toyed with that interest and power. She'd written it into her story. Had the story taken his already inappropriate interest and forced him off the deep end into a full-fledged obsession?

She needed to write him out of the story. But her journal was in her backpack, and her backpack sat on the table in the kitchen, and that table sat in front of the front windows. He would spot her if she went to get it. And her bones were so tired, she felt as if she couldn't move. She just needed to sleep.

As she lay there on her stomach beneath the window, she considered how she would actually end the story after she finished her assignment. Maybe there would be no end. She'd write the rest of her life. But the fact that Manny's part of the story had gone haywire was concerning. Did that mean what she'd written for Eva's life could go wrong too?

Her headache turned full throttle; it felt as if a strap was wrapped around her forehead, squeezing tight. As she lay on the floor, listening, waiting for pebbles to break the glass, waiting for Manny to leave, her head became thick and dreamy. Her eyes closed, and her breathing slowed.

So tired. *I have time.* Her thoughts became mushy, and her mind drifted to a soft cloud in the sky. *I'll worry about … everything … in the morning.*

The Flores File: Video
Interviews
NOW

Jennifer Palmer: I just stood there, waving the ticket. I was breathless. I couldn't believe it. She did say she was going to win, and I guess she just put it out to the universe that it would happen.

Jeffrey Slater (*Aspen Times* reporter): I got the call about it at maybe three in the afternoon? When I saw the jackpot size, I immediately drove over to Jennifer Palmer's house and knocked on her door.

Jennifer: We didn't say anything for a couple days. And when the Lottery finally released the news and it was out, it was, what? Kind of overwhelming. Seriously. I know some states let you keep yourself anonymous. I'm not sure why Colorado doesn't... Oh you know, all the media calls, the photos, the conversations about how I knew what numbers to pick. Everyone thought that I had somehow ... cheated. You know, a new person ... like I'd rigged the thing. By then, all that suspicion centered on my girl, too.

Jeffrey: She slammed the door on me. Jennifer did. That made me think for sure she rigged the thing. I went on the *Today Show* about it. It was national news. A new employee at a gas station wins the lottery? I mean, come on... I'm trying to get a book deal about that and all the weird stuff in Paonia and Eva's disappearance. Buncha publishers are interested. It's gonna be huge.

Sheriff Rawlings: When Sophia became the main suspect in the disappearance of Eva Flores, why sure, I questioned. The lottery? The rumors about Eva's stepfather? The fact that this businessman suddenly signs the deeds of property to a seventeen-year-old girl. Did she blackmail him? Have some sort of control over him? It still doesn't add up.

Jennifer: For the most part, Sophia wasn't even there for all the craziness. She was gone for a few days after Eva's wilderness thing —now, don't get all suspicious. She was looking for Eva, helping her friends. Things like that. It was just me and Dylan swept up in everything. I wouldn't say ... well, yeah, I was kinda bummed out. Sure. Sure. I called her, but she was busy.

Ethan: I was kinda mad at Sophia when she told me she won. But once the news got big, it was a madhouse in town.

Morgan: Sophia did get weird around that time. Not to talk bad about her, but yeah, I'd say she was high on her own power about that time. Different. Way different.

Ethan: Yeah, we didn't talk too much for a while. [Clears his throat.] She, um... Yeah, well, let's just say we had a falling out about that time—right before Eva's big event.

Flores File: A TikTok posted by Eva Flores

May 1

[Close up of Eva wearing lip-gloss, light makeup, and a baseball cap that says Yeti.]

Oh my god, guys. I'm super-excited about this new event I'm doing this weekend. I moved to the middle of the mountains, and I'm getting a bunch of other guys to take me there for some outdoorsy fun. Before you know it, I'm going to be dancing on top of a mountain. Next, I'll climb a fourteener! [Laughs.]

34

Sophia
SURPRISES

Then: May 4

On Friday, Ambien paced in front of the class, the sound of his shuffle a ticking clock of anticipation. It was two o'clock, the last period of the day. When the bell rang, the selected kids would get their belongings, jump into their cars, and go on the wilderness trip. Chris Piirto, Ethan, Eva, Morgan, annoying Riley, and that Aidan guy, too. Practically the whole English class.

Sophia hadn't said a word yet about the lottery to anyone else—not even her mom or Dylan. She put the ticket under her mattress until the end of the week, for after the Wilderness weekend.

And though Morgan and Ethan knew the big news, her friends looked right through her for most of the day. They gave her the cold shoulder, and it crushed Sophia more than she thought it would.

She hadn't told anyone about Manny either. She had no idea how the art show had gone, and she'd ignored his incessant texts.

She wiped all of that out of her mind. Tonight would be

the night they went on the wilderness trip, and right then, she was solely focused on crushing Eva. Like a hunter hiding in the weeds, Sophia watched Eva's every move in class, knowing that soon, Eva would be hers. She watched the way Eva would shift in the seat, push her short hair behind her ear. The way the kids admired her and expressed sympathy about her parents' pending divorce.

Word had gotten out that she'd kissed Eva's stepdad and that he gave property to her, so more eyes were darting to her than usual. But by then, most people assumed that if they stared at Sophia long enough, she might slam them into a locker. Sophia had never really slammed anyone into a locker, but she appreciated the way that fear kept most people from looking at her wrong.

"Now, most of you are excited for the plans, but I have two surprises before the big event," Ambien said, a smirk climbing up his cheek. "Mrs. Evans asked me to be the chaperone on this weekend's nature excursion."

Eva sat up straight, smiled, and silently clapped, while Ethan, Sophia, and Morgan sank into their seats with defeat. Sophia could barely handle once a day with Ambien, let alone all night.

Ambien raised his hands. "Thank you, Eva, for inviting me. It's an honor."

An honor? He had no life, clearly, if he thought it was an honor to go on a lame high school trip.

"And for the next surprise…" He stood and gazed at the class for a long moment, all for extra drama, with his hands in the pockets of his tan chino pants. "As you know, I'm not your traditional teacher."

Sophia rolled her eyes.

"At the beginning of this project, I promised you that it would be different, and you would work together as a team."

Sophia hadn't even remembered that this was supposed to be a team project. She had been grouped with her friends and that Aidan kid, but they'd never actually worked together on a project. It was like they were doing their own things. And that was fine with her. Obviously.

"We're going to have some fun. We're going to swap projects." Ambien turned his attention to Sophia. "Ms. Palmer. You will be trading projects with Mr. Voinovich."

Sophia's spine felt stiff, and her brain felt like it had been sucked out of the top of her head.

"*No.* What? Why?" Sophia's voice sounded like slicing knives.

Aidan chuckled and smiled at the ceiling. The bump on his nose looked more pronounced.

"He hasn't even done anything on his own project." Sophia threw her hand at Aidan, slumped in his chair.

"Aidan? Is that true?" Ambien asked. He raised his brows over his glasses, and the class silently watched the exchange.

"I've been workin' on stuff." Aidan sniffed and scratched the side of his face.

"You have?"

"Yeah. Sure." He didn't sound convincing.

"I'm not switching." Sophia lifted her black backpack off the floor and clutched it in her lap.

"Why would that be, Sophia?" Ambien asked.

"Why should I? This is *my* story. *My* hard work. No author gives up their story to some weird dude who happens to sit nearby."

"Let's be kind."

"I'm not letting *anyone* finish my story."

"I'm afraid that's not your choice." Ambien stood stiff, like a piece of wood, at the front of the room. This was his game, and he was the game master. He wanted to make everyone do what he wanted.

Sophia glared at him.

Ambien turned away. "Let's see now… Eva, you and Holly switch projects."

Eva clenched her paper tight to her chest and glared at Holly, who sat next to her. "I don't think that's a good idea," she said.

A tiny smile crept up Holly's cheeks, and she held out her hand, waiting for Eva to give her the paper. Slowly, begrudgingly, Eva slapped it on Holly's desk, placing it so as not to touch her former good friend.

"Ethan, I want you to take your story—"

"I didn't do a story."

"What'd you do?"

"Nothing." Ethan slumped in his chair, twirling his pen between his fingers.

"No comic strip? No story?"

Ethan shrugged and shook his head. His project had been talking during class and being fully invested in Sophia's story. In fact, out of everyone, he had always felt the most like her partner. Sophia almost spoke up, telling Ambien that he had been collaborating on her project. But Ambien kept talking.

"Well, that's too bad, Mr. Switalski. This class is a key credit for graduating."

"I've got plenty of credits." True, Ethan took summer classes at the community college. He probably had enough to graduate already and could afford to blow off the course.

"Morgan, you'll switch with Chris Piirto," Ambien said. Her face contorted and Sophia turned to look at the shaggy-haired boy with the smug smile. Sophia rarely saw him without his face suctioned to Amanda's. He handed his one-page story over to her. Morgan clutched her paper tight to her chest.

"I'll get a bad grade if he finishes it," Morgan said. Finally, she handed her paper over to him. She read his paper silently before rolling her eyes and dropping it onto her desk. She sunk deep into her chair and covered her eyes with her hand. "Oh God."

"What?" Ethan asked.

"It's a freaking love story about Amanda Toch."

Ethan tried not to laugh. Morgan read it out loud to him in a quiet voice. *"Her mouth tastes like flowers,"* she said.

Aidan looked at Sophia and gave her a wistful smile. He extended his hand. "Hand over that baby."

Sophia frowned and looked straight ahead, her fingers digging into the backpack that held the magic journal.

"Riley told me stuff about that book. That you've been writing your future," he said.

Panic squeezed Sophia's chest tighter. *Did he know? Would the power of the story work for him too?* She refused to look at him and instead focused her attention on Ambien.

"This is so not fair," Sophia said. "To us. And our education."

He gazed at her with an uptilted chin, pausing before answering. "On the contrary. Each of you must understand character arc. You must know plot development. And you have to bring continuity through to the end. It's *harder*. But you guys are capable. And, like I said, I'm nontraditional."

Power trip. That was all he cared about. She had no character arc. She had no conflict. She had just written what she wanted to happen in a make-believe world and watched how it unfolded.

"Plus, it requires trust." Ambien sat on the edge of his desk and folded his arms across his chest. "See, I notice what happens in the hallways. I hear the conversations, the whispers, the cutting comments on social. You bite and gouge each other. Sure, those jabs start as harmless ripples, but after time, they grow as big as ocean waves, and they lead to a toxic environment. You're a group that most definitely needs to let go of control. You need to build trust in your peers by believing they'll keep good guardianship of your story and that they'll give you the ending you deserve."

"Why the hell would they do that?" Sophia snapped.

"Yeah, why would *she* want to help *me*?" Eva asked, nodding at Holly, who just blinked innocently.

"You'd be surprised how vulnerability changes you, leaves you hoping … just hoping you'll see the best in each other. In yourself. Who knows? You might see yourself in their story?"

"How will we be graded?" Morgan asked. "When it's not all your own work?"

"You'll be graded by the care you take in each other's work."

"Bullshit," Sophia said under her breath. Morgan looked at her blankly, as if she didn't know her.

"Excuse me, Miss Palmer?"

"Nothing." She looked at the floor.

Ambien continued to instruct other kids to swap projects. Some sighed and others whooped with delight.

"One thing is for certain: You *will* fail if you don't switch and collaborate," Ambien said, looking directly at Sophia.

"I'd rather fail," Sophia said quietly. She wanted to keep that book forever. To write her whole life. She was *never* giving it to this sociopath. Maybe she could type it up and give him the pages. *If he finishes it, will what he writes come true?*

"I guess the lottery, The Wheel, *and* your house aren't enough," Morgan whispered.

Sophia clenched her jaw tighter, obstinance settling in her. They weren't really talking to her at that point, and Sophia was going to pretend she didn't care.

She gazed out the window and actually gasped. Outside, Manny Flores was pacing on the grass. A chill swept down her back.

He must just be waiting for Eva.

Then he stopped moving and gazed inside the classroom— directly at Sophia. Her window seat put her just six feet above him on the grass below. Their eyes locked and Sophia's heart raced.

Manny licked his lips and stared at her like a hungry lion.

The edge of one side of his mouth lifted in a half smile, and he tilted his head down, a move that made his gaze far more intense. He slowly mouthed the words: *You owe me.*

She *owed* him? Baffled, she shook her head and glanced at Ambien, who continued to drone on, clueless.

Then Manny touched his chest and pointed at her. This time mouthing the words, *call me.*

She looked away, rattled, to find Aidan looking at her with a mirthless smile.

After a moment, Eva, who sat two rows ahead, also noticed her father outside on the lawn. Surprised at first, she weakly waved to him. Sophia watched as Manny Flores scowled and pointed a threatening finger at her. She had never changed her story in her journal. She had never fixed it. Now, as she felt his heavy gaze still on her, she worried.

Flores File: Voicemail from Manny Flores to Sophia Palmer

May 4

Hey, beautiful artist. Why aren't you returning my calls? Starting to make me think you don't like me... Making me a bit worried... [sing-song voice] Where'd you go? I had some big-time clients I wanted to show you off to... Didn't make me look so good, you know?

But hey. I'll let you make it up to me. Use your imagination. Or I'll use mine? [laughs low]
I know, I know ... you probably just want Eva and her mom out of the way. So it can be just us.

But, hey, don't you worry your little head off.

Listen, I'm headed out of town for a business meeting this weekend. So I'll have to catch you later. Maybe I'll pop by and see you, just to say bye.

I really want to taste those lips again.

The Flores File: Video Interviews
NOW

Aidan Voinovich: Sure, they were surprised to see me on the trip. That kid Virgil gave me his spot.

Virgil Harrison (Sophomore): [Laughs.] Gave him my spot? Yeah, under serious duress. I couldn't really do anything about it, though.

Principal Gloria Evans: Frankly, I was impressed that Eva Flores wanted to organize a school-sanctioned event. She wrote a very nice proposal, indicating that she thought it would infuse some energy into the school and create unique bonding opportunities for our students.

Manny Flores: I wasn't surprised that everyone wanted to go on that trip. My daughter. She's ... beautiful. Right? She's hot. Right? I mean, if I hadn't been married and she wasn't my daughter...

Holly Stephenson: I can't tell you anything. Because Eva never talked to me after Senior Bust. I was drunk. I was ... mad... Eva kind of took stuff from me. My dignity, really. I'm not trying to talk bad about a dead girl. [Pauses. Rubs her face.] I mean, she's probably dead, right? But I was really glad to get out of that friendship. It just ate me alive.

Rick Griffith (local historian): I did find it odd that Ms. Flores took the group to the base of the West Elk Mountains near Kebler Pass. That's the place I was talking to you about. The place folks like Star say is haunted.

Kayla Godfrey, student: Yeah. And I don't want to go back to that place. Ever.

Wicked Games

BY SOPHIA PALMER

Elsa organized a party in the wilderness, where she took a handful of handpicked fans. They were selected specifically so she could prove herself and win their affection. For Elsa realized they provided the oxygen for her blood. She gave them nuggets of entertainment to attract them, and she fed off of them. Her adoring fans were fat, juicy fish, and she was the leech attached.

They arrived in the forest, near a river. Low clouds hung at the base of rocky snow-capped peaks in the distance, and drizzle hung in the air. Elsa, uncomfortable outside of her heated and air conditioned home, rubbed her arms. She was fearful for the first time in her life.

35

Eva
THE FLOAT

Then: May 4

E va couldn't shake the strange, ominous feeling about
the weekend, as if the trees themselves would gobble
her up and the river might drown her. Still, she got
into the car of a sophomore as part of the assigned carpool
plan for the trip.

Her stomach still felt sour after seeing the way Manny had
pointed at her during class. He'd eyed Slut Sophia too. It was
so bizarre that he'd stand outside their classroom window.
Why wouldn't he just text her or call her? Eva knew he
wanted her to make the videos from the trip worthwhile,
enough to get her more gigs, like commercials and sponsorships. And his gesture was a threat to make sure it happened,
or else.

The pressure pounded in her head. *That's what this is about,*
she told herself. *Just big numbers from her posts.*

But she knew in her heart that he was losing it. In the last
week, his behavior had grown even more disturbing, a dialed-
up version of how he'd behaved in the past.

The week prior, he'd thrown his weight around, or rather

thrown *her* around, when she'd told him she wanted to cancel the wilderness trip. She complained that she wasn't in the mood and felt ill. After all, she'd organized the event weeks earlier. But that was before.

Before her stepdad had taken a left turn and given away her mom's bed-and-breakfast dream to Sophia Palmer. Before he just handed over The Wheel to Sophia Palmer. Before he started screwing her.

Eva had stood in the kitchen of their house, crying, telling him that she needed a break because she was having a hard time after seeing him with Sophia and everything else. The reality, though, was more complex. She wasn't actually sad to think her parents might break up. Not really. It was the pressure, the constant treadmill of performing. She felt sucked dry of energy.

He hadn't even allowed her to finish her explanation when he pushed her into the kitchen table. "Our marriage is none of your affair," he said in a booming voice.

He'd always loomed over her physically, a subconscious threat. He'd only twice struck her before.

Now, riding in the car with music blaring, the memory of it made her chest tighten even more.

The girls' dramatic chatter about rumors of pop stars and people at school faded into a whirring sound in her mind. Another wave of nausea hit her. TikTok might have started out as a fun diversion, but once the algorithms noticed her, it became a feeding frenzy and her life had transformed. Now, it wasn't so much about fear of being humiliated and trolled by millions of people, but a true fear of failure. She hadn't noticed—not until the day he pushed her into the table—that the fear really stemmed back to her stepfather.

She never really let herself think about the nagging drive for success, but it had probably always lingered in the back of her mind. She knew that if she let him down, if she wasn't able to get the multimillion-dollar sponsorships anymore, she'd pay. In more than one way.

She looked at these girls in the car. They were strangers. It didn't seem fair that she couldn't pick the people who went on the trip, but that was the rule Principal Evans set. She wouldn't even let Eva put Lydia on the invite list. "Lydia's name wasn't drawn in the lottery," the woman had said in that nasal voice. It disappointed her. Lydia had always backed up Eva—a sort of kind of gun in her holster.

But Lydia couldn't come, and now Eva was stuck with these nameless girls without her sturdy sidekick.

What was worse, Sophia—of all people—was going to be there, as well as Sophia's obnoxious minions, Morgan and Ethan. Also on the list were Riley Neuman and that kid Aidan Voinovich, both of whom Snap-stalked her practically every day.

As the car weaved around corners, Eva felt a bit of acid rip up her esophagus. She swallowed the nausea and nerves and managed a fake smile as the girls took selfies and talked nonstop about how amazing this would be. The car turned towards the put-in on the river.

Eva was not a strong swimmer, and being in nature was about as comfortable as sleeping on cactus. But she had no choice. Eva *had* to fake it. Ever since she'd made it big on the app, she was always *on*—a never-ending job interview.

The car zipped down the two-lane road too fast, careening around tight corners. The plan was to float on paddle boards from just above Somerset for about three miles down to the new Elk Lodge, where they'd stay the night. Clearly, the girls had been on the river often, and offered to lend her a PFD.

"What's a PFD?" Eva asked.

"You're kidding, right?" asked one of the girls, a blonde who wore a nose ring. Her laugh sounded airy and high-pitched, and it twisted Eva's insides to hear it.

"Personal flotation device," said the sophomore girl

behind the wheel. She wore dark braids and a red bandana on her head and clearly was a new driver. "Super key ... you know, to survive."

Eva realized that she didn't even know these girls' names.

The girl explained then that she'd borrowed her mom's BMW for the occasion, and she turned around briefly in the seat to look directly at Eva. "We have a waterproof bag for your phone, too," she said.

"Dakota!" the blonde said. "Watch where you're going."

Eva's stomach twisted further as the driver, apparently named Dakota, drove haphazardly, momentarily weaving off the road and nearly careening into a yard littered with junk cars, lawn mowers, and shiny hubcaps.

In the back seat, the girl with sandy brown hair knotted atop her head gazed intently at Eva, as if she wasn't human. Eventually she spoke up. "The float'll be super cool." She licked her lips. Eva nodded and flashed a quick smile. She thought the girl's face looked slightly like that of a pug dog.

"I have video skills, too," the driver said, turning around again, pulling the steering wheel with her.

"Dakota, will you freaking pay attention?" the blonde shouted. The driver recovered and erupted with a hysterical honking laugh. *Dakota. That was her name.*

Eva blinked, wondering if maybe she wouldn't drown but instead would die when this car went flying into a crooked little junk house on the road.

As it turned out, the float down the river started out peaceful, albeit a bit chilly with the drizzle and the snowmelt spring runoff. The girls donned wetsuits and PFDs, and the river guide, a brawny woman named Rita, instructed the girls in a feather voice. She showed Eva how to properly stand on the board and hold the paddle to get the most push. The girls probably assumed they were getting to know Eva, the real Eva, because she had shared about her move last fall from Boulder and how her kitten Molly had died at the same time.

It was the bare minimum Eva ever gave people—even Holly and Lydia. Enough to make them *feel* like they knew her, while maintaining a safe distance from everyone. The truth was that the move to Paonia had been pure hell, worse than she had revealed.

She had screamed inside their all-white living room, complaining that she didn't want to move to a dumpy town. And her stepfather slapped her across the face, pushed her down on the sofa, and hovered over her, panting. The reaction was bizarre to her, as if she'd lifted a door to see a strange, dark side of him. Lying there beneath him, frozen, Eva felt dark fingers of fear, a premonition of sorts that something bad may soon happen. She tried to tell her mom, who shut it down immediately.

"How dare you lie about something like this," she had told her daughter. For two weeks, she refused to talk to Eva.

Eva didn't understand the reason for the move. Her stepdad had said he was "done with traffic." *That* was his one stupid reason. Oh, and the fact that he saw low home prices in Paonia, and Colorado real estate promised to be the next gold rush for him. Though she never voiced it, Eva suspected he was running from something—or someone—in Boulder.

Her stepdad had been representing a young model in town, and apparently the business relationship fell through. Now, Eva felt even more pressure to boost her TikTok numbers.

Eva pouted and sulked for weeks before the move, but once she got to Paonia, she tried to pretend it was a good thing, to grace the small shitty town with her presence. She would blend seamlessly into any environment, urban or wretched nature, she had decided.

But no one knew how she really felt.

About the time she moved to Paonia, Eva realized she didn't care if she had true friends. She wanted devotees, people she could mold into what and who she wanted. She couldn't afford friends. Friends were ... unpredictable. Could tarnish her reputation with a tweet, a negative post, a video of her saying something dumb. Anything could be used against her.

On the river, she floated past a herd of deer drinking from the water, and at one point, a hawk swooped across the rippling surface, gliding effortlessly across the air. For a moment, on a smooth section of the river, Eva actually kind of enjoyed the scenic float.

Then Dakota, the infamous terrible driver of her mother's BMW, started talking again. "You could have your pick of any guy at our school, Ev."

Eva hated this girl's decision to shorten her name, as if they were tight friends. The girl wore a pink wetsuit and a price tag hung off the back. She had clearly bought it for the occasion.

Eva looked at the water as she dragged her paddle deep by her board, pretending not to hear. Rita trailed just behind her, instructing Eva to press down on the top of the ore, tighten her core, and stroke deeply next to the board. It was over-whelming to Eva, but she didn't let it show.

"You probably don't want to share the limelight and all your money with some stupid boy!" the pug-faced girl said, a grin still painted on her face.

Eva didn't know all the details of the finances behind her fame, but she did know that she'd sometimes get twenty-five grand for a sponsored post, if it was good, and she had the potential to get multimillion dollar deals like Justin Floyd did for his mountain biking tricks.

Eva thought about how TikTok was only part of the problem. She remembered one night when her mom had gone out, how Manny had asked her to dance for him. She did, and then he asked that she just wear her tight jean shorts and a bra, and then he took photos of her.

He shot the pictures while lying on the ground in front of her. She felt weird about it and said no at first. *What, are you gonna tell some Hollywood director you can't be in a bra? Just like a swimsuit, Eva,* he had told her.

At one point, he began massaging her shoulders, telling her she was too uptight. Uncomfortable, she had put her shirt on and said she had to go to the bathroom. She complained she was sick and didn't come out for hours.

The next day, she told her mom that she was uncomfortable with the way he was touching her and the way he wanted her to strip down for the photos, and her mom told her that she was being "dramatic."

"Don't fuck this up for me, Eva," she had said.

Eva's mind returned to the present when the four girls came upon the first big rapid. The river was swollen with water. She tried not to show fear, but it was in her eyes. "I thought you said it was mellow," she said with more bite than she intended.

"You've got this Eva, just paddle through," Rita said before her board rolled through the rapid.

Eva's heart thumped inside her chest and she found herself bracing for the waves that knocked her side to side. She sat on her knees and held tight to the paddle, pushing to maneuver around jagged rocks that jutted out of the water in front of her.

Rita and the girls shouted something, but she couldn't hear over the roar of the rapids, which extended ten or twenty yards downriver. The waves jostled her board from side to side, and Eva held her breath. The water had pushed her board sideways, then spun her to float backwards.

Icy water rushed over her thighs, sweeping her off the board and swallowing her into the river. The cold froze her bones momentarily.

She fell beneath the water, holding her breath with puffed-up cheeks, her body spinning in the water, as the current took her another twenty yards. She came up, gasping for air, glimpsing the white board and paddle floating out of reach.

"You're okay!" the pug-faced girl shouted.

"Swim to the shore, sweetie," Rita said.

Eva wished she'd just hidden in the bathroom after school instead of coming on this trip. *Why am I here, doing this? What do I have to prove?* She couldn't move her legs, she couldn't breathe, she couldn't see straight. *I am going to die,* she thought before going under once more.

When she came up for air, her knee slammed into something hard, waking her, forcing something to rip open inside her, releasing her muscles.

She doggy paddled to the river's edge, where Dakota sat on her green board, completely dry, and held the top of Eva's board with three fingers. It floated calmly next to her.

Shivering, Eva stumbled onto the shore before collapsing into the tall weeds.

"You okay?" Dakota asked. "Kayla, get me the paddle." The girl who yelled about Dakota's bad driving skills—who apparently was named Kayla—tossed the paddle to the shore.

"I'm cool." Eva's voice sounded icy, as she climbed back onto the wet board. Her kneecaps bounced from the cold, but she forced confidence onto her face. She grasped the paddle and stood, wavering back and forth in the rocky current. She looked up to see relief spread over the faces of the three younger girls.

"Oh god, Eva," the pug-faced girl said before cackling.

God, how Eva wished she knew her name, too. It was too late to ask.

"I cannot even—" Dakota said.

"If you had drowned, like, I wouldn't even know how to save you," Kayla said, turning to look at the others. "What about you guys?"

Rita nodded. "That's why I'm here. School wouldn't let you girls go out on your own."

Dakota rolled her eyes. "We've done this a thousand times. We didn't need you."

As they continued to float, the girls spoke over each other, and they moved faster downstream than Eva. The rush of the current made it so she couldn't understand what they said, and for a moment, she was glad of it. She was tired of being *on*.

Then she considered whether these girls would have saved her if she had really been on the verge of drowning. She wondered whether social media fame would've even mattered. If she drowned, it might simply become one more way for them to become stars themselves.

She could imagine the headlines:

"I saw Eva Flores die in front of me."
Nature crushes social media phenom.

She stared, glassy-eyed, at her board. The girls' chatter mixed with the loud rush of the river. She caught Rita gazing at her from about ten yards away in the river, looking concerned.

Immediately, Eva flashed a confident smile. "It's cool."

Fake. Everything she did was fake. There was no escaping it. Real emotions were not an option.

She remembered her stepfather's intense gaze outside the classroom earlier that afternoon. The nature trip would let her expand beyond makeup and clothing brands, beyond snack foods and soft drinks. She'd get sponsorships from kayak companies and paddle board makers and she'd find a whole new network of moneyed people and a wider audience, he said.

She'd only go deeper into the social media persona. Her stepfather had decreed it. And she knew what happened if she didn't abide by his decree.

36

Morgan
ANTICIPATION

Then: May 4

The pop music blared, and Morgan drove with clammy hands on the steering wheel. The Highlander ripped past abandoned coal mines, with their steel structures and walkways that extended high in the air for five hundred yards. She worried about going to the wilderness event, but covered it up with conversation about how Chris Piirto's story would ruin her grade in Ambien's class.

"I won't get an A," she said, staring blankly out the windshield.

"You gotta be dead not to get an A in his class," Ethan said, leaning his head back on the headrest. "The hard part for you will be not making Chris and Amanda break up in his story."

"How do I finish a story like that? I mean, it's all about sleeping with Amanda. So many details I *did not* need to know," Morgan said. "I'm so screwed."

"Go kiss her and find out firsthand," Ethan said, smiling.

Morgan frowned. She couldn't imagine kissing Amanda. Her lines of sexual orientation ran straight—though she'd

251

never even kissed a boy, either. Morgan shook her head when she saw Ethan smiling, and she realized that Ethan was just trying to rattle her. She changed the subject. "What do you think'll even happen this weekend?"

"You mean the story?" Ethan shrugged before she could answer. "I'm so over Sophia's power trip."

"As if winning the lottery isn't enough," she said. "I still can't believe she won." Morgan definitely regretted giving Sophia the journal, and she vowed to herself that she was going to stay mad at her throughout the weekend. Sophia needed to beg for forgiveness from her and Ethan.

"Over it," Ethan agreed, nodding.

"What do you think it *is*, anyway?" She glanced at him.

"What?"

Morgan braked the car to slow to the speed limit through the little town of Somerset, which equated to a handful of run-down houses. "The magic. How do you think it works?"

She'd been giving it a lot of thought over the past few days. She was not one to believe in magic. She understood formulas and coincidence and laws of similarities. What was happening with Sophia went outside the solid boundaries of physics, reality, and everything she understood to be true of the world.

She sighed. "Maybe it's the journal—"

"It's not your stupid journal, Morgan. It's something else. She tell you anything?"

Together, they listed off a number of things that had happened over the past couple months that could be relevant. Hendy firing Sophia's mom. The sale of The Wheel. Her house. Senior Bust. Manny. The fake Instagram.

"Dylan said they took pictures in a graveyard?" Morgan asked. Why Sophia wanted to take pictures of a place where dead bodies were buried was beyond her. But Morgan always appreciated this quirkiness about her friend. The antithesis of herself.

"We went to get a look at that crappy car…" Morgan turned and pointed her finger at Ethan. "In that *haunted* place! The place with that curse! The place *we're going to now!*"

"Curse my ass," he said.

"She fell in mud … in the middle of the field … and she was all spacey and it was creepy there. The *same exact* place—"

Again, anything paranormal chucked rocks at Morgan's need for explanations. She remembered the bad feeling she had gotten when they went to Anthracite Creek that day. She'd felt as if a thousand eyes watched them from the trees that day. Morgan grimaced. "Why exactly are we going back there?"

"I have no idea. Eva planned it all," he said.

"You mean *Sophia* planned it," she said, banging on the steering wheel. "By writing the story."

"Maybe we need an exorcist," Ethan said with a chuckle. He looked out the window at the river.

Morgan knew he was joking, but she didn't like hearing that. Past the railroad tracks, Morgan pressed on the gas again. Drizzle hung in the air and the tall grass waved in the breeze.

Ethan pointed to the river off the highway. It was rushing, and the air looked chilly. "Eva's gonna freeze her ass off down there," he said.

"Shouldn't Sophia be done torturing her by now?" Morgan asked, hoping it was true. This story was changing her friend, and one reason Morgan had decided to go to this event was to keep things from getting even more out of hand. Even though she knew that Sophia had no keeper.

"Maybe it'll be simple: Eva'll just puke on her paddle board," Ethan said, nodding, his gaze still trained out the window.

Morgan worried it was going to be a lot worse than that.

37

Sophia
GOTTA TAKE A SELFIE

Then: May 4

A female guide, Eva, and three sophomores floated up to the lodge on the river, and by the looks of the drenched Eva, Sophia knew her story had played out. A dark, curious part of her wondered if Eva had nearly drowned, if she had reached out blindly in the water, grasping for logs, for boards, hands, rocks, anything to save her. An even darker part hoped it was true.

As Sophia stood off to the side, below the looming jagged peak of Anthracite Mountain, her nerves buzzed. She watched as the guide and the four girls, clad in wetsuits, pulled the paddle boards out of the water and moved carefully over slippery rocks. The sophomore girls prattled on about Eva's fall in the water.

"She was seriously so brave." Dakota Rawlings squeezed water out of her dark braids. She was the ultimate camouflage animal, taking on the same color, voice, and style of those around her. Her freshman year, Dakota took on the biker look, then went for a homeless look with unwashed hair and big old moth-eaten sweaters, although everyone knew she had a line of BMWs and Mercedes at home. After Eva's arrival, she had donned the TikTok wannabe look.

"I can't believe you've never been on a board." Kayla Godfrey nudged Eva with her elbow. She was a toned-down version of Dakota.

Eva grinned and shook her head. She pulled her wetsuit down to her waist, revealing a pink bikini top and a tanned, flat stomach. "It was insane."

"She did quite well," the guide said, patting Eva on the back and moving away from the kids.

"Seriously, my heart," Dakota said, awkwardly tugging her wetsuit down, just to be sure to also show off her tiny waist too. *Look at me! Look at me!*

Behind her, Nessa, a mousy sort of girl with sandy brown hair knotted atop her head, nodded furiously. She was glued to Dakota and Kayla and rarely said much beyond *coooool*, as far as Sophia knew.

"I knew I was in good hands," Eva said, wringing out her hair as phones recorded them.

She and the others posed for photos with one bent leg, hands on hips, wetsuits pulled down to waists.

A wicked part of Sophia beamed at the story of Eva's near-death moment. She had *made* that happen. The power of the pen had always referred to how journalism exposed people and situations. But *she* actually controlled the future.

That knowledge thrummed inside Sophia's chest, and she wondered if fear had gripped Eva like a vice, forcing her to confront the fact that her life had been one giant fraud. If perhaps she felt momentarily guilty or sad or remorseful that she had made a habit of stomping on regular people to achieve her fame.

The girls took selfies, and the other kids who had been invited on the wilderness trip stood on the shore. A few of them peppered the girls with questions. Phillip Hackett took a video of them.

"I swear, Eva," Dakota said. "You go down as a badass in my book."

Badass. That was not what Sophia had written in the story. She wanted Eva to suffer. To be humiliated. To see the side of her that was weak. Eva was supposed to realize that her grit and skill was lacking—in spirit, in depth, in everything. This would be the trip that would ruin Eva, and her followers would see her for the weak person that she was. This would be it.

But it wasn't. The three sophomores plus Aidan, Riley, Chris Piirto—they all clamored over her as if she was the moon and they were wolves. As if they needed her energy to survive.

Eva gave a fake half smile to Aidan and turned away from him. He continued to watch her keenly, with narrowed eyes.

The group began walking into the lodge, and Ambien stood at the doorway, welcoming everyone. Sophia passed him, then noticed how overly warm he was toward Eva, who entered the house behind her.

"You look cold, Eva!" Mr. Ambien said. Sophia rolled her eyes.

"Yeah," Eva said from behind Sophia.

"You know, I asked your dad to be a chaperone—"

Sophia's heart stilled. *Manny? Here?* She slowed her pace to listen to their conversation.

"What?" Eva's voice sounded icy.

"But he said he couldn't come…," Ambien said slowly.

Sophia's muscles froze.

"Oh," Eva said.

"And I was just going to say, it would've been nice to have another guy here... I was going to talk to him about real estate, since I just bought a fixer-upper."

Sophia retreated from them, and the smell of rainy drizzle swept into the lodge from the open door. She wondered if her river scene had actually added to Eva's alluring persona.

Maybe that dab of humility had made her seem more human, more approachable, *more like them.*

Sophia stuck her hands in the pockets of her ripped baggy jeans and walked into the kitchen. She grabbed an apple off the kitchen counter and bit into it hard. Through the open doorway, she watched the other's commotion, and a dark thrill coiled inside her. She knew there were more opportunities to ruin Eva. And the first would come that night.

Wicked Games

BY SOPHIA PALMER

Elsa asked her followers to make her a raft, so she could see the river and all of the wilderness around her. They spent all their energy making the very best rafts for her, and for themselves.

Together, they climbed onto the boats and began to float down the river. The river was peaceful and smooth for some time, until eventually, they came upon some rapids. Her followers had spent more time building Elsa's boat than their own, and the rapids nearly crushed their boats. They nearly fell into the water and were nearly swept downstream. Elsa watched. She could always replace those followers with others, she had decided.

The Wilderness, however, didn't feel the kind of love for Elsa that her followers did. The Wilderness overturned Elsa's raft instead, tossing her into the icy water. The cold stole her breath. She gasped and spun in the rapid, and realizing she couldn't swim, she considered that maybe she wouldn't survive. That maybe this time, her fame and wealth wouldn't save her. She clamored for something to grab onto and finally grabbed hold of a stick. Clinging for her life, she gasped and shivered and crawled out of the water, feeling defeated. A handful of followers looked at her with disappointment and glee, and she knew word would spread that she had failed her own personal test.

She came to the river's edge to shelter, warming herself and changing into fresh clothes. Afraid she looked weak and fearful to her followers, she decided to go into the cursed forest alone, and come out the next morning a survivor.

She would not let anyone come with her, because they would see her cry, because they would see her crumble under the knowledge that she wasn't worthy of a crown. She also knew they would spread stories to their friends and ruin her fame and glory back home. Which was exactly what would happen either way.

She trudged off into the forest alone.

The Flores File: Video Interviews
NOW

Dakota Rawlings: Eva? She was totally different when we were out there on the river with her. She was kind of... I don't know. Checked out?

Kayla Godfrey: You should have seen her face after she fell off the board. It was... I shouldn't say this because she's probably dead now. [Pauses and puts her fingers to her mouth.] But ... it kind of felt *good* seeing her suffer.

Dakota Rawlings: She was so freaked out. And not that I was happy about it, but I guess it was the first time in the whole trip that she felt *real*. Authentic, you know? Like, the rest of the time, it was like she was always performing or something.

Kayla Godfrey: I still can't believe all that went down right after we were all dancing in the lodge. She just kind of flipped out and ran off.

Dakota Rawlings: She seemed like she had a lot going on in her head. But you couldn't really poke through.

Kayla Godfrey: Holly warned us before the trip.

38

Sophia
CONNECTION CARDS

Then: May 4

The fire crackled in the massive fireplace, and the lodge felt cozier than Sophia expected. Elk heads mounted on the wall seemed to stare down at them with glassy eyes. The room was as big as her entire house. Everyone settled into big chairs and sofas to eat dinner on paper plates. This was *not* the wilderness. But it was typical Eva to plan some "adventure" in the comfort of a cozy lodge.

Ambien read off the agenda for the weekend. Tomorrow, they'd all hike at the end of the day to a camp spot in the woods and do a night of tent camping. Ambien nodded to the backpacks lined up along the wall.

"Now if it were up to me, I'd let you do what you want. But..." He sighed. "Principal Evans told me to remind you this is *not* Senior Bust. Okay? Just be cool."

On Sunday, he said, they'd break off into small groups for a variety of planned activities: Eva, Phillip Hackett, Chris, and Amanda would go rock climbing with a guide. Then Eva and the sophomores would go fly fishing.

"The girls got to go paddle boarding. Why do *they* get to

do *two* activities?" asked Phillip in a whining voice.

Ambien shrugged. "Everyone had the opportunity to get on the river, but you complained you'd be—"

"Yeah, too cold, I know," Phillip said, rolling his eyes.

"And lastly, Sophia, Ethan, Aidan, Riley, and Morgan—you all will go mountain biking with me," Ambien said.

Sophia rolled her eyes. *That* was her group. She should have had more control over the weekend.

Even across the room, Sophia could feel the coolness from Ethan and Morgan. They refused to make eye contact with her as they chewed their hamburgers, and she felt momentarily invisible to them.

She shook off the loneliness. They'd come running back to her like usual, eventually. And she took comfort in the fact that Ethan would get peace soon.

Ethan's dad was probably loading everything into his truck right then, headed off to the cabin in the woods alone. She had written that he'd forget to bring Ethan altogether, allowing her friend to stay at his house, able to finally breathe free without his dad's doomsday fears. Maybe his dad would even die, because he'd go and eat too many granola bars in that cabin, hunkering down for the end of the world. She couldn't remember exactly what she had written.

After dinner, Sophia had to work extra hard to banish the amused smile that snuck up her cheek as she and the others watched the endless TikTok dances. The girls—Eva, Dakota, Nessa, Kayla—wore half-shirts and self-tanning lotion on their stomachs. They giggled and gaffed and flopped around each other, watching the takes of their videos.

Sophia hunched into an oversized leather chair, humored by the annoying antics of Eva and her underlings. *Waiting. Waiting.* Ethan and Morgan sat next to each other on another couch, heads together, looking at his phone. Another pang of loneliness stabbed Sophia, and she looked away.

Ambien moved in and out of the room, dipping his curly-topped head low, offering brownies and chocolate like a servant.

It's coming, Sophia thought.

After a few takes, Eva finally collapsed into a big chair and sighed a laugh. "Oh my gosh, this has been *amazing,*" she said, emphasizing the last word.

The other girls agreed and asked about when she was going to upload the footage, and whether they could view it again to ensure their butts and stomachs and hair looked good enough for prime time.

"I'm so happy you organized this," said Dakota, who lay flat on her back in yoga pants and crop top, her hands raised in the air. A mirror of Eva's head-tilt mannerism.

"Yeah, this is awesome," said Kayla, who could have been Dakota's twin with matching black leggings.

"I swear, high school is *so* much more fun now that you're here," Nessa said, nodding furiously.

Sophia scoffed. She glanced at Aidan, who sat against the wall on the floor, flipping through an Elk Mountain history book. Riley, of all people, sat next to him, looking over his shoulder. The appearance of them together surprised Sophia. *Are they friends?*

Over the course of an hour, Riley and Aidan whispered to each other, pointing at the book. At one point, Riley stood and looked out the window, craning her neck to look up at the tall red cliffs beyond the lodge. When Riley came back to her seat on the floor, Aidan was gone. Sophia didn't notice when or where he'd disappeared.

"Can we do something else besides watch you guys twerk?" Sophia asked suddenly. The low tone of her voice startled even herself.

"What?" Eva asked.

"I said, isn't there something else we're gonna do besides watch your little show?" Sophia twirled her hand in the air.

Eva stood up and walked slowly to stand in front of Sophia, her arms crossed over her chest.

"Why're you even here, *Sophia?*" she asked. Eva glanced around the room, acting. "Oh wait! You're looking for my stepdad, right? Because you're looking to screw his brains out again, right?" She put her hands on her hips. "Because *I* certainly didn't invite skanks here."

Sophia gazed up at Eva with a blank stare, her eyelids heavy. She willed Eva to feel afraid, to worry that Sophia was as cruel as she looked. That with one punch, Eva would fall to her knees. Maybe she'd have a flicker of worry that Sophia might actually break her jaw. That would shut her up.

Sophia felt the weight of the other kids' gazes on her, heavy like an invisible blanket, burning with suspicion. Her own silence surely confirmed what they all assumed about her. *Stalker. Copycat. Obsessed. Scary.* Chris Piirto and Amanda Toch, who rarely acknowledged anyone outside of their attached bodies and lips. Phillip Hackett, who cut Eva's lawn. Dakota, Kayla, Nessa. They all watched the two girls, probably hoping for a catfight.

Yet despite their attention, Sophia felt so giddy she almost laughed. She knew that Eva was going down, and that Eva would be the one to feel small and insignificant when the night was over. But she remained quiet.

"Oh yeah, that's right. I forgot, you're here because you're *my stalker*, too," Eva said, throwing a hip out and flipping nonexistent hair over her shoulder. Old habits died hard.

A tiny smile crept up the side of Sophia's mouth and she simply tilted her head, amusement filling her face. She, Morgan, and Ethan were there as witnesses. A testament to the power of her story. The others were there for their obsession or adoration for Eva, and they'd soon witness that she, like everyone else, was flawed.

Ambien must've sensed the tension because he entered the room with gusto, handing a cooler of soda to Chris, asking him to hand them out. The teacher turned around and swiped a deck of cards off one of the many decorative wood console tables. "I brought these Connection Cards," he said in a teacher voice.

Sophia rolled her eyes.

He pulled a card out of the deck. "This one will get you talking," he said, before reading the card aloud. "What's the most selfless thing you could ever do?"

They looked at each other blankly for a couple seconds. It was clear from their expressions that they were resistant to a teacher leading the evening.

Yet the question nagged at Sophia. Everything about this trip was for and by Eva. It was an Eva-sponsored event—albeit spawned by the writings of Sophia—but it was indicative of all that was Eva. "Me TV." Self-centered and self-indulgent. She didn't care about these people, and Sophia was curious to see how this question would challenge her, publicly, about whether she knew what it meant to serve other people, instead of just sucking everything up for herself like a starving anteater.

"What?" Kayla chuckled.

"No, really. What is the most selfless thing you or someone else could do?" Ethan asked. His eyes met Sophia's, and Sophia shrank under his gaze. *He thinks I'm selfish.*

"The most selfless thing you could do is save someone," Eva said. "That's easy."

This has to be uncomfortable for her, Sophia thought. *She isn't used to deep questions.*

"No, because you're getting satisfaction and a hero status if you save someone or something," Sophia said. "So it benefits you."

"So you volunteer," Kayla said.

"Same thing. You feel good," Sophia said.

"You kill bad people," Aidan said.

"You're a hero!" Morgan said quickly, leaning forward.

"The most selfless thing is to be a single parent," Ethan said, glancing at Sophia. "You're taking care of someone, putting them before yourself. That's your job."

"Unless you're a crappy mom," said Kayla, the sophomore.

"Or dad," said Chris.

"There's no such thing as selflessness," Sophia said.

"Who made you the all-knowing?" Eva asked. "Like you know?"

"And why are we even talking about this?" Holly asked.

Ambien had walked out of the room. So Sophia reached down and took another card off the deck, then gazed at Eva steadily. "Do you believe social media presents an existential threat to humanity?"

"What?" Eva scoffed. "Dramatic question."

"I think yeah," Amanda Toch said slowly. "Yeah, it does. All these girls are killing themselves over likes and—"

"Yeah, and we're all concerned about what filter looks best," Kayla said.

"It's not that bad." Phillip Hackett waved his hand. He knew the filters made his acne look better.

"I'm personally addicted," Ethan said. "All those algorithms... I'm like a trained monkey."

Morgan leaned forward. "No, it's keeping us from having real conversations. We're not talking to each other, just comparing ourselves. Plus, we're more divided than ever."

"New question," Eva said, standing up and taking a card from the top.

She read it and put it back on the pile.

"No, you gotta read it." Aidan stood up, walked across the room, and snatched the card off the deck before reading it out loud. "What is your deepest, darkest fear?"

"What?" Eva huffed. "You're ruining the vibe."

"You don't have any fears?" Sophia asked.

"Well, yeah, everyone does." Eva's eyes narrowed. An owl hooted in the distance.

"What are you afraid of?" Sophia's low voice sounded ambivalent.

"What are *you* afraid of?" Eva countered. The room grew quiet, and they waited for the answer.

Sophia thought about it for a moment. *Really* thought about it. Perhaps only Manny had struck true fear in her. But it was irrelevant because her story relieved her fears. It would give her control over her future. That, she realized, was her biggest fear. Loss of control.

"Spiders," she lied. "You?"

She knew Eva's fear without her even saying. It was being alone. Having no approval from the outside world. She *needed* those likes and that adoration to breathe, to survive. And here she was getting it. Would she admit it?

"I don't…" Eva paused and exhaled. "I don't like nature." She shrugged before glancing out the window at the woods.

"Sometimes we have to face our fears," Sophia said, gazing intently at her. She willed Eva to say the lines she scripted. "Why don't you face yours now?"

Eva bit her lip, then defiantly jutted her chin like a scorned child. "Yeah. No problem. I'll do it. Some day."

"Do what?" Kayla asked.

"*Some* day?" Aidan scoffed.

Eva paused and looked out the window for a few moments before suddenly standing up. "You know what? I'm not afraid. I'll go to the forest."

"Now?" Kayla asked.

"Yeah, why not?" Eva said, placing her hands on her hips.

No one else had to prompt her to say it. *It is written, and so it will be.*

"Really? You're gonna do that? Why?" Aidan grimaced.

"Because" Eva said, "I'm *not* afraid."

39

Eva

DARE

Then: May 4

E va stood in the living room with the group staring at her. *I am not afraid of the woods. I am not afraid of the woods.*

She looked at Sophia, who leaned back in the thick leather chair, enjoying the lodge that her family had paid for, on the trip that she had organized. Had this bitchy social recluse really been screwing her stepfather? Just looking at Sophia's smug face, the way she attempted to intimidate everyone, judge everyone, made Eva angrier. She was going to show her. She wasn't going to turn away from a challenge.

Sophia had always been hard to read, but early on Eva had thought she sensed a softer side of her beneath the seemingly calloused exterior. That's why she'd hung out with her when she moved to Paonia. Well, part of the reason. Sophia didn't fall all over her, which was somewhat of a relief. But it also bothered Eva. She'd gotten used to some level of interest in her—even when it came in the form of backbiting and brutal cutdowns below her posts.

But now, Sophia was different. It was as if something hot

and fiery raged beneath her skin.

They made eye contact, and she cut Sophia with her eyes. How dare she insinuate that Eva was selfish. A mirage, yes, but not selfish.

She wondered if Sophia could possibly fathom how absolutely miserable she was in this position, how controlled she was, how incapable of doing anything other than this, of *being* this. She had no idea.

Sophia assumed Eva's life was perfect, that social media stardom was so amazing. She got free gifts from admirers, and always felt that rush of dopamine in seeing the number of likes climb on her posts. But the flip side was a crushing sense of obligation, so intense that it smothered her at night, waking her from dreams, turning her breathless and anxious. She had no career future, no choice; she had given everything over to the app.

The only thing that fed her was seeing others lap it up. That was it.

She had to admit she got a jolt of pleasure when Lydia and Holly had jumped to attention and did what she said, whether it was taking her advice on what boy to date or which TV show to watch on Netflix. She loved seeing these sophomores grovel to sit near her in the cafeteria and ask her opinion on dance moves and clothes. When boys checked her out at school and professed their love, it always ignited something inside her gut. It was a fire that burned, and they provided the fuel.

Still, these people didn't necessarily like *her*; they liked the *idea* of her. No one really knew her.

She stood up, her thin frame stark against the dark sky outside.

"You're gonna do it?" That girl from the river, Kayla, leaned forward on her elbows.

"That's what I said, didn't I?"

Sophia's eyes narrowed. *Sophia. Smug Sophia.*

"Just have to get my jacket," Eva said, before darting up the winding staircase to the bedroom. She rummaged through her suitcase, searching for a light jacket, hoping she'd packed one. She grabbed her embroidered jean jacket with the peace sign and dashed back down the stairs.

Not for one instant did she wonder why she spontaneously decided to do this, when she knew in her heart she was terrified of the dark, terrified of the forest. Not for one instant did she consider this might be the last time she'd see those kids. That she'd never see her mom or Manny again.

Yet she strode past the outdoor fire pit, through the tall grass along the river shore, up the rocky hill, and into the thicket of trees. Her feet crunched the ground beneath her, and a breeze fluttered small wisps of her hair. The hoot of an owl reverberated in her mind, making her feel uneasy. But still she kept walking, knowing the others surely watched her from the window as she hiked up the hill alone.

In the moonlight, the branches of the trees appeared to stretch, to reach out to her, falling in line behind her as she made her way up the rocky path away from the lodge.

Her mind spun. She had just left a warm and cozy setting in the lodge with adoring fans. She could have easily said she was sleepy and retired to bed. Instead, she was trying to prove herself to them, trudging up the hill in sneakers, leggings, and a lightweight jacket.

Why? Because they thought she was selfish. Because they thought she was afraid. Because they had asked her to. Because she needed to prove *something*.

A voice, tucked down in the deepest part of her, seemed to speak to her. It didn't sound like her own voice, but it was familiar and compelling. It drove her legs, her actions, her will. She was to go to the forest in the dark. This was what she felt obliged to do. More than any of the things she'd done recently, she knew that she had to do this. The voice told her so.

Wicked Games

BY SOPHIA PALMER

Elsa ran into the woods, determined to prove that she indeed was fearless, that she indeed could overcome the forest.

But the forest crept up on her, bending its branches to touch her as she climbed a narrow path, lit only by the moonlight. The fingertips of the trees brushed her hair and tickled her back, and fear traced its way up her spine.

Alone. She had never been truly alone. And the word grew thorns and wrapped itself around her torso, squeezing her. Panicked, she ran farther into the darkness, knowing that alone, she would be left to her essence to survive. Not charisma and charm. Not flattery and falsehoods. Not entertainment and adoration. Her chest heaved.

She stood atop a mountain with expansive views of the valley below, and in that moment, she saw her true size in the world. She was just a speck on the infinitely huge earth, smaller than the trees and sky and mountains and universe. She realized that what she projected to the world was huge, a glittery gold mirage. Yet she really was but a small and vulnerable snail without a shell.

Why, oh why, had she taken the people up on this challenge? Why had she thought that she could survive in the world without the full weight of her followers behind her?

She slumped on the ground, hard and cold, shivering, wondering how long she'd have to stay to prove she'd survive. An hour? All night?

A low growl emerged from the bushes, and the hair stood on the back of Elsa's neck. She froze, unable to move her limbs. In the clear light of the full moon, the leaves on the bushes began to shift. She rubbed her eyes, and shook her head. She had to be imagining this.

But no, the leaves began to look more like thorns, and they grew sharp claws. The stems extended long like arms. Slowly, one branch reached out and scratched her neck. She recoiled and screamed, before standing up and jumping away.

It wasn't her imagination. The bushes reached out for her, growling, hissing, and the trees curved downward, blocking the light of the moon. Soon, she was eclipsed into darkness, and several pairs of glowing yellow eyes emerged from what looked like a long dark tunnel between the trees. Flesh-eating, peering eyes, amid thorns and thin laughter.

She screamed, as the forest enveloped her. Momentarily, she wondered what her followers would think of her if she were consumed by the terror of the forest. If they would still love her. Then, as teeth and jaws emerged with the eyes, she realized it didn't really matter. And she ran.

The Flores File: Video
Interviews
NOW

Ethan: Eva just ran up the hill in the dark with those thin little shoes. I knew that Soph had written it, but I was still kind of blown away.

Kayla: It was such a fun night until Sophia Palmer started getting all up in Eva's hair. She pretty much ruined it. We waited for a while, but eventually I fell asleep right there on the sofa.

Dakota: It was the weirdest thing she could have done. Run off like that. We called her name, but she just kept trucking up the hill. She kind of waved her hand at us, like, just hang on, I'll be back. But she didn't come back.

Nessa: I think eventually Aidan went after her.

Aidan: I didn't go after her.

Riley: Sophia went after her. I'm telling you. She was bad news. She was the one to kill Eva Flores.

Wicked Games

BY SOPHIA PALMER

Jane knew her power and was given everything she wanted. She had piles of gold in her backyard and decided perhaps she might share it with her two friends who hated Elsa as much as she did. She decided to help her friend Earl out of a very bad problem. He was afraid of the world, afraid of his own shadow. So she cast a spell to fix all of Earl's problems....

40

Sophia

TRADING PLACES

Then: May 4

T he grandfather clock ticked like a metronome and the fire crackled in the stone fireplace. Two hours had passed since Eva marched up the hill alone in the dark.

Sophia sat reading a horror book under a blanket while the sophomores snuck off to their shared room.

In the main lodge, Ethan and Morgan played chess at a corner table. They never looked in her direction, never acknowledged her. She even stopped next to their table and asked who was winning. Neither of them answered her. It was as if she didn't exist, and that pissed her off. They were being selfish.

She dragged her blanket to a new spot on a recliner a few feet away. "Guys, are you ever gonna get over it?" Sophia finally asked.

After a moment, Ethan leaned away from the chessboard to look Sophia in the eye. "Are you ever going to write a chapter about my dad?"

"I did." Sophia put a piece of gum in her mouth.

Ethan looked genuinely surprised. "Well, what'd it say, Your Majesty?"

"I sent him away."

He frowned. "What?"

"To that cabin. Alone with his crazy head. And I made him forget about you." She popped her gum and looked back at her book. "Happy?"

"You *what?*" Ethan's voice thundered, and Morgan shushed him.

Sophia flinched. "I sent him off to do his thing ... without bringing you into his shit anymore." It was simple. So simple. Why did he seem so mad?

"So your solution to my dad's OCD was to send him away to a cabin where he'll go crazy all by himself." A vein in his temple throbbed. His voice sounded way too loud for the room. Phillip Hackett, Chris, and Amanda looked up from their conversation on the sofa, but Ethan didn't notice. "What the hell are you thinking? You win the freaking lottery, and I get abandoned?"

"I was just trying to help, like you asked," Sophia argued.

"He's my dad. I want him chill. Not *away.*" He flung his hand out.

Sophia sat there, speechless. She had thought she was doing the right thing when she wrote it. But really, she didn't put much effort into that part. She'd been more concerned with doing harm to Eva than considering what might make Ethan whole.

"*You* wanted him away. Not *me!*" Ethan stood up from the chess table.

"And while we're at it. How about me?" Morgan asked, rising to stand next to Ethan. She crossed her arms over her chest.

"What *about* you?" Sophia asked, feeling defensive.

Morgan scoffed. "That's what I figured."

Sophia paused, swallowed, and pressed her lips together.

"You're kidding. You still didn't write anything?" she asked, throwing her arms up in exasperation. "I'm your friend. Who has ... who has defended you and your awful ways to ... to ... everyone."

"So I didn't get to it yet, okay?"

Morgan let out a disgusted guffaw, and she shook her head. "After everything, that was my one small ask. One." Morgan spun around and began marching out of the room and up the stairs.

"Seriously, Soph." Ethan closed his eyes slowly in exasperation. "You let this whole thing get to your head."

"I didn't write anything because I didn't think you needed help," Sophia yelled to Morgan as she climbed the winding staircase. "You've got everything..."

Ethan gestured to Sophia, still curled under the blanket on the chair. "You didn't need to win the freaking lottery either, but you didn't forget about *that*, did you, Soph?"

Then he followed Morgan upstairs.

"E!" Sophia called to him. She stopped yelling when she realized that Phillip, Chris, and Amanda were curiously watching the scene. The three of them looked high, though, so hopefully they wouldn't remember.

She kept the rest of her thoughts to herself. *I hate your dad sometimes, E. I'm sorry. But I do. I hate that he makes you so upset ... and I just wished him away.* Sophia had never felt so alone. Even the air felt chillier.

The clock struck midnight. Sophia figured that Eva would be back by then. The story had been simple. She purposefully left it open, allowed Eva to change, to fight, to find her way back to the cabin. She had no idea what really would appear in the forest because the story was so fictionalized, so unreal. She wanted Eva to see what she was without her fan base, wanted Eva to look closely at herself and pay her dues.

But now that two hours had passed, she worried. What if a mountain lion or bear really did attack her? What if Eva didn't really survive?

Sophia didn't know how she felt about the answer. Numb, maybe? She stood and trotted up the stairs to her bedroom, where she picked up her black backpack from the bed. She was curious to know what she really wrote, if she wrote more hate into that story than she should have. Her hand dug deep into the backpack, but the journal wasn't there.

She pulled out her phone and texted Dylan, who undoubtedly was still up playing video games on his phone.

Sophia:
is my brown leather journal in my room

Three dots indicated he was replying.

Dylan:
no
Sophia:
maybe i left it on the kitchen table
Dylan:
Aidan came by and took it

Blood rushed to Sophia's face, and she dialed Dylan.

Before he could say hello, she blurted into the phone. "Why would he come over?"

"He said you were doing a project together." Her brother's voice was slower than normal this late, but it still had its familiar sing-song ring to it.

"No, no, we aren't."

"You were gonna switch stories, and he asked for it."

"He *what?* And you gave it to him?"

"Well, sure."

Aidan, with *her* journal. Aidan, with the murder-y cat shirts and the bloody comics. Aidan, who surely was capable of way darker shit than Sophia could have ever... And now, Eva was...

Blood pounded in Sophia's chest, her temples, a *whoosh whoosh* drowning out every thought, every sound. She sat speechless on the phone before she spat cutting words that she would always regret, words that distorted her to Dylan, and to herself. "You fucking idiot. Do you even have a brain?"

She heard herself, and everything quieted.

"Oh my god, I'm so sorry. I'm so sorry."

Dylan was quiet.

"Dylan?"

He didn't respond.

"I didn't mean. I didn't. I just ... he's a bad kid ... and that story is important..."

"G'nite, sis." His voice was small, and she heard tears in his throat. He hung up.

A heaviness fell over her, and she held the phone in her lap. It had always been Sophia and Dylan against the world, and she'd been the person to always defend him, to see his disabilities as his greatest assets. He had such a gentleness and sweetness to him, and no one was going to stomp on that. Except her, apparently. She called him back a couple times more, but he didn't pick up.

She caught a glimpse of herself in the mirror over the dresser. Her features looked the same. The longish nose, the hard dark eyes with dark lashes and matching arching brows, the pink mouth that turned down on the edges. That was the hard exterior that others saw. That kept them away from her. But inside, she held kindness, right? Morgan, Ethan, Dylan, and her mom saw that kindness. A softer version of herself.

But she didn't feel soft inside. She felt as if writing in that journal had been a sort of wet cement poured inside her. With each page written, a little more filled up her insides. And now, she was as hard as concrete.

The thought startled her. She stared at herself, but the fear and worry that swirled inside that last soft part of her heart didn't change her expression. And she hardly recognized herself.

Sophia had challenged Eva earlier about the idea of self-lessness. What was true selflessness? *What do I know about being selfless?* Everything that had transpired over the last several weeks was about finding control—over what she wanted, not what anyone else experienced or needed.

Her face felt hot, and her stomach twisted.

She set the phone down and remembered the task at hand. *Aidan.* He had her journal. He might have already written in it. The thought closed her throat off. *I have to find him.*

She ran through the house, searching for him inside rooms, opening doors on sleeping kids. Finally, she came back downstairs to where Phillip Hackett was conked out on the leather sofa.

"Aidan. Have you seen Aidan?" Sophia asked, and Phillip awoke with a jolt. His brown hair looked smashed on one side, and red marks streaked his acne-pitted face. He'd been sleeping on his arm.

"Wha?" he asked.

"Aidan! He has my journal!"

He gazed at her blankly before grimacing and slowly standing up and stumbling up the stairs.

"Aidan, where is he?" Sophia asked.

"Why the hell would I know?" he muttered under his breath.

Sophia, though, darted out the glass doors of the lodge and began racing around the exterior of the building. She slowed as if she was looking for a lost dog. "Aidan?"

She squinted into the dark toward the bank of the river

and saw a hunched figure sitting down low in the weeds. She trotted over to the person. "Aidan?"

He turned, but it wasn't Aidan. It was Ambien. "Oh, Mr. Thomas," she said, breathless.

He swiveled to see her, surprised. He held a bottle in his hand.

"I told Aidan I didn't want to trade projects. But he stole my journal," she said. "He can't do that."

"He probably wanted to ensure he didn't fail, Ms. Palmer," he said.

"No," she said. "No... He took my story." She felt as if she were hyperventilating. This meant everything. He could undo her lottery winnings. Make the house and The Wheel disappear. He could make things happen to Eva that she hadn't intended.

He patted a large boulder next to him, but she stood stuck to the dirt. She didn't have time to sit.

"Where is he? Have you seen him?" she asked.

"Sit."

"I don't have—"

"No, sit." His voice was sharper than she'd ever heard before. She dropped down onto a rock.

"Aidan expressed concern about you and your willingness to throw this project away," he said.

"That's not—"

"*And,*" he said forcefully, "he said he had great ideas for your story."

"He read it?"

"I think he did."

"How?"

Ambien shrugged. "He wanted to kill off some characters."

"Who?"

"He said he hated both the female characters."

"I'm the—" Her chest heaved with anxiety.

"*But* I told him that was the easy way out of stories, that arcs are far more compelling when you don't just eliminate difficult people. You make them grow. Evolve. Change."

"What?" she said through a sharp exhale.

"Listen," he said. "I can tell he has a good grasp on your characters and plot, and I know he'll do what's necessary for your piece." He patted her knee. "Don't you worry."

Fear consumed her. "Don't *worry?*" she asked sarcastically. "You have *no* idea what he's doing."

"I've never seen you so into schoolwork."

"I might die. I literally … and *she* might die." She stood up, fingers splayed, heart pounding, chest heaving.

"Now, come on, it's just a story." He took a swig of his drink.

She turned away. She could hear Ambien's voice chasing her. "It's just an assignment."

She had to find Aidan.

41

Sophia
LITERATURE REVIEW

Then: Early hours of May 5

In the kitchen, Kayla told Sophia that she'd seen Aidan head into the woods, so Sophia set out in the dark to find him.

It wasn't long before her breath burned in her chest and her thighs ached. She ran over the roots and the jagged rocks dotting the spongy trail, and the pine tree branches extended overhead, casting shadows on the moonlit ground. She was not the kind of girl who ran. Ever. But she propelled herself as fast as possible, yelling Aidan's name in breathless, hoarse spurts.

Her feet pounded over pine needles and roots, and she scrambled over large, moss-covered rocks. The path twisted and turned up the hill. Around a bend, about three-quarters of a mile into the woods, something rustled amid the mess of tall grass and thorny bushes off to her right.

She slowed her pace to listen, her heart thumping and a shiver running up her spine. She peered down a steep hillside off the edge of the trail. She hoped it was Eva or Aidan, and not a bear or mountain lion. "Eva?"

There was more thrashing. "Is that you?" Her voice was urgent, and she squinted to see in the shadows of the pine and aspen trees below the trail. "You down there?" Hope stirred inside her. Maybe she'd find her safe, and maybe Aidan's words wouldn't have meaning, whatever they were.

"Ev—" she said again, after a figure rose in the bushes below.

The person moving toward her had long, stringy hair, not Eva's short-cropped style. The girl was shorter too, heavier. She stomped her way up the ridge, ducking beneath tree limbs, scrambling over logs, and clawing at the ground to reach the trail.

"Who's there?" Sophia asked.

"It's Riley," she said in that shrill voice.

"Riley? What are you doing—"

"She's with me." The bodiless voice hung in the air behind her. Familiar, like scorched earth.

She spun around.

Aidan. He stood just a few feet away behind her on the trail, and in the filtered light of the moon, Sophia could see the pockmarks on his skin and a smirk on his face. His eyes were dark pits in his skull.

"Oh, there you are," Sophia said, sighing relief. "Kayla said you were up here. Why'd you come out here?"

He held a hand behind his back. Sophia strained to see.

"That don't matter. Why're _you_ up here?" he asked.

"Looking for Eva."

"Ain't your story over?"

"What?" Her voice was sharp, and she heard Riley move in the bushes again below her.

"Your _journal_," he said. "It's supposed to be all _magic_?" He enunciated the last word and then scoffed.

Sophia felt a tinge of panic run through her. Riley must've heard her talking to Ethan about the journal. Sophia quickly glanced back over her shoulder to see Riley rising from the gully.

Sophia pointed at Aidan. "My journal. You stole it. It was a present, and you can't take it."

"A present?"

"From Morgan. It was her grandma's."

"Bullshit," Riley said from behind. "That thing's brand-new."

Sophia took a step toward him, knowing he held it behind his back, and he took a mirrored step backward, as if they were dancing.

"Uh, uh, uh, uh, uh…," he sang, wagging his finger. "It's my turn. Teacher says."

His taunting tone took Sophia back to the days when kids would tease her brother. Inside the lodge, she had been the one who ripped her brother to shreds, had become that kind of cruel tormenter. She had been the one crushing his soul. Her chest squeezed tighter. She needed to stop this, stop herself, reverse time. She gritted her teeth as anger, impatience, and desperation tore at her.

"Give me my goddamn journal!" she screamed at him. "Did you write in it? Did you?"

Riley emerged from behind and she felt something draw down her back, like a pencil or a stick. She turned and saw the glimmer of a hunting knife. Riley's fingers wrapped tightly around the thick plastic handle. Stunned, Sophia stilled.

"We didn't really like the arc of the main characters," Riley said. Sophia could smell her minty gum.

"Yeah, your story sucked."

"I mean, we asked, did the narrative hang together or collapse into a mess of self-contradiction?" Riley asked. "Did I feel like I learned something or is it a story that makes me wanna just slit my wrists?"

"I didn't ask for a review," Sophia said. "I wrote the story for *other* reasons."

"Oh, we know that," Riley said. "But still, in our analysis, it was certainly wrist-slitting reading."

Aidan put a flat palm out. "Hang on a sec, Miss Palmer, while I read for the class how we... how we..." He paused.

"Tried to rectify," said Riley.

"Yeah, how we fixed your shitty story." He put his hand out, mimicking Ambien's gestures. He cleared his voice.

"*This* is literature at its finest," said Riley.

Sophia waited, anxiety heaving her shoulders, the prick of the knife in the middle of her back. "Feel that?" Riley whispered to her. "It's sharp. Right. Next. To *your* weak, little spine." Riley slowly enunciated every word.

Aidan opened the journal, held it with one hand as if he were reading from the Bible, raised the other hand in the air, and read dramatically from the journal.

Wicked Games

BY AIDAN VOINOVICH

When Elsa got to the forest, she got scared. But then she realized that she wasn't scared of the forest really. She was just scared of not being perfect. Her fans changed into a big tall giant monster that was filled with all the faces of her fans. And it was coming after her in that forest. With a big-ass knife. And big giant hands that would kill her.

That monster was kind of green and gooey and also hated that girl Jane because she was just as bad as Elsa and she was selfish and cursed everything in the first place. Jane was the one who kinda fucked everything up and thought she was better than everyone else. She always looked down on everyone. So that monster came after both of them.

The girls screamed and stuff and ran real fast into the forest. The monster magically undid all the spells that Jane created. So she didn't get rich, and didn't get property, and her friends didn't get nothing.

And then the monster had big fangs and told them they were stupid because the monster had control of everything. He said everything that the girl Jane wanted was not cool, and he said that Elsa had made mistakes by rejecting really nice people and being all bitchy and stuff.

Then blood spewed and girls screamed and the monster killed both of them. First Elsa and then Jane.

42

Sophia
AIDAN VS. SOPHIA

Then: May 5

Sophia's heart pounded. "Where's Eva?" Her voice was shrill. "What'd you do to her?"

Aidan just shrugged.

"You're the one who sent her out here into all this big scary danger," Riley sang.

Sophia's mind raced. *That was it?* She was dead? They killed her? They wrote the rest of the story, then killed Eva, and now they would kill Sophia too.

A latch unlocked inside her, and she barreled toward Aidan, ramming her shoulder into his chest with a thud and tackling him to the ground. She straddled him and pinned his shoulders down with biting hands.

"Where is she?" Sophia roared above him, her face inches from his crooked nose.

A wry smile made its way up his cheek. "I like seeing you like this, Soph. Straddling me." He growled. "I bet you're a hot—"

With a swift move, she let go of his shoulder and punched

him in the mouth. He squinted and cried out. "You bitch!" He pushed her off him, and Riley lunged at her from behind.

"Get off him!" Riley's acidic voice scraped at the insides of Sophia's skull.

The knife struck Sophia's back. Stunned, Sophia froze for a moment and looked at the blade, poking a few inches into her back hip. It didn't hurt—until Riley yanked it back out.

Searing pain rushed through Sophia, and she cried out. Riley backed up, a look of surprise on her face.

Just as Aidan scrambled to his feet, Sophia lunged at him again, swiftly kneeing him in the nuts. He let out a low, breathless grunt and rolled onto his side, striking a large moss-covered rock. His movement revealed the journal, which had lain beneath him. Quickly, Sophia grabbed it and skittered away.

"Drop it, Sophia." She didn't even sound like Riley. It was as if, for years, she had been a fuzzy TV screen. Suddenly, Riley was clear as day, in focus and crisp.

Like a child, Sophia kicked out at her with one foot to keep her away as she tried to look at the journal. She spotted the change in handwriting and attempted to tear a page out of the book. Then Riley's knife swung through the moonlit air and caught Sophia's wrist.

She dropped the journal.

Backing away from Riley, she looked at the cut on the soft side of her wrist, visible below the blood-soaked edge of her jacket sleeve. She felt stunned at first, taking in the clean slice that soon began to ooze a steady river of scarlet. After a few seconds, her wrist and hand were slick with blood and the cut began to burn.

She forgot about the stab wound to her hip as she covered her wrist with her opposite hand, then looked back at Riley.

"You're fucking crazy," Sophia said.

"You bet I am. I'm your worst nightmare." Riley kicked

the journal behind her and confidently swung the knife in the air.

Aidan slowly climbed to his feet, groaning. Still hunched over, holding his nuts, he looked up and registered what was happening. "Dude, Riley, what're you doing?"

"Delivering justice," Riley said, glancing back at Aidan.

"A knife? You brought a *knife?*" He stepped away from her.

She had her back to him, and she glanced at him over her shoulder. Riley looked emboldened in the moonlight, which shone like a spotlight on her amid the dark and eerie pine trees. She crept toward Sophia, preparing to pounce.

Behind her, Aidan stood still with a gaping mouth and wide eyes. Slowly, he backed away from the two girls. Instead of determining which side to take, he clearly was contemplating whether to run.

Fear seized Sophia, and she spun on her heel and took off at a dead run up the hill.

The Flores File: Text messages obtained from Sophia's phone

May 5

12:26 a.m.
Morgan:
wya?

1:01 a.m.
Morgan:
yes im still mad
but now worried

1:17 a.m.
Morgan:
eva's still not back.

1:35 a.m.
Morgan:
soph!
u looking for eva?

1:47 a.m.
Morgan:
kayla said you went to woods.

1:50 a.m.
Morgan:
thats it
were coming to find u

43

Eva
MIDNIGHT VISIT

Then: May 5

Eva felt as if the trees would swallow her, and she found herself hyperventilating and running aimlessly up the trail, deeper into the forest. Her feet thumped over spongy moss, over rocks checkered in gray lichen, as she followed a staircase of steps made of uneven tree roots.

The air grew cooler, and the scent of moist dirt and pine swirled around her head.

After a few minutes, she found moonlight pooled in an opening between the trees. She left the steep edge of the trail and headed upslope, wading through a small clearing. Eva sat down on a downed tree, feeling somehow that this random midnight hike was more than just about being alone in the woods. It made her question everything about herself. Which should have been good, but after having to show up every day like you know yourself, it was terrifying.

Tears began to ripple down her cheek.

The forest was quiet outside of the oceanic hum of the wind through the treetops. She sat quietly, rethinking her life. She didn't really even remember her mom's presence in her life until she was sixteen. That's when Manny began taking a keen interest in everything she did, the way she looked, the way she moved, how she presented herself to the outside world. Her mother seldom said anything. Instead, she busied herself with decorating their house and watching those reality TV shows about making fat people thin.

Eva heard a rustle in the bushes at the edge of the clearing, and she sat up straighter, holding her breath. Her heart thudded against her chest. Then in the moonlight, a figure emerged, urgently pushing through the brush. She couldn't move.

It was a man. And, immediately recognizing the physique and swagger, she exhaled. "Manny... er ...Dad!"

"There you are," he said, but his voice didn't sound warm. And his appearance in the clearing made absolutely no sense. She was at least a mile into the woods.

"What're you doing out here?" She stood up and crossed her arms over her chest, the chill seeping through the fabric of her jean jacket.

"I tracked your phone," he said. "Kids called me because they were worried."

"Oh," she said, feeling relieved. She unconsciously patted her phone in her pocket.

"Why're you here, hiding?" He stood a few feet away from her, wearing a puffy coat and stocking hat. He repeatedly rubbed his hands together and balled his fingers into fists.

"I'm not hiding. I was trying to prove that—"

"You don't need to prove yourself. You need numbers," he said. "This?" He waved his hand around the moonlit grassy opening. "This is not getting you followers and likes."

"I ... I ... wanted... I was facing my fears." Her throat felt as if cotton were stuck in it, preventing words from forming correctly.

"You don't get it, do you?" He walked in a large circle around her, an unfamiliar move. "You're beautiful. You're hot.

300

With that ass and face..." He nodded to her, scanning her body. "And your sexy moves... You had the potential to be big."

It always made her feel uncomfortable, the way he noticed her body. The way he'd stare too long and run his eyes up and down her when she danced.

"I'm still gonna be big." But her voice was soft, and even she didn't believe it. She wanted out.

Manny spoke over her. "I don't believe you anymore. All anyone is going to talk about now is how my daughter ran off into the woods and sulked. That she was a scared little girl who couldn't handle life."

"Why does that matt—"

He raised his voice to quiet her. "And now, I have to turn to other means. I thought I found another brilliant young star. An artist. The next Njideka Akunyili Crosby. But now, even she's disappointing me."

He circled behind her slowly, and she followed him with her chin to keep track. It made her uneasy, the way he was rounding her as if he was hunting her.

Then she noticed the silvery glint of the blade in his gloved hand. Her heart clenched tight, and she nearly couldn't breathe.

"Why do you have ... that?" She pointed to his hand.

He held it up, almost tenderly. "To give you a story that people won't stop talking about."

44

Sophia
HUNTED

Then: May 5

Sophia's shirt was damp with blood, and though it was only an inch long, the wound went deep. So deep that the fleshy fat beneath her skin protruded from the cut. Each step tugged at the edges of her injury, and it felt as if her skin was tearing open like a paper bag.

Riley was faster than Sophia thought she'd be. As she caught a glimpse of her in her peripheral vision, Sophia remembered seeing in the school newspaper that Riley had been a top contender on the track team. Was it distance running? Or sprints? She didn't know, and she didn't have time to ponder it. Numb to her injuries, Sophia ran like her life depended upon it. Which, she had a grave feeling, it did.

Riley's footsteps crunched the dead leaves, edging closer and closer with remarkable speed. Sophia knew her only choice was to go off course. If she stayed on the trail, she'd be tackled and likely stabbed to death by this angry rat girl who, apparently, held a serious grudge.

With one jerking motion, Sophia leapt into the bushes and careened down the hillside, running and tripping over decaying logs, bushes, and gatherings of rocks. She cried out in pain as her wrist and hip struck stray branches, and she reflectively attempted to cover her hip with her hand. Her fingers slipped along skin slick with blood.

The incline sped her pace and she stumbled over a root and struck a low pine branch. She fell hard to the ground. Branches sliced her arms, and rocks gouged her knees. She scrambled to keep going, knowing that Riley was right behind her, ready to attack.

Except she wasn't. A good hundred yards from the path, shrouded in the shadows of the trees, Sophia was alone. Or at least she hoped.

She listened for breaking branches and movement through the bushes above. Even the slightest, deftest movement would be heard down there.

Sophia's lungs burned, and she momentarily wondered why she never bothered to do any kind of exercise at all. She paused, listening again, holding her breath, trying to hear above the pounding of her heart. After a couple moments, she turned and ran farther down the hillside, away from the two local psychopaths.

The moon had risen higher in the sky. She had to get back to the lodge. But she was completely disoriented and had no idea where she was.

The sun normally would be a guide in the forest. But she had only the moon. And she was being hunted. The story foretold this. And if things played out as expected, she would be dead soon.

Burning pain wove its way into her waist and wrist. Dark, sticky blood shone on both her shirt and on her hand. Panic squeezed her.

She suddenly stopped running. This wasn't like her. She wasn't the type to be afraid. To be hunted. She always figured if someone broke into her house, she would greet the invader in the kitchen doorway with a baseball bat to the head.

She spotted a rock the size of a brick and picked it up. Whoever messed with her, she'd knock them down. The rock gave her comfort, and she willed herself to draw on the fearless spirit that had seen her through plenty of situations. But as she made her way through the forest, she recalled the rocking terror of Aidan and Riley's attack, and it shook her insides.

These were people she looked at every day amid coffee grounds and donuts at the cafe, inside dusty classrooms and crowded hallways at school. Now her stupid story had turned everything upside down, unlocked some sort of gleaming greed and devilish want inside everyone, including herself. She wished none of it had ever happened.

With each step over the roots, the decaying logs, and the dead leaves, she thought of Eva, envisioning her lying dead at the bottom of a ravine, her body splayed unnaturally from a fall—or a push. She'd prompted Eva to do this trip, to run to the forest, with the stroke of a pen. Deep regret tore at her insides, ripping the soft parts of her heart.

She stopped and spun around, panting, wondering where Eva was in this sea of aspen and pine trees. Just before she began to move again, she heard something. Voices, a murmur. Male and female.

It had to be Aidan and Riley. She slunk down low, gripping the rock close to her hip. She followed the sound of the voices. *They'll be sorry they ever messed with me.*

She slunk low to the left, scrambling quietly up the hillside. She ducked behind wide-leaf berry bushes and pine trees, watching two people off the steep trail above her. They faced off in a grassy moonlit clearing upslope of the ravine's edge.

It wasn't Aidan and Riley. The short hair and tiny frame were a dead giveaway. It was Eva!

"Sometimes I think I loved your future more than you did."

The voice was unmistakable.

Instinctively, she knew Manny Flores was not out there to help. She could feel him in her blood, like the rotten smell of something dead. *Why is he out here? At this hour?*

She watched. The way he circled Eva made her nervous. Her story had switched on a lever that changed him, made him obsessive and creepy. Or maybe he'd always been that way. She stayed low, watching from the bushes.

"Your fans deserve better. They are disappointed in you," he said to her.

"No, *you're* disappointed in me." Eva's voice sounded thin — nothing like the overconfident girl that Sophia and the rest of her classmates knew.

"Think of me as all of your fans. Think of me as an amalgam of them all."

A blend of her fans. Just like Aidan's story. The monster. A chill ran up Sophia's spine.

"And you're afraid of them. Of me. Of being what you're supposed to be." He stopped directly in front of Eva. So close he could take her hand. But he didn't. Instead, he reached up and touched the side of her face.

"I'll miss you," he said—so softly that Sophia had to strain to hear. Eva's knees buckled, making her entire body sway.

Manny's hand crept up to Eva's throat, and with his other hand, he drew something that glinted in the light. Eva cried out and placed her hands on top of his. Shock flooded Sophia. *He's going to kill her.*

Sophia bounded from the bushes and ran toward the two of them. "Stop!" She wielded the rock high over her head. Manny turned and Eva wriggled out of his grip, falling backward onto the ground.

Sophia raced across the uneven meadow, roaring in anger, the rock in hand. When she neared him and coiled her arm back to hit him, he ducked to the right and struck her outstretched arm. The rock fell out of her hand. As she watched it tumble away, a thunderous blow struck her jaw, throwing her onto the ground. The pain reverberated through her whole face. It reached its jagged fingertips to her ear, her eye, inside her skull. She couldn't see straight for a moment, and when she gazed up at Manny, she saw double. Two of him, holding the rock above her with one hand and a knife in his other hand.

A scuttling noise told her Eva was still nearby, trying to escape.

"God, Sophia, and to think I loved you so much that I wanted to crawl inside your veins."

Sophia tried to make sense of the words. They floated around her head, crashing into each other, and she grasped for them.

He tossed the stone away and turned back to Eva, who scooted on hands and feet like a crab, away from her stepfather. She looked to Sophia, who mirrored her fear and surprise.

When Sophia could see him clearly—just one of him—she sprung from the ground and charged him—much the same way she had Aidan earlier. It took him by surprise, and she pushed him backwards like a football player might press an opposing team's defender. Off-balance, he gave ground but still gripped the knife. He was raising it to stab her when Eva jumped up and bit his hand.

"Ow! You bitch!" he yelled, and his weapon fell to the ground. Then she too pushed behind Sophia.

"Harder," Eva whispered, as her stepfather staggered backwards. Sophia glanced at her and pushed in a way that kept him on his feet. Sophia could take down a guy in the blink of an eye, flatten him onto his back. And that's what she wanted to do to Manny.

But then, over his shoulder, she saw what Eva was doing. They were pushing him backwards, across the outline of the trail towards the edge of the ravine. Sophia had just climbed a similar one. He wouldn't die, but he'd struggle to get up. And that'd be enough time to get away.

With one last shove, Manny toppled off the edge with a thud, tumbling and rolling, hitting trees and crashing into bushes. Eva watched, holding her hand over her mouth, flinching with each crunching roll.

"Come on," Sophia said, grabbing Eva's hand. "We've got to get out of here."

45

Sophia
THE HUNT

Then: May 5

In the shade of the trees, it was hard to figure out what was the path and what was just worn earth from animal tracks. They ran swiftly through the dark in the silence, careful to tread lightly and make the least amount of noise possible.

Adrenaline flooded Sophia, dulling the pain that would otherwise consume her body. If she let herself, she'd note the throbbing jaw, which was surely bruised, the swelling headache folding across her skull, the dizziness, the tearing pain in her hip and wrist.

She was out of breath, and after a few minutes of running with Eva trailing her, Sophia slowed to stop, squirming to check the wound on her waist and her wrist.

She winced in pain. Eva caught up to her, panting. Her damp hair stuck to the sides of her face. "What're you doing?"

"Riley cut me," Sophia said.

"What? Why?"

"Because she's crazy," Sophia said. "We got to get outta here."

Eva reached into her jacket pocket and retrieved her phone. She threw it into the bushes. "He'll track me."

Sophia noticed a cut below Eva's jawline and the dark crimson stain it left on the collar of her jean jacket. It was a clear reminder to Sophia that Manny literally was out for blood.

The moon lit their way, and Sophia worried that Manny was somewhere behind, following their movements. Eva kept asking about Riley, babbling on about some text messages she kept sending her. "I wonder if she was trying to get me."

Sophia didn't answer. She was too out of breath and didn't want to explain the journal to Eva.

"I'm so thirsty," Eva said through labored breaths. "Did you bring water?"

Sophia shook her head. She hadn't come prepared, and her mouth was parched too. Another reason to get back to reality.

Along the way, they must have veered north, because when they emerged into the moonlight, they stood along the bank of the river—but at an unfamiliar section. The lodge wasn't across the water. Sophia figured it was probably around a couple bends and close enough to walk once they got across the water.

They clambered down a hillside, and Sophia stopped to take off her sneakers. Eva followed suit, and with shaky hands untied her shoes. Her breath sounded shallow, barely audible above the rush of the brook. A series of rapids formed white-caps to their right.

"Should be shallow enough here to wade through ... maybe up to our knees," Sophia said before pointing down-stream. "The currents below get pretty sketchy down there, though." She paused. "Can you swim?" Elsa couldn't swim in her story.

She didn't look back at Eva, just listened for a response. Eva grunted a yes.

JENNIFER ALSEVER

Sophia stepped onto a couple of big boulders and searched for more protruding rocks, to avoid the frigid water if possible. She looked back to see Eva following behind slowly, her shoes in both hands. The water gushed over the rocks, and Sophia leapt from rock to rock, wincing with each step. She'd almost reached the far side when her foot slipped off and she splashed down into the water. The biting cold water rushed over her shoulders and its strength threatened to sweep her away. But Sophia caught her footing and clambered to the shore.

Eva stood frozen on two rocks. "I can't," she said.

"Just go!" Sophia couldn't handle her being a wuss. She *had* to cross the river. She glanced back at the bushes, her heart pounding over the rush of water. *Was he there?*

After a few deep breaths, Eva hopped from rock to rock, fingertips flexed. Her dancer's athleticism paid off—until she came to the same slippery rock that got Sophia. Eva screamed as she fell in the water, submerging fully before gathering her footing. She crawled onto the shore.

Sophia reached out a hand to pull her up from the ground, and Eva took it. Strands of wet hair covered Eva's face, obscuring her small nose.

Together, Sophia and Eva lumbered, barefoot, in heavy, wet clothes. Eva's teeth began to chatter.

"Wh-wh-ere. Is. Ma-a-a-nny."

"I dunno." Sophia glanced over her shoulder, searching for him. She thought she saw something rustle the bushes across the river, and her spine felt stiff, her throat choked off air.

She picked up the pace. She didn't have energy for talk, and she knew she needed to get them both warm. She had to get them to the lodge—and finally she saw it, maybe just a football field away.

Sophia kept her sight on the lodge, and she noticed that chills began to wrack Eva's entire body, like mini earthquakes.

Sophia stopped. "You gotta take off some layers. Too heavy."

Eva sat amid thorny bushes, blood rushing down her neck, dripping onto Sophia. In slow motion, she bent her arms to remove the stiff jean jacket. Sophia took off her own and threw it on the ground, and then tugged Eva's bloody jacket off her body, too. She threw it on the grass.

"I-I-I … can't go hhhh-ome," Eva said through chattering teeth. "He'llll k-k-kill me. And no c-c-c-ops. He knows them all."

Sophia didn't respond.

"I c-c-can't go into the lodge. N-n-not yet," Eva said.

46

Morgan
RECLAIMING PROPERTY

Then

Ethan and Morgan didn't even bother turning on their headlamps when they went to search for Sophia in the woods; the moon gave the ground a candlelight glow. As they walked, Ethan talked about a guy he'd met on a dating app, chattering away as if he were on a casual afternoon hike.

"He's older than me. Well, they all are," he said, through huffing breaths. "But he's gonna drive all the way from Salida to meet me."

"You think dating old men on some app is a good idea?" Morgan asked gently.

"Not many options here."

"There's that guy Deeter who lives on Delta Street." She knew it was a ridiculous suggestion. Deeter was a nineteen-year-old drunk who'd crashed his moped into a ditch and knocked out his front teeth.

"I heard he's raising rattlesnakes in his backyard," he said.

"I should've written about him in my story." She laughed.

"You know, getting a bad grade on something won't kill

you," Ethan said. "You don't *actually* have to do everything perfect to be happy."

Morgan thought about it for a moment, wondering if that was possible. She firmly believed that any deviation could cause catastrophe. If she didn't get into a great school, maybe she might live? She shook off the thought. Of course she needed to be accepted to her top three.

They came to a point on the trail where the tree branches dipped over like a canopy, blocking out the light of the moon.

Ethan stepped onto a large boulder. "Maybe I don't need anyone. I got you and Soph."

"If we *find* Sophia." The anxiety that had scratched at Morgan for two hours reappeared. She was mad at her friend, but she loved her. Enough to wander through the trees looking for her in some creepy forest. She cupped her hands around her mouth. "Sophia!" she called out to the trees.

Ethan called her name too.

No response.

They walked in silence, passing aspen branches and scrambling over rocks for a few more minutes. Morgan's anxiety made her chest tighten. She wanted to turn around. "Maybe she's not out here."

Someone leapt out onto the trail a few yards ahead of them, startling her. She yelped and stumbled backward.

Aidan darted past her and swung wide to avoid Ethan on the trail below.

"Hey! Where're you going?" Morgan asked.

"Back … to the lodge." He was breathless and sprinting fast.

"Hey!" Ethan grabbed Aidan's shoulder to stop him.

Aidan spun back and shrank away from him. "Get off."

Morgan pointed. "Hey! That's Sophia's journal."

If Aidan had written in the book, his chapters would probably make for an incredibly foreboding prophecy. Morgan felt the blood drain from her head.

"No it ain't," Aidan said, pulling away and tightly gripping the journal.

"Yeah, it *is.*" Morgan pointed at the book. "That's the book I gave her."

"She was looking for that, dude," Ethan said. He stuck his hand out. "I'll get it to her."

"Naw," Aidan said, turning away and beginning to run down the hill again.

Ethan trotted after him and gruffly grabbed Aidan's skinny arm. Aidan pulled away, but Ethan managed to rip the journal from his hands.

The struggle forced Aidan to stumble backward onto the ground. He kicked a grimy sneaker at Ethan. "That's mine. Mr. Thomas said it's my turn. It's *my* turn!"

"What are you, nine?" Ethan asked, kicking back with a stiff hiking boot. He mimicked him in a childish voice. "My *turn!*"

Ethan handed the book to Morgan behind him and stood on guard, ready to pound Aidan if he tried to get it. Aidan scrambled to his feet. Ethan moved in front of him, blocking the way to Morgan.

"Get lost," Ethan said, using his fingertips to give Aidan's chest a push.

Morgan opened the book and began flipping through to read the last few pages in Aidan's handwriting.

She read the last two sentences out loud. "*Then blood spewed and girls screamed and the monster killed both of them. First Elsa and then Jane.*"

Morgan stopped and looked up at him. "What the heck, Aidan?"

"It's just a stupid story," Aidan said.

Morgan scoffed and read a line from his chapters. "*When Elsa got to the forest, she got scared.* Wow, brilliant writing."

"Doesn't matter. I heard what you guys did with that

story." He tossed his head at them. "And it's gonna bite you in the ass."

Morgan felt her body stiffen. "What'd you mean?" She looked at the pages and scanned his words. "What's this monster, anyway?"

"It's whatever you think it is. You know, like … like…"

"A metaphor," Riley said from behind them. She'd stealthily appeared up the trail, chasing a weird chill up Morgan's spine.

"Spooky much? What're you doing here?" Morgan asked.

Riley extended her hand. "We'd like our journal back."

"*Your* journal?" Ethan asked with a chuckle. "I think not."

"What were you doing up there?" Morgan asked, her eyes searching the trail ahead.

"Who knows?" Riley asked, tossing her head in a taunting fashion. She slowly removed a hunting knife from her pocket and gripped it firmly in a defensive stance. "Now, give me that freaking journal, and no one gets hurt."

Morgan's heart dropped into her stomach at the sight of the knife and the dark smudge on the white handle. She stepped backward, away, down the trail. "What the hell, Riley."

Aidan's eyes looked bigger. "Dude," he said. "Riley … not again." He stumbled backward before taking off at a dead run down the trail, away from them.

Ethan watched him go.

"Give me my journal," Riley said through gritted teeth.

Ethan didn't appear fazed by her and with one hand, he ushered Morgan behind him for safety. "I'll crush you if you get near Morgan. I don't care if you *are* a girl."

Morgan hugged the journal close to her chest, knowing she had to protect the story in order to protect her friend's life, and Eva's life too. Her gaze steadied on the ground as she pored over her options.

How the hell did this magic work anyway? Could she

undo what he had written? Could she write more to change the outcome? Maybe say it was all a dream? No, the "it-was-all-a-dream" thing was such an overused, easy, empty cliché ending, she thought.

"You think I'm a nobody," Riley said. "But I want a story, too."

Ethan scoffed, still not backing down from the looming girl.

"Like, yeah, I'm gonna write a story that would fix my folks," Riley said, tossing her head defiantly.

"Fix them," Ethan repeated. "How could anything fix them after the mistake of making you?"

"See? In my story, bullies like you get what you deserve. And I'll get to be…" Riley took another step closer, not at all intimidated by Ethan.

"What do you get to be, Riley?" he asked, puffing up his chest.

"Powerful." She stepped closer to Ethan, who stood twice her size. "I'll chop you to pieces."

Riley really does sound like sociopath material.

"Morgan, looks like we've got our own little Paonia Butcher here—" Ethan glanced over his shoulder at his friend.

That turn of the head provided Riley with a momentary opportunity. She caught Ethan off guard and took a swipe at him. The knife sliced through his flannel down to the skin on the side of his stomach. He looked down, stunned. "You cut me!"

"You bet your ass I cut you. Now tell your little bitch friend to give me the journal or like I said, I'll cut you into tiny pieces."

Riley had just cut Ethan! Anger boiled inside Morgan. Her heart pounded and after a momentary pause of indecision, she stepped in front of Ethan.

Then in an instant, Morgan wound back and punched Riley in the face.

47

Sophia

FAVOR

Then

S ophia told Eva to hide in the backseat of her car while she snuck through the front door of the lodge. The legs of Sophia's stiff, wet jeans rubbed against each other as she ran up the stairs to the bedroom.

Breathless, she changed clothes. She stopped to inspect the cherry-red mark on her jaw in the mirror and briefly studied the red linear wound on her hip and then the slice across her wrist. *Freaking Riley.* They hurt, but she wouldn't die. She shoved her belongings into her duffle bag, then gathered her phone, wallet, a metal water bottle, and a blanket off the bed.

Wearing sweatpants and a hoodie, Sophia sprinted down the stairs, out the door, and back to the car, still barefoot. The car smelled like cool water and a little fishy, but the warm air from the heater felt inviting. Eva lay across the backseat in a ball, shivering and whimpering.

Sophia retrieved some fresh clothes from her duffle and a clean down jacket and passed them and the blanket back to her. Inside the dark car, Sophia could make out a wet curl that fell toward Eva's face, and the button nose that made her so pretty.

Eva didn't look at her as she sat up slowly and wiped her eyes and rubbed her face. She let out a shaky exhale and rubbed her throat where Manny had grabbed her, before beginning to strip down to put on the clothes.

Sophia paused and took her keys out of the ignition, realizing she didn't know where to go.

"You okay?" Sophia asked as she looked away.

Eva didn't answer as she dressed, only grunting a few times. Clothed, she rolled her eyes and rested her head on the seat with a long sigh. "Of all the people. You."

"What, you surprised I'm your knight in shining armor?" Sophia asked, turning around to look at her. She winced again from the stab wound. "You're welcome."

Eva scoffed and shook her head, irritated. "Thanks." After a moment, she breathed the next words. "No, I mean it."

"Heroes come in all shapes, ya know," Sophia said.

After a moment, Eva muttered under her breath, "So do sluts."

"Excuse me?" Sophia had just saved this girl's life, escaping the hands of a psychopath who wanted them both dead. She had always wanted Eva to disappear, and if she had waited quietly in the grass, she would have. But Sophia was *glad* that she hadn't let Eva die. She was *glad* she was alive. But it still didn't mean she liked her. Even in crisis, Eva just couldn't help from being *So Eva.*

It took a moment before Eva responded. "Uh ... you went and *fucked* my stepdad." She looked at Sophia. "Surprised you didn't help him murder me."

"I didn't fuck him."

Sophia's wrist burned, and she wondered briefly if Riley really would have stabbed her to death if she hadn't run. She'd totally underestimated Riley and her inner rage. She had two attackers to look out for. Her eyes scanned the riverbank, searching for signs of either of them. She slunk down into the driver's seat, fiddling with her key, as thoughts poked along the edges of her mind. She had no idea where they should go.

They should call the cops, but Eva asked her not to do that, not yet.

"Wasn't that your plan? He leaves my mom, you two get rid of me. Live happily ever—" Eva said.

"I *said*, I didn't fuck him. And wouldn't ever want to," Sophia said, gazing at the dashboard.

"Right."

"I just pretended to be into him. To mess with you." Sophia peered at Eva between the two bucket seats.

"Wait," Eva said, frowning. "You led him on because you wanted to—"

"To mess with you, yeah." She took in Eva's gaping stare and waved her hand at her. "Oh, as if you haven't spent all your months trying to ruin my life because I didn't play into your *bow down to me* bullshit."

"You ... seduced ... my stepdad." Eva's jaw hung slack, and she spread her fingers wide.

Sophia sniffed and looked away. He had nearly killed them. She had to call the cops.

"So you ... could mess with me." Eva's voice sounded flat.

Sophia waited a few moments to answer. "Yeah, basically."

"You're a fucking psychopath."

"And *you're* not?" Sophia snapped. "At least I don't make fake Insta accounts of other people."

"I ... you ... deserved... Why were you out in the woods anyway?" Eva threw her hands up and strained her neck to peek out the front window. "Where's everyone?"

"I was looking for Aidan. Everyone else? The lodge, I guess."

"Aidan? *He* was in the woods? Why?"

Sophia didn't want to tell her about the journal. "Maybe I worried something bad might happen. Which, I was right. You're welcome."

Eva scoffed and turned to face the side window again. "Right. You came out there to protect me. You *hate* me."

"Maybe." Sophia scratched her head and considered her words.

Eva pointed a finger at her. "You know, I'm a *nice* person. You? You're mean. No one likes you because you're mean. Everyone is afraid of you."

That was the way Sophia had wanted it, and for years she'd never seen that as a drawback. Unlike Eva, she didn't care if people liked her.

"So?" Sophia said. "At least I don't go around trying to make people like me, trying to control what they think, what they wear, how they feel about themselves. At least I'm real. Not putting on some phony idea of who I should be for everyone else."

And she certainly didn't have to explain herself to Eva. This girl couldn't possibly understand why being authentic, even if it was not entirely friendly, was better than being fake.

"Listen, we *should* be worried that your freaking psychopath dad—"

"No. No-no-no-no," Eva said, scooting forward on the seat. "You don't know me. You judge me, just like you judge everyone else. But you have no idea what's inside my heart."

"Omigod." Sophia rolled her eyes.

Eva's voice choked up. "You have no idea what it's like ... like ... to live with Manny. To be productized by your own family... To be..." She sputtered and shook her head and looked out the window. "Forget it."

Sophia had never considered that this was anything but what Eva wanted. She figured that Eva controlled the game. But maybe...

The silence between them must've clearly bothered Eva, because she gasped and buried her hands into her face.

In the dim sliver of moonlight shining through the window, Sophia noticed faint lines that crossed Eva's wrist.

"You cut yourself?" Sophia asked bluntly.

Eva looked at her wrist, covered it with her hand.

"Did you ... actually try to…"

Eva looked away. "Just … once."

Sophia nodded slowly. How had she not noticed before? Because she wasn't looking. Because Eva looked perfect on the outside.

"How'd you hide those?"

"Makeup." Eva sniffed and covered her wrist with her hand. "Filters. Distraction… You know." She exhaled long and hard. "Some days, I did just want to die, you know?" She looked at Sophia and spoke slowly. "But after, when they stopped me. Maybe I didn't want it that bad. Otherwise, I would've done it right."

"Yeah," Sophia said, not sure what else to say.

Eva gasped, and emotion and tears garbled her voice. "Funny. He was already killing me. Deciding who I was and…" She paused. "And then, he… Forget it."

"What?"

Eva swallowed emotion and remained quiet for a few seconds. "He's a monster."

Sophia looked at the lodge outside, grinding her teeth. She had been so stupid. So, so, stupid. She noticed a crack in her windshield, weaving low like a crooked river.

Eva laughed bitterly. "I don't even know why I even went out there to the woods." She shook her head, pressing the palms of her hands into her eyes. "Prove you wrong, I guess."

Sophia knew she should tell Eva about the journal. *But would that do any good? Would she even believe me?*

Yet Eva had shared some serious stuff, and Sophia felt

some sort of obligation to open up to her too. Eva already thought Sophia was a heartless shell of a person. Telling her about the journal would make Eva hate her more.

"I have to ask you for a favor. A huge one," Eva said.

48

Ethan

RUN LIKE HELL

Then: May 5

E than led Morgan, journal under her arm, away from the fuming Riley. They made their way to the base of the trail, outside the lodge.

When they were a distance away, Ethan slowed and patted her back. "Dude, you never fail to surprise me."

"Remind you of elementary school?" she asked. He'd never forgotten the day she'd pulled bullies off of him on the playground. They had been tight ever since.

"Skinny noodle Morg is an ultimate fighter." He chuckled, and he could see a small smile slide up her cheek. His wound throbbed and felt as if the pain radiated through his veins and whole torso, but laughter felt good after all that.

"Riley's pretty unhinged." Morgan said. She stopped, turned around, and squinted. Surely, she was expecting Riley to come barreling down from the trail, teeth bared like a little rabid squirrel.

"What if it's all a metaphor, like they said?" she asked.

He didn't have an answer for her.

They continued walking. The light from the lodge glowed like a warm respite amidst a snowstorm. He knew his wound would still throb and burn even if he was inside, but somehow, he felt like maybe he'd be safer there.

"Does the journal even work if Aidan writes in it?" she asked.

"Don't know, Morg."

"Does it work if we destroy what he wrote?"

"Can't say."

If he could, Ethan would undo all of this, get his friend Sophia back—both physically and emotionally. She'd gotten so weird, so hard, so unattached to him over the past couple weeks. Ethan had never felt so lonely. He needed Sophia, Morgan, and his dad. He needed them all.

Morgan was always the one who had a fierce bookish sense about what to do. Right from wrong. She always seemed to keep him on track. She was the one who had suggested the summer credits at the community college in case he needed to graduate early.

Now, she looked to him—of all people—for a roadmap on how to undo this weird spell.

He shook his head. "I don't know, Morg, okay?"

"I wish there were … rules. I am good with rules. Coloring in the lines. Following six-step scientific experiments. Solving differential formulas," she said.

"I get you." His tone was soft.

"We should call the police," she said.

"Chill."

"But what if we're too late and Soph is—" she said.

"I don't know, Morg! But how the hell are we gonna find her in—"

"What if they're trying to kill her right now? What if she's hurt and needs help? What if—"

"Guys! Stop arguing." A hollow, bodiless voice floated on the breeze in the parking lot outside the lodge.

The two of them snapped their mouths shut, and with wide eyes they both spun to follow the sound. "Sophia?" Morgan asked.

49

Ethan

SELFISH

Then: May 5

Morgan and Ethan stood, mouths gaping, squinting at Sophia standing by her car. She waved her arm for them to come over. Wordlessly, they jogged to the vehicle.

"What's up?" Ethan said.

"Shh!" said another voice. It wasn't Morgan's, and it wasn't Sophia's either.

Ethan peered through the open window of the car and saw someone inside. The person was clearly female. Small and folded inward with knees to chest. When she moved slightly, he made out the short wavy hair.

"Dude, you found Eva?" he asked.

"Looks like it, dumbass," Morgan said, crossing her arms and gazing sternly at Sophia. "Why are you wet? And why are you with *her*?"

Ethan looked closer and saw that Sophia's hair hung in wet clumps and her jaw chattered. He grasped his friend's arm firmly. "You fall in the river?"

Sophia let out a tiny yelp, and he let go.

"My wrist." Sophia said, squeezing her arm. "Riley cut me."

"Dude! Me too," Ethan said, pointing to his torso. "She went freaking nuts up there. Until Morgan opened a can of whoop-ass on her."

He nudged Morgan with his elbow, and she smiled proudly. Blood had soaked an uneven circle through Ethan's t-shirt. He didn't seem to register any pain at that moment, unable to take his gaze off Eva in the back seat. It was as if she were a live, two-headed zebra sitting in the car. He'd never seen her like that before, curled up like a little kid.

"Just so you know, I'm still mad at you though," Morgan said to Sophia, crossing her arms. "But I'm glad to see you, too."

"What happened to *her*?" Ethan threw his head toward Eva.

"I'm right here, you know." Eva's voice sounded raspy, as if she were teetering on the edge of a breakdown. "You can actually talk to me."

"Get in," Sophia said, shivering and motioning to the car. She glanced around before sliding into the driver's seat. Morgan sat in the back seat next to Eva. Ethan climbed into the front passenger seat.

Ethan was dumbfounded.

Inside, Sophia turned up the heater and put her hands up to the vents.

Eva's hair was wet and she was curled under a blanket in the backseat, with her knees to her chest.

"What *happened?*" he asked.

Sophia's attention suddenly sprung to Morgan. She pointed. "Oh my god, Morg! You have my journal?"

Morgan lifted it from her lap. "Yeah, Ethan got it from Aidan. You should see the shit he wrote in it."

"I already know what he wrote."

"journal?" Eva asked, her eyes darting between them.

"So how do I stop it? The story?" Sophia asked, ignoring Eva.

"E and I think it all started with the curse here," Morgan said.

"Yeah, you got mud on it from this place. It's got a weird vibe here—"

"The mud…," Sophia said quietly, half to herself.

"So you gotta find out how to stop it all." Morgan sounded urgent.

"I don't know how to stop it," Sophia said.

"Stop *what*?!" Eva practically screamed. Clearly, she wasn't used to being ignored.

Ethan and Morgan looked at Sophia with surprise.

"She doesn't know, okay?" Sophia said with a shrug.

"I'm here, you guys, sitting right here." Eva's voice sounded more like her sharp, normal self. "What're you talking about?"

Sophia let out a long exhale. "Long story."

Ethan and Morgan glared at Sophia. "Did you write that you went for a midnight swim in the freezing river?" Ethan asked. *The stupid journal. Sophia and her stupid journal.*

"Soph, you gotta fix the story," Morgan said. "'Cuz Aidan says you're both gonna die."

"We're gonna die," Eva repeated, her throat sounding as if there was peanut butter stuck in it. "Why? Did you see my stepdad out there?" Her breath grew labored, as if she was going to hyperventilate.

"Your *stepdad*?" Ethan asked, incredulous. "What the hell are you talking about?"

Sophia let out a long sigh and threw her head back. Ethan wondered if Sophia should keep her mouth shut. This was their secret. Eva was the enemy.

"Okay, fine." Sophia exhaled dramatically. Ethan clenched his teeth, knowing once again Sophia held all the power of what they would or wouldn't do. And she clearly had just made a decision.

50

Sophia
SECRETS

Then: May 5

Sophia revealed everything to Eva, sharing her worst thoughts about her, how she used the book and its power to destroy her. Eva listened and flipped through the book, scanning it briskly and flipping pages with a furrowed brow, as if it held the secret to the meaning of life.

With each of Sophia's explanations for each chapter written, Eva seemed to shrink. At the end of all of Sophia's revelations, a silence opened up in the car. Her face felt hot.

"It was messed up, okay?" Sophia finally said.

Eva's voice was quiet. "I had no idea you hated me so much."

"You get it, though?" Sophia asked. "Why I hated you."

Morgan and Ethan looked like they were watching a tennis match, and their attention bounced between Eva and Sophia.

"I tried to be your friend."

"Eva, you only wanted to be my friend because I didn't fall all over you," Sophia said. "I wasn't following you like a puppy dog and doing everything you wanted me to do. You wanted to control me like Holly and Lydia—"

"You're wrong. I liked you. I did. I wanted to be your friend."

"Right, because everyone is trying to be my friend." Morgan smiled and rolled her eyes.

"I liked you because you didn't pretend. You were who you were—no apologies," Eva said.

"But when I didn't want to be your friend…"

"I got mad. I lied. I know." Eva's voice sounded sheepish.

"In a huge fucking way," Ethan said. It felt good to have an advocate like Ethan, even if he was mad at her.

"So I hated you," Sophia said simply, shrugging as if revenge was an obvious reaction to being burned.

"We all kinda do," Ethan said.

Morgan kicked his arm from the back seat. "Did," he added.

"The bigger question, you guys, is what the hell do we do with these last pages." Morgan ran nervous fingers through her hair, putting it into a ponytail and then removing it a few seconds later, only to do it again. "Do you have a pen?"

"Yeah, carry one everywhere," Sophia said, sarcasm dripping from her voice.

"Well, *I* keep one in *my* car. Along with wet wipes and hand sanitizer," Morgan said.

"He wrote we're going to die." Eva looked at Sophia. "Everything you wrote has happened. Everything Aidan wrote except for the death thing has happened. My stepdad tried to kill me."

"Yeah, go through that part?" Ethan said.

They explained to him about Manny's arrival and the attack, and how the event mirrored what had transpired in Aidan's story.

"Dude, how big was the rock?" Ethan asked, gazing at Sophia. She shrugged.

"*He* was the monster in the story," Eva said quietly, more to herself than anyone else. "He represented my fear." She paused and looked at the other three. "How would Aidan know that?"

"He said your character needed more depth," Sophia said.

"He knew Elsa was you, obviously," Morgan said.

"He probably didn't know that the monster would be Manny," Sophia said. "It never works out like you expect. The book and real life seem similar, but I don't know exactly how."

"Where'd he hit you? Like, in the jaw? I don't see a mark," Ethan said.

"So where's he now?" Morgan asked, warily glancing out the window.

Eva tossed the journal at Sophia, and the corner hit her in the temple. "You and your stupid games," Eva said.

"He's not gonna be that way forever." Sophia made the promise even though she didn't know if it would be true.

"It's not too far off from how he really is," Eva said quietly.

Morgan exchanged looks with Ethan.

Eventually Morgan said, "E, you gotta get that cut checked out. You too, Soph."

Ethan nodded. "Let's go to urgent care then, for all of us."

"No … you guys really need to get out of the car," Sophia said, giving a silent look to Morgan.

Ethan and Morgan sighed and slowly climbed out of the car. "Dude, I can't believe you really saved her life. Wow," Ethan said, half to himself.

"What're you gonna do?" Morgan asked. She didn't meet Sophia's eyes.

Sophia didn't answer for several seconds, only stared at her hands in the dim light. Her chest felt tight. She knew what she had to do.

"I'm still super-pissed at you," Morgan said with her arms

crossed over her chest. "But I don't necessarily want to leave you here to die."

"Go," Sophia said. She didn't look at her friends. "Just don't say anything to anyone about this yet."

Morgan and Ethan gazed at her for a few quiet seconds before they walked back to the lodge.

"And now," Eva said. "We're going to die."

The Flores File: Video
Interviews
NOW

Sheriff Rawlings: We found the two jackets near the river. One belonged to Ms. Palmer and the other to Ms. Flores. Each jacket contained both girls' blood.

Mr. Thomas: Of course I helped with the investigation. But honestly, Sophia looked for Aidan that evening, not Eva. And she and Eva weren't even friends, if I recall. She appeared bored at the event.

Ethan: For maybe a while after the wilderness trip, I didn't really talk to Sophia. I had stuff happening with my Dad. But I can tell you this: Sophia didn't kill Eva.

Riley: Everything points to Sophia. She hated her. And she was tormenting her. [Points to a blue jumpsuit she's wearing.] I don't know why I'm the one wearing this and she's not. [She motions to the chain-link fence behind her at the Adams Youth Detention Center.] And why *I'm* in this place and *she's* not.

Ethan: I had to have five stitches in my back because of Riley. Cost me a thousand bucks. We called the cops on her and Aidan that night, say … oh around four in the morning. She was outside sitting on the patio when Sheriff Rawlings came over.

Morgan: Riley was sitting there with the bloody knife right there in her hand. She was literally caught red-handed.

Riley: Now I'm the one in anger management classes. Pretty f-ed up, right?

Aidan: I didn't see nothing. I don't know why Riley went and stabbed Ethan. She hated homos, I guess.

51

Sophia
RESPITE

Then: May 5

"You sure you want to do this?" Sophia turned around to look at Eva, lying in the back seat. She felt like a chauffeur, but it was important that Eva stay out of sight.

Eva nodded but didn't look at Sophia. With that, Sophia started the car and backed out of the lodge parking lot.

Sophia made sure Eva was covered from head to toe with the blanket and then drove up a winding dirt road. The car jiggled, and she wasn't sure it was going to really make it up the steep incline.

Sophia stopped the car on the side of the road. She looked at the clock on her dash. It was five o'clock in the morning. *Screw it.*

"Wait here," she said, leaving the car running.

Eva lay in the back seat, fully covered, while Sophia strode up the road with her phone as a flashlight. She came to the lean-to cabin with firewood stacked outside. On the porch, she banged hard on the door, rattling the four metal locks that lined the edge.

The knock set off an alarm of yapping dogs and thumping inside. Ethan's stupid rat dogs. Her breath was unsteady and her body was wound, impatient. She didn't care what time it was.

The door opened, and Ethan's dad appeared. Tim Switalski frowned and blocked the doorway, wearing blue sweatpants, a camouflage hoodie, and a stocking cap. He held a rifle in one hand, the door in the other.

"Sophia," he growled. She knew he didn't like her, and without Ethan's support or presence, she wasn't likely to get very far. But Ethan's dad was her only hope. The dogs kept barking, and the sound made Sophia want to scratch her ears off. She must've made a face, because he kicked at the scraggliest one and shouted for him to shut up.

"I know this is your, um, hideout." She glanced back at the dense forest, knowing her car was left running with Eva hiding in the backseat beneath a blanket. *I shouldn't have left her like that.*

He nodded.

"But I need help."

52

Eva

ARMAGEDDON

Then: May 5

"W hat's she running from?" Ethan's dad was burly, redheaded, and an exact physical replica of his son—plus some thirty years.

Eva sat down in a chair and folded her arms across her chest. "Why does everyone talk about me like I'm not sitting right here in front of you all?"

Eva gazed at this man as he dabbed Sophia's stab wound with a sterile pad. He had virtually every kind of first-aid treatment you could need inside a box the size of a small suitcase.

Sophia looked down as he kneeled by her side. He shoved the little white dog away with his elbow.

Eva inspected the small cabin, which smelled like fresh-cut wood combined with rubbing alcohol. Lit by a kerosene lamp in the corner of the room, the one-room hut felt like a kid's fort. A tattered sofa that looked like it came straight from a dumpster. A countertop with just two glasses and two plates. A two-person wobbly table with a single folding chair.

"You're in good hands with Ethan's dad," Sophia said.

339

"It's Tim. Quit calling me *Ethan's Dad.*"

"Yeah, um, well... If there's one person prepared when the shit hits the fan, it's Tim Switalski," Sophia said.

Is this really happening? A memory came rushing back to her: the knife against her skin. Her stepdad's scrambled, hateful face. A wave of nausea rolled through her, and she exhaled loudly. *Yes, this was really happening.*

Back in the car, Sophia had told Eva her plan in all of two minutes. This was a man known to stockpile guns, gas masks, and food and water. He was the ultimate in being prepared. The idea of betting on a strange man—a classmate's dad who'd been going off the deep end? Probably not the smartest idea.

But what choice did she really have? If she went to the police, her mom would never forgive her, never accept what she alleged as truth. In a way, what had just transpired felt strangely good. Quite simply, she wanted *out.* She wanted offstage, away from the constant approval from thousands of strangers. She wanted to turn off the running commentary that her ears were too big, her smile lopsided, that she had no talent. Some days, she couldn't even look in the mirror.

This was her way out.

"How'd this happen?" he asked, rustling in his box of supplies. "Where's that anesthetic..."

"Eva's stepdad tried to kill her," Sophia said.

"Why's that, 'zactly?" He appeared unfazed by the explanation.

"Because he's a total psychopath," Sophia said.

"And he must've come after you, too."

"No. Different psychopath," Sophia said. "But if Eva goes home, he kills her. So she's staying here for a while."

"Staying here," he repeated slowly. He filled up a syringe and gave Sophia an unwavering stare.

Eva winced in sympathy as Tim plunged the needle into the soft part of Sophia's hip. She caught Sophia's eye and noted the absence of loathing revenge, the lack of judgmental aloofness. Somehow they were now tied together. A shared secret.

Later, the three of them sat at the table with hot coffee. As the soft light of early morning brushed the cabin floor, Sophia asked Tim for advice. "I'm trying to end something. Ya know? It started a long time ago, when people were real mad."

"She has a journal that makes everything she writes come true," Eva interjected quickly. Enough of the dancing around. She was exhausted. All she wanted was to sleep, and now the sun was rising. Sophia needed to spit it out.

"That so," Tim said.

"Yeah, so there was a curse and a fire down in Kebler," Sophia said, nodding down toward the pass.

"Oh, the old Ute story," he said.

"Yeah," Sophia said, "and it did something…"

His nod was barely visible, and he fell silent. He looked at her with a blank expression that was unreadable.

Sophia continued to explain what had happened, and the story was a jumbled mess, so much that Eva could barely follow. "What do we do?" Eva asked. "Sir?"

"Hell if I know," he said, scratching his nose and standing up from his seat.

"Okay," Sophia said quietly. After a few moments, she leaned forward. "I have to tell you, sir. Ethan really wants you home. *Needs* you home."

Eva had never seen her act deferential to anyone. It was as if she were in a play on stage.

For the first time all morning, Tim stood with a stiff posture. He clenched his jaw, and his eyes narrowed.

"He wants you to be…" Sophia spoke carefully. "Settled… Safe." She looked up at him with pleading eyes. A new expression Eva had never seen on Sophia's face.

It was as if she hadn't said anything to him, because he

turned to Eva and pointed to the gross twin mattress with piles of blankets. "You can sleep on that bunk over there, Eva."

Her whole body ached, and the worn blankets looked inviting. She listened as he gave her long-winded instructions: where to find the jerky, the canned food, the water, the firewood, the hiding place beneath the floor, the loaded Glock G19. She listened from outside her body. *A Glock G19.* Eva watched in a dreamy state as he explained how to shoot the gun. *I'm so not prepared for this.* She tried to pay attention, tried to memorize the details that might save her life, before tucking the gun beneath the mattress and exhaling loudly.

Sophia gazed at Eva for a long minute with a soft expression. "You don't have to do this, you know," she said.

"No." Eva looked at her hands. "I can't take it anymore."

As Sophia and Tim left the cabin, Eva crawled onto the bed and listened to their muffled conversation just outside.

"You won't tell the police?" Sophia asked.

He scoffed. "You think I trust them?"

She listened to their fading footsteps and watched through the window as they disappeared into the woods. She felt so suddenly alone. So suddenly naked without a phone. She froze, listening, waiting for something to move out there, to stomp up the stairs to get her. But nothing moved in the rising sun. The only sound was her labored breath.

Flores File: Text message obtained from Sophia's phone

May 5

7:20 a.m.
Sophia:
you back?

Ethan:
yes

Sophia:
know you're mad but i need help

Ethan:
oh how im dying to help u

Sophia:
create a distraction

Ethan:
why

Sophia:
its the only way out

Ethan:
what

Sophia:
riley and dont mention eva

Flores File: Text messages
obtained from Sophia's
phone

May 5

5:15 p.m.
Sophia:
ma, ill be late
helping e w stuff

Mom:
How late?

Sophia:
late
save me dinner pls?

Mom:
Where've you been? We need to talk. This is not okay.

Sophia:
go look under my mattress

Mom:
why?

Sophia:
lottery drawing yesterday

7:15 p.m.
Mom:
OMG!! We won! Sophia! Call me. I called you. We won $6 million!

7:30 p.m.
Mom:
Answer the phone!

7:45 p.m.
Mom:
Sophia! Dylan and I are having a dance party. This is crazy. What do we do? Come home!

8:30 p.m.
Sophia:
ikr?
cant believe it
call lottery office in am?

8:33 p.m.
Mom:
Can you talk? I called you. We won't be able to sleep. This changes everything.

53

Sophia
REWRITING HISTORY

Then: May 5 Sunrise

Tattered stickers covered the back bumper of Tim Switalski's Jeep. "Water is for Everyone." *Trust the Government. It worked for Sitting Bull.* "Prepare for 2021: The World Ends.*

Then, one bumper sticker in particular struck Sophia. Fight Fire with Fire.

"I'm going to stop and get a gallon of water in case they poisoned my tap…" he said. She only half listened to him, turning the bumper sticker line over in her head. *Fight fire with fire.* The curse had started with fire. Would she be able to end it with fire?

"Don't go to a doctor about the stitches…"

Maybe she could burn the journal. She'd rewrite it and then burn it. *Would that stop Manny from killing them?* Her stomach cramped and her wounds ached again. She had to fix this. Fast.

"Hey—you got some matches I can have?" Sophia asked suddenly.

"Sure, sure." He climbed into his car, pulled out a rubber

storage bin, and removed a box of matches. "Take the whole thing. I got twenty more." She took it and nodded quickly.

"Um, thanks again."

He nodded and sniffed. "I'm gonna go search the perimeter for the feds now and then head home to get some supplies."

~

The sky behind her began to glow a bright yellow on the horizon of the mountains. Sophia parked her car on a dirt road leading to a dense thicket of pine trees. Sirens rang in the distance, and she ducked in her seat as the Sheriff's SUV swooshed past on the highway below.

For the rest of the day, she studied the journal—and waited.

She'd scribbled over Aidan's chapters, tore them up into tiny pieces, and shoved them into the back of the book. She needed a new ending and had terrible writer's block. All she could think of was, "And then they lived happily ever after."

She also needed to write for her friends, Ethan and Morgan. *Would any of this even work?* Before she had the chance to write anything, her phone dinged with a text message from Morgan.

Morgan:
you ok?

Sophia:
yes

Morgan:
change the story?

Sophia:

what?
not yet. why

Morgan:
I just got accepted to harvard

Sophia:
congrats

Morgan:
did you write that in?

Sophia:
no

Morgan:
i was just saying that
I didn't really get in to hrvd
going to cornell

Sophia:
are you still mad?

Morgan:
yes

Sophia waited for her to respond. She didn't. So she texted Ethan.

Sophia:
ur dad may come home

Ethan:
u ok?

Sophia:
yes

Ethan:
good
now fuck off

Regret pulsed through her. She'd been a terrible friend. *So selfish.*

She considered Ethan's dad and how he became who he was. She started Googling things like "end of the world mental health" on her phone and found that plenty of people who have had a history of traumatic experiences can be fatalistic. Tim had endured so much trauma. When his wife left him and Ethan, it must have pulled the pin on the mental grenade.

She'd judged him without taking the time to understand him. As she wrote, everything came pouring out. Her rage, her sadness, her feelings of abandonment and powerlessness, her revenge—and her misunderstanding. She wanted everyone to be okay. She wanted Eva to live. She *had* to live.

She sat, waiting, in her car for hours within eyesight of the lodge at Anthracite Creek. She sat until her butt hurt, until her legs cramped, her stomach twisted. Until evening, when all the vehicles at the lodge were gone. She drove down to the lodge and parked and then carried the journal and the matches to the field.

An old, rusted metal bucket sat near the barbed wire fence in the field. She trotted over, picked it up, and carried it back to the spot where she'd laid the journal. Some liquid sloshed in the bottom, probably left over from a recent rainstorm, so she tipped it over before she set it down.

Exhaling, she scanned the tops of the cliffs beyond her, looking for any ghosts, any eyes peering down at her, laughing at what she'd created. She squatted down quickly on her haunches, readying herself to do this, to end the curse. Then her eyes stopped on the river. For a moment, Sophia gazed, frozen by fear, at the grassy bank, expecting to see Manny looming, waiting, ready to stab her to death. *No, I'll kick his ass this time,* she told herself.

But he wasn't there.

She needed to get this done. She stood up and hurriedly tossed the journal into the can, and then lit the match and tossed it in, too. She never expected the *whoosh* that followed, so strong it threw her back and singed her hair. She knocked over the pail and kicked out her legs, screaming and frantically patting her hair.

By the time she looked up, the flames had leapt from the overturned pail to the grass. The tall, knee-high blades glowed orange, and the flames spread and twisted like the fire was alive. A breeze blew the flames just so, as if directed by an invisible hand.

She screamed, dancing about, fretting about what to do. She kicked dirt at the fire. She considered how she could get water from the river. She had no container to get water to the fire, outside of the metal pail, which would surely scorch her. She could *not* set the valley on fire. *This can't be happening.*

Her chest and forehead squeezed tight with panic. People who lit forest fires went to jail. She would go to jail.

With her heart thumping inside her chest, she ran to her car, started the engine, and peeled out of the grassy lot. Foot slamming on the gas, she drove a quarter of a mile down the road, glancing in the rearview mirror as the flames grew like a monster and crept closer to the lodge.

The liquid. Of course she'd ignored the smell from that pail. It was probably gasoline in there and she just hadn't noticed it. She banged her hand on the steering wheel and screamed again.

She yanked the steering wheel to the left, skidding into the dirt driveway of a nearby Victorian-style house. There, she tucked her hair into a winter stocking cap and raced to the house to bang on the front door. A woman wearing a fleece vest answered, and Sophia pointed. "Fire!"

The woman jumped with surprise. "Oh my god!" She turned away and ran into the house, surely planning to call for help.

Sophia took the opportunity to run back to her car and drive off, hoping the alert would save the land while somehow keeping her anonymous.

The Flores File: Video
Interviews
NOW

Mr. Thomas: Certainly. I was initially concerned when I couldn't find Eva the next morning at checkout. Some of the kids said she had left early. [Pauses, covers his mouth with fingers.] Yes.

Becky Flores: My baby never came home. [Sobs.] Something terrible happened that night. I feel it in my bones. [She leans into the camera.] Because a mother knows. We just do.

Mr. Thomas: Who told me she left? Let's see ... Ethan, Riley, Aidan. They stayed up the latest. Eva's bed was made. Sophia's belongings were gone.

Dakota Rawlings: What happened to her ... I never would have thought. I mean, I was literally shook. But I guess, it's like, now she'll live forever, in what? Martyrdom. Which is good if you die?

Mr. Thomas: I forgave the assignment after the weekend. Eva's disappearance. Riley's arrest. A forest fire. It was a lot. Too much.

Nessa: The whole night had a weird vibe. I couldn't quite figure people out.

Lydia: I still miss her. I like, cry, every day. Every. Single. Day. She was my other me.

Dakota Rawlings: I heard … [leans into the camera with a conspiratorial look] that somebody got a movie deal about her life story. Is this what this interview is for?

Sheriff Rawlings: Carol Lincoln called the fire in quick enough. But it could've been a disaster. We assumed arson, and the way Sophia Palmer was snooping around, she was a suspect. We found bits of a journal in a can. Earlier, we had found the jackets there with the blood. We found all kinds of ties between Sophia and Eva. Sophia transferred money out of her bank account. Sophia Palmer has been and still remains our prime suspect.

54

Sophia
UNDONE

Then: May 6

Sweat dripped down Sophia's forehead as she sat beneath bright lights inside a boxy interrogation room. Sheriff Rawlings, a rail-thin man with a face like a blade, paced in front of her, peppering her with questions.

"Why were you in the vicinity of the lodge after it nearly burned down?"

"Did you light that fire?"

"Where is Eva Flores? When did you last see her?"

"Why is Eva Flores' blood on your jacket? And yours on hers?"

"Did you hurt Eva Flores?"

"Riley said something about a journal. What is the story of this journal?"

"You do know that arson is a federal offense? And so is murder. I could arrest you right now for both."

Her heart thumped against her bones, but she slumped in the hard plastic chair for two hours, revealing nothing. "I don't know anything. I didn't do anything. And I won't talk until I get a lawyer."

He finally released her instead of waiting for her to get an attorney—although she wasn't about to call Paonia's only lawyer, Hendy. After the interrogation, she drove straight to Ethan's house.

She banged on his front door with her fist for several minutes before Ethan finally sauntered to the door. He opened the door with disgust, but she brushed by him and slumped onto the tattered mustard-yellow sofa. Filled with boxes and piles of dirty clothes, the room smelled dusty, as if the curtains and windows hadn't been opened in years.

"I'm too young to go to jail."

Visibly shaking, she told Ethan everything that had happened later at the cabin with Eva, everything that happened inside the Sheriff's interrogation room.

Ethan stared at her with a stony expression.

She exhaled a sigh and rolled her eyes. "So, I almost died because I fucked everything up. You guys too. I suck. We good?"

"You were a real bitch."

She shrugged and nodded faintly and waited for him to accept her Sophia-esque apology.

"Yeah, guess we're okay."

They sat side-by-side with feet up on the coffee table, inching their heels between piles of magazines and books.

"Did your dad ever come back to the house?" Sophia asked, examining the piles of camouflage clothing, the clear bins stocked with water purifiers, the dozens of jars of Jif peanut butter, the axes and camping stoves.

"Yeah. But he's going back up to the cabin. Said I'd be fine here by myself."

Sophia didn't respond.

"He's out back, burying more rice." He paused. "For no fucking reason."

"You gonna get him to talk to some sort of specialist or something?"

He shook his head. "Dude, you know I've tried before. He's gotta be willing to get help."

His face was blank, but Sophia knew he hid a pinball machine of emotions inside. Sophia's stomach felt sour. She had missed her opportunity to help with her story.

A couple moments of silence passed before Ethan spoke again. "Eva should just come home and call the cops and stuff. You're gonna wind up in jail."

Her throat tightened with that reality. "Hope not." But Eva. She made a promise. She told him what Eva had said about her stepdad. "Even without the journal's story, he'd probably kill her."

"So now what?" Ethan asked.

"Can you get us on the dark web?"

Ethan's face lit up. That was just the sort of thing that he'd know how to do. A computer challenge. "What kind of illegal stuff are we looking for?"

The next day, Ethan invited Morgan to his house. She marched into the house pretty talkative, but once she saw Sophia leaning against the kitchen counter, she scowled and crossed her arms over her chest.

Sophia held out a palm. "So I was shitty about your grandma, okay?" Sophia said. "I fucked up."

After a long pause, Morgan's face softened and she rushed to hug Sophia, who awkwardly patted her back. The torn edges of their friendship apparently had been hard for Morgan, who desperately needed order.

"You know, I shouldn't have even asked you to get me into those schools. I guess I wanted … perfection," Morgan said.

"You know you're perfect in all the ways that count," Sophia said in a sarcastic sing-song voice.

"What, did you google that response?" Morgan asked, incredulous.

"Read it on an inspirational poster in Mrs. Evans' office," Sophia said.

"Hey, I wanted to give you this." Sophia reached into her back pocket and handed Morgan and Ethan each a check from her lottery proceeds. Morgan squealed when she held the check in her hand. Ethan studied the check while nodding his head and beaming. His shoulders seemed to relax a bit.

After a few moments, Morgan's face crumpled into embarrassment. "Oh Soph, I'm so sorry."

Sophia frowned. "I hand you a check and you apologize?"

"It wasn't my grandmother's journal. I lied."

Ethan and Sophia exchanged a wry smile. "I had no idea!" Sophia said.

After her scribbling and burning of the journal, Sophia didn't ultimately get all of her wishes. Tim didn't change. The bank took over The Wheel and her house because of Manny's debts. Somehow, though, the lottery winnings didn't disappear, and she and Eva were both alive. Being alive meant more than any other stupid wish.

All the while, volunteer search teams searched for Eva in the Kebler Pass area. Over the next two weeks, the mood of the town became more somber, as if a drizzly fog had descended over it. Hordes of reporters camped out at local bed-and-breakfasts and interviewed people on camera at nearly every corner. Sophia ducked the cameras and questions, and she knew that she was the prime suspect.

Graduation came and went with little fanfare, and girls in town wept over Eva's absence. The police told the press about the blood on the jackets and the strand of Sophia's hair they found. Sophia didn't know evidence law but she figured it looked pretty bad and might soon take her down. The police questioned Sophia twice more, searched her bedroom, and interviewed her friends. But with no body, they had no case.

Sophia continued to make secret trips to the cabin after the sun went down, checking on Eva and stocking her up with food, water, toilet paper, books, and clothes for several weeks. Tim came and went as well. To ease Eva's loneliness, Sophia would stay longer some days, playing cards with her. She began to share more personal stories, and Eva did too, getting to know the road that had taken each of them to this ultimate destination. Each time, Sophia asked Eva if she wanted to come home and call the police. Each time, Eva said no.

Sophia's mom often asked where she went and why she bought so many new clothes online and didn't seem to wear them. Sophia gave vague answers about photography and excitement about the lottery winnings.

Fortunately, her mom never saw the guy with the handlebar mustache who showed up at the house in a van with out-of-state plates. And her mom wasn't there when he handed Sophia a manila envelope. She also didn't notice right away that Sophia took out a million dollars from the account, nor did she know that she bought a Honda Accord.

Jennifer Palmer did notice, however, that the Sheriff seemed to drive past their house too slowly and too often. Sophia noticed too, and she watched the way her mom's jaw clenched and her chest seemed to rise and fall in steep heavy movements as she gazed back at him through the window. "How dare he assume you did anything," she'd say. "The gall of that man."

Despite being flush with cash, Sophia's mom remained grounded. She still worked at the gas station, but she did enroll in community college.

When Sophia pulled up to Tim's cabin with the purchased car one evening, Eva looked rested. Her hair was slightly longer, showing her natural reddish-brown color at the roots, and she pushed a few strands behind her ear. Eva held a duffle bag and watched plaintively as Sophia walked toward through the lush green foliage and trees.

"I was starting to think I'd live here forever," she said when Sophia got closer.

Sophia rolled her eyes.

"Come on, I got something to show you," she said before leading Eva back through the woods and down to the dirt road.

There, the silver car sat parked along the side of the road. Sophia motioned toward it.

"I checked it out and it runs pretty good," she said. "It's yours."

"Wow." Eva put her fingers to her mouth and frowned. "It's…"

"I put the title in your new name. There's cash under the back seat, and when you set up the bank account, I'll wire you the rest of the money." She handed her a flip phone. "Burner phone."

Eva gazed at the phone. "I don't know how to work this kind."

"You'll figure it out."

Eva looked at Sophia and shook her head. "Wow. Just … wow," she said. "And to think I've hated you forever."

The feeling was mutual. But Sophia didn't respond. Maybe this was a kind of atonement, maybe, for almost killing her. For hating her. Trying to destroy her.

Those few weeks of isolation softened Eva—just a tiny bit. She still had that annoying Eva voice. Yet there was something else. The only way that Sophia could describe it was a tad more authentic. She moved a bit slower, and she didn't always wave her hands so dramatically. She no longer had an audience. There was no longer anyone else to control but herself. She had only focused on hiding, surviving, and thinking about who she wanted to be.

"It'll be weird," Eva said after a moment. "You know… I've always been this … character. It's like I have something new. A blank slate, maybe."

Sophia nodded, shoving her hands into the pockets of her overall jeans. "You sure about this?"

Eva nodded and looked at the car again.

"Your mom's *super* worried. We can call the cops and protect you from that asshole."

Eva shook her head and looked down at her sneakers. "The attention … it's kinda what she craves. So no, thanks."

Sophia stared at her, wondering what was inside her head. She'd never know the girl's entire story, so she just nodded and quickly walked around to the passenger side of the car, opened the door, and jumped in. "Drop me off at Anthracite Creek. Morgan's giving me a ride home."

Eva climbed into the driver's seat of the car. She put two hands on the steering wheel.

"I don't know what to say," Eva said.

"Yeah," Sophia said.

Two weeks after Eva drove off into the sunset, a figure brushed past Sophia as she examined tomatoes in the grocery. She glanced up to see it was Manny. Her heart nearly dropped into her stomach. His brows dipped in the shape of a V.

She had no idea whether he remembered what happened in the forest and in the gallery or, most important, whether he still planned to kill her and Eva. *Did the fire rid him of his intentions or memories? Or did it do nothing at all?*

Either way, his presence choked her breath. She spun on her heel and nearly ran to the checkout counter.

In the parking lot, she frantically searched for her keys inside her purse. He approached at a brisk pace, and she gripped the metal keys, ready to stab him if necessary. Fear blazed through her brain.

She turned to look at him and held herself steady with a wide stance.

"What do you want?" She practically screamed at him.

"You know what I want," he said, more gently than she expected.

"You … tried to … kill her." Her voice squeezed out of her throat. *There it was—out in the open.* She *so* wanted to ruin him, to scream it to the world. But Eva…

"Me?" he scoffed. "I think we both know the real story." His brow flickered, and he turned and walked to his car.

His response swam between Sophia's ears. It was confusing, jumbled. *You know what I want… I think we both know the real story.*

Yes, she knew the real story! He attempted murder. If Sophia hadn't been there, he would have succeeded in killing Eva. She wanted to ask him if he remembered. If that was really him, a monster. If that monster went away when she burned the pages of her journal.

But she said nothing. She gnawed on her lip, her entire body buzzing with anger. And she watched him drive away.

Sophia never again saw Eva's mother, who hid away in her three-story farmhouse like a hermit. She claimed Sophia had destroyed her, and she subsequently landed a book deal that fingered Sophia as a murderer.

Upon news about the upcoming book, Sophia painted nonstop for twelve hours.

Worried, her mom entered the tent and sat on a chair next to Sophia for a long time, quietly watching her swirl the paint into thick circles on a canvas.

"Everyone thinks I killed her," Sophia said finally. She let the paintbrush rest on the canvas and turned to her mom. "I didn't, Ma. I didn't. I swear."

Her mom nodded and brushed Sophia's hair over her shoulder.

"Do you want to talk about what happened?" her mom asked softly. Sophia hadn't heard her mom talk to her in that gentle tone for years. She'd usually treated her as another adult unless she was scolding her.

Sophia shook her head. "I just … want people to stop … telling stories about me and…" She stopped, as rage burned behind her eyes.

"You want some advice?"

Sophia bit her lips together and nodded. *Yes. Please. How do I get this to stop?*

"You just gotta figure out what you can control." Her mom nodded and paused. "That usually means just controlling how you *respond* to things that life throws at you. The rest of it? You gotta leave that up to grace."

Sophia grabbed hold of that advice as if it was a lifeline. She resumed her armor-plated demeanor to endure the sting of suspicion, acknowledging that no one would ever know her story. She worked on her car and spent hours painting and shooting photos. Tourists bought her work, but mostly because she was tied into a sensationalized story of a beautiful social media star who had disappeared.

One afternoon, Sophia and Ethan walked into The Wheel, now owned by some Denver hipster, and ordered coffee.

Lydia approached Sophia at the counter. "Nice car out there," she said, tossing her head to the front door. It was like déjà vu from months earlier, when E and Sophia worked there. "Did you use it to hide Eva's body?"

Sophia didn't respond. She sipped her coffee and floated past Lydia to a table in the corner. She put her feet up on the chair next to her. Ethan followed and sat down, clearly rattled.

Lydia stood with hands on her hips and a smug, angry scowl, and Sophia glanced up to see a group of girls in the corner. One held up a phone, recording the exchange.

"Dude, you shoulda punched her in the face," Ethan whispered.

Sophia rolled her eyes.

Sophia knew what hate felt like and what power did, and she didn't want either anymore—even if people never really knew her story.

Denver Post
NOVEMBER 30

Father of Missing Social Media Star Arrested

PAONIA—Police on Tuesday arrested the stepfather of a missing social media star on felony charges in connection to a separate case involving a teenaged Los Angeles girl.

Manny Flores, 44, formerly of Paonia, was charged with three counts of sexual assault on a child and one count of kidnapping in connection to an incident in which he claimed to be the new business manager of a 16-year-old actress. Just six months earlier, Flores and his former wife, Becky Flores, spoke to journalists and led search parties in Paonia to uncover the whereabouts of his missing stepdaughter, Eva Flores. Eva, 17, had risen to fame on Instagram and TikTok, and Flores acted as her manager. She disappeared in May during a school sleepover event.

Flores' attorney Hendy Ferguson said his client is innocent of the assault charges and he will fight all charges against him. "This girl is a liar," said Ferguson, "and she is well known for making up wild stories."

The Flores File: Video Interviews

NOW

Dylan: I still work at Don's. I got a raise. But I'm a millionaire. [Grins proudly.] Oh, and we got a house that's big enough for Mrs. Ratner to live with us. She paints with Soph.

Jennifer Palmer: So when does this movie come out? You'll show that Sophia had nothing to do with it, right?

Ethan: Man, feels like high school was forever ago. So ... before you leave, you gotta go to the Renegade shop downtown—the old Wheel. They're selling some of Sophia's art there. It's dope. By the way, the police didn't find nothing on Sophia, so you know you gotta clear her with this movie. Right?

Morgan: I've been at school since August. I heard that Eva's mom hired some private detective to stalk Soph for a while. [Pauses.] I think her dad moved. Somewhere ... like L.A. [Stops, listens, leans into the camera.] What? Her mom's the producer of this documentary? [Folds her arms across her chest and chuckles.] Omigod. Of course she is.

Becky Flores: Do you see now? Sophia Palmer murdered my girl. I won't rest until that girl is behind bars.

Star Caperson (local psychic): Sophia made paintings with starry backgrounds and outlines of a Ute tribe member and a silhouette of Eva. She gave the picture to the owners of the lodge there at Anthracite Creek. I think it was a great way to, you know, honor the spirits... Because ...[sings the word] I haven't seen the ghosts of the chiefs up there on the hill since. [Pauses, taps her chest near her heart.] You just don't know what's inside... You don't know everyone's truth.

Sheriff Rawlings: Hmmmm ... so anything else you should know... Good question. [Scoffs.] Whelp, since your video team called me about *The Eva Flores Story* movie, I got another search warrant to look at Sophia Palmer's place. And I figured this here would give you all some more fodder for your story. I hope it helps.

[Tosses a file folder onto the table. He flips it open to show a printout of an email.]

An email found on Sophia Palmer's computer
OCTOBER 28

To: Sophia Palmer
From: Elsastory@gmail.com
Subject: Gift

Sophia:
Just wanted to tell you I was thinking of our convo that one night. How we debated about what's the most selfless thing a person could ever do. Remember?
So I'm enrolled in community college for marine biology! I'm off social media. And I'm thinking about all that, and I realized that I figured out the right answer to that question.
The answer is <u>you</u>. You did the most selfless thing a person could ever do. You knew the finger would be pointed at you. You had nothing to gain and everything to lose. Still, you helped bury Eva. And for that, you gave me one thing that I never could seem to find before: myself.

Elsa

Don't forget your free gift....

Or go to www.jenniferalsever.com/free-book

Acknowledgments

This story had its starts and stops, but when it finally poured out of me, it was thanks to the many people that have come into my life. I'm grateful for my editor Kate Angelella, who brings enthusiasm and always another perspective on my work. As always, I'm better because of you. Thank you Diane Telgen, my lovely copy editor. You are my dictionary, grammar teacher, cheerleader, and detail-oriented eyes. A big dose of gratitude goes out to Nicole Hower, my talented book cover designer who deftly captured the tone of this story with unique images.

Thank you Kevin O'Donnell for your continued support of my wacky ideas and wild imagination. Thanks also goes to my boys, Brendan and Jacob, for schooling me on the TikTok world and the mindset of young people today. To Ingrid and Astrid McGinley for dancer tips and crucial feedback. To Thomas for helping me identify weak spots in the manuscript and for the encouragement. To Jaden Barbella for allowing me to borrow her phrases and deep knowledge of cars. To Molly Blevins for her style inspiration, and to her mom, Carolyn Blevins, for being a valued early reader. To Cheryl Cooney and Kali Renay for endless questions, long lists of revisions, and feedback. To Jeni Lowry for your second sight. To Eliza Klearman for your character development inspiration and keen eyes. To Nicola Farrer for your keen eyes and attention to detail. HUGE. To the girls at Rachel DeLong's yoga retreat at Kebler Corner in Paonia, thanks for the camaraderie, space, and inspiration. And to all the people who have supported me in my writing adventures. I love you all.

Also by Jennifer Alsever

Extraordinary Lies

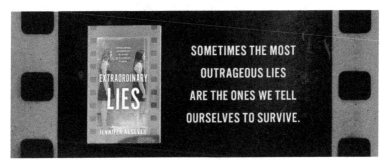

SOMETIMES THE MOST
OUTRAGEOUS LIES
ARE THE ONES WE TELL
OURSELVES TO SURVIVE.

San Francisco 1971.

Two girls from opposite worlds —each of them with unique gifts. Brash and bold Charley can touch a hand and glimpse a person's dark secrets and dangerous future. The refined and shy Julia can stir a deadly energetic force that uproots trees and crushes cars in a moment of rage.

When they join a group of teens for a summer of psychic tests at the Stanford Research Institute, the experiments quickly turn deadly and more sinister motives emerge. Truth and lies intertwine, and soon, ambition and war outstrip science in a race to manipulate their gifts.

If they are to survive, the unlikely duo must figure out a way to work together. Can Charley and Julia do this and control their innate powers that have long been exploited—and suppressed—by the rest of the world?

If you like Cold War spy novels, page turner books and supernatural suspense, then you'll love Jennifer Alsever's enthralling paranormal thriller.

Inspired by true events!

Get your copy of Extraordinary Lies today!

"Imaginative and thrilling all at once. A truly captivating page turner from start to finish." – MATT MOORE, FILM PRODUCER AREU BROS. STUDIOS

~

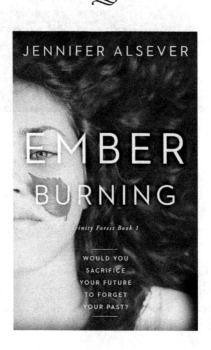

The Trinity Forest Series: Ember Burning, Oshun Rising & Venus Shining

When Ember Trouve first ventures into Trinity Forest, she goes looking for escape. What she finds there is something much more dangerous than even the urban legends could have predicted.

The forest's candy-coated wickedness draws her in like a spider's web, promising a new, exciting life… with just a few fatal strings attached.

What Ember chooses next will challenge her very notion of reality. In a series of events that will turn her and her friends' lives upside down, Ember travels through the looking glass into a world of fame, wealth, and deadly vengeance. She will have to fight like hell to reclaim a life she once wished away in order to save the boy she loves and the family she only now realizes she's always had.

Enter into a world a breath away from our own, filled with witchcraft, deception, and romance and download the entire series today!

www.jenniferalsever.com

"An absorbing, stellar series introduction with elements of fantasy and horror." --Kirkus Reviews

2018 Gold Medalist: Best YA Horror/Mystery Moonbeam Book Awards

Semi-quarterfinalist: 2017 Publisher's Weekly BookLife Prize

Finalist: 2019 Dante Rossetti Book Awards

2018 Gold Medallist: Best YA Fiction eBook Independent Publisher Book Awards

Honorable Mention: 2019 Writer's Digest Best Indie eBook

CPSIA information can be obtained
at www.ICGtesting.com
Printed in the USA
BVHW092332210922
647507BV00015B/90